Return *to* Cattail Marsh

Linda Panasuk

NEWMAN SPRINGS PUBLISHING
320 Broad Street
Red Bank, NJ 07701

First originally published by Newman Springs Publishing 2021

ISBN 978-1-63692-166-2 (Paperback)
ISBN 978-1-63692-167-9 (Digital)

Printed in the United States of America

To my mother, Geraldine, who always supported all my dreams, and my Nana, Thelma, who inspired and believed in my abilities

PROLOGUE

"WHERE'RE WE GOING?" MICHAEL CALLED after Cate as he stood up on the pedals of his mountain bike. Right, left, right, left—his whole body moved with each push of a pedal.

Cate's thick auburn hair swung around like the tail of a thoroughbred as she turned to look back. "The marsh," she yelled.

"Why?" asked Michael in between panting breaths.

Cate braked her bike, put her foot down, steadying herself, and waited. "Come on." She impatiently waved Michael on toward her. "That's where he'll be."

"Why'd he be there?" Michael asked as he pulled alongside Cate.

"Because I was supposed to meet him there."

"When?"

"The day he disappeared."

"That was two days ago. He wouldn't still be there."

"Maybe something happened."

"Why were you meeting him?"

"Because…"

"Why?"

"He said he had something to ask me."

"*That sneak.*" Sweat beaded up on Michael's forehead as he recalled his locker room conversation with Ryan the day of his disappearance.

"I'm going to ask Cate to the spring dance," he'd revealed.

"You are?"

Ryan gave Michael an awkward grin as he moved several fingers across his forehead, sweeping his wet blond hair in place. "Do you think she'll go with me?"

5

"Not if I ask her first!" Ryan may've thought Michael was joking, but he wanted to ask Cate to the dance too. After all, she was the prettiest girl in their high school freshman class. The nicest too.

"I should've gone," Cate said as she sniffled and wiped her nose with the sleeve of her shirt. "Cheerleading practice ran long."

"So you didn't go? You don't know what he wanted?"

Cate touched Michael's arm. "Did he tell you?"

"No." Michael's response was quick. He turned away from Cate and went silent.

Finally, he mumbled, "it's not important now," and turned back around. Cate had tears running down her cheeks. Michael jumped up and off his bike, letting it crash to the ground with a thud.

"Don't cry. We'll find him," he reassured her. Then, he hugged her. He had never done that before, but it seemed like the right thing to do.

"I know it's silly." Cate backed up out of his hug. "I just keep thinking he's still out there."

"He can't be."

"What if he was upset with me?" Cate pulled at the roots of her hair with one hand, moving a strand back off her face, exposing her high cheekbones and greenish-blue eyes.

Thoughtfully, Michael spoke, "How could he be mad with you?"

"It's my fault."

"What's your fault?"

"What if he ran off because I stood him up?" Cate pointed at herself.

"He didn't run away," Michael said with certainty.

"How'd you know?"

"He's my friend too. He wouldn't do that."

Cate pushed herself up onto her Schwinn with a leg. "Let's go."

"We're still going?" She didn't answer as she pedaled away. "Wait up. I'm coming."

Cate made a sudden turn off the paved road, causing her to lose balance and almost topple sideways. Catching herself, she rebounded and propelled her bike, down the long dirt trail. As Michael lagged behind, she came to a stop at a rickety foot bridge at the edge of the marsh. This was the spot. The spot where she and Ryan were to have met. The spot where he'd once kissed her.

Cate gingerly walked across the haphazard bridge and came to a stand on the soft, mushy edge of a small fishing pond surrounded by skunk cabbage, ferns, and cattails. The murky pond surface was littered with floating green lily pads with cup-shaped white flowers in full bloom.

She moved along the water's edge, looking down for any sign that Ryan had been there. There was not one blade of broken or bent grass—not one shoe indentation left in the mud. Cate winced as a large dragonfly swooped by her ear and landed on a lily pad as if to mock her. "He's not here," she yelled back across the bridge.

"You really didn't think he'd be here." Michael bellowed as he approached.

"I knew it was a long shot." Cate closed her eyes and took a deep breath in. The smell of mud and decaying vegetation permeated the air. Tears welled up in the corners of her eyes once again.

Michael tapped her on the shoulder. "I think we should head back to town. Meet up with the search party, see if they've had any luck."

Cate turned to face him. "There's nothing here. No sign of him at all." She threw her arms up in disgust. "Doesn't it bother you?"

"Of course it does. I just think, coming out here was a waste of time."

"A waste of time!"

"Yes. He was last seen in town. Not out here."

"You're right. But this was our place."

"Your place?"

"Yeah. We...we liked each other." Cate coyly conveyed with pleading eyes.

Michael looked down at his feet. "Oh." He burrowed the toe of one of his tennis shoes into the mud.

"Ryan never said anything to you?"

Michael looked back up into Cate's sad eyes. "Let's go." Then he turned and ran back across the bridge. Cate followed and watched as he jumped on his bike and took off like a gale of wind.

Uprighting her bike, Cate hopped on and pedaled until they were riding side by side. "Michael." He stared straight ahead. "Michael." Not even the turn of his head. "What's wrong?" Still nothing. They rode in silence until they reached the edge of Meadowbrook.

"Look." Michael pointed to a telephone pole. Cate turned to see. There was a poster with Ryan's yearbook photo and the word MISS-ING in bold black letters. As they pedaled down Main Street, every telephone pole had the same poster on it, foot patrolmen walked the sidewalks, and groups of parents with children called out Ryan's name. Together, they joined the search, making their way up and down every street in Meadowbrook. Having had no luck, at dusk, they split up and went home. As darkness set in, Cate and Michael were in the safety of each of their homes, and Ryan was still out there.

CHAPTER 1

EMILY THOMPSON LIFTED A SWEATING glass of iced tea to her dry, parched lips as she fanned herself with the latest issue of *People* magazine. Not even the gentle breeze that rustled the once vibrant maple leaves was a relief. Her husband, Nicholas, seated next to her, wiped his damp forehead with a tissue. There was no escaping the sweltering August heat. Trying to make the best of the day, they slowly rocked in their favorite white cane chairs on their backyard deck.

"I can't do this another second," exclaimed Nicholas.

"Do what?" Emily looked up from her magazine.

"Melt." Nicholas lifted his arms above his head, showing off his sweaty, stained underarms. "Look."

"What choice do we have? The electric company is doing rolling brownouts."

"Let's head to the shore. With an ocean breeze, it'll be cooler."

"How about Atlantic City? It's midweek. I bet we can get a comp room at one of the casinos. I'll call Sarah. We'll make a trip of it."

"I'd prefer if it was just us."

"But...it'd be fun to have company." Emily's face lit up as she flashed her husband a big, bright smile. The same one that had enticed him to ask her out on their first date.

"Please, Emily. Just this once, let me have my way."

"As you wish." She nodded in agreement. Nicholas asked for little; it was the least she could do, but it was so unlike him. "I'll make some calls." It must be the heat, thought Emily as she walked away shaking her head.

"I'll be here melting." Nicholas chuckled.

Before his retirement four years earlier, the last place you would've found Nicholas Thompson was in a casino. He had worked too hard as a civil engineer to gamble or, as he had mentioned a time or two, "throw his hard-earned money away." His retirement brought on many changes to their daily routines—some positive, like trips to Atlantic City, and some not, like tripping over each other. Their three children, Cate, Todd, and Paige, were all grown and self-sufficient, and before there were grandchildren to dote on, Emily and Nicholas wanted to reconnect with one another. It was their time to focus on themselves, to rekindle old friendships that had slipped by the wayside while working and raising a family, and a time to just enjoy each day. Some days were horrifying as they rediscovered one another, and others were exciting, like finding a shiny new penny as a child. It took some effort to learn to respect each other's space, but when the adjustment period was over, they laughed together harder than they had in years and fell deeper in love than ever before.

The Thompsons were lifelong residents of Meadowbrook. In fact, they were high school sweethearts. Crazy in love and impatient to marry, they took the plunge the June after Nicholas graduated from Rutgers University. Twelve months later, their first daughter, Cate, was born and followed by Todd five years after and another girl, Paige, three years after that. Finances were tight in those early years, but love, laughter, and respect got them through then, and it would get through retirement too.

After two nights in a casino hotel room with an ocean view overlooking the Atlantic City boardwalk, Emily and Nicholas headed back home. Emily, exhausted from dinner, a show, and playing blackjack to the wee hours of the morning, began to doze off just as dusk was settling in. They had just driven over the most eastern tributary of the Cattail Creek River, which flowed east toward the US Atlantic Ocean, when she was jolted awake by the sudden and erratic turn Nicholas made onto the Parkway off ramp.

"What're you doing?" Emily asked as they continued down the ramp and merged onto the local highway that lead to Meadowbrook. Nicholas accelerated. "Why are you speeding up?"

"There's an idiot on my tail. He's been on my ass for the last ten minutes. I'm trying to shake him."

"If he's in that much of a hurry, just pull over. Let him pass." Nick conceded to his wife's better judgment and slowed the car, pulling it onto the shoulder of the highway. Once the oversized black pickup sped by, he eased their car back onto the darkened roadway.

"Look," Emily shouted. "The truck. It just did a one-eighty."

"What the hell? It's headed straight at us. Hold on, Emme!" Nicholas called out as he tried to divert their vehicle out of the path of the oncoming truck. Quickly, he maneuvered the car onto the road's shoulder. The truck veered close to the driver's side as it passed. With perseverance in mind, Nicholas drove the car back onto the pavement. The truck stopped, circled around, and then barreled like a speeding train toward them. Having no other options, Nicholas swerved their vehicle into the oncoming lane. Thankfully, the lane was empty. The truck followed their lead, caught up to them, and nudged at the Thompsons' car bumper several times. Nicholas floored the gas, causing Emily's head to wrench backward. The large truck's engine revved once again as their car sped away. Then *bang*, a thunderous sound rang out as the truck rammed their vehicle. The impact forced them to spin off the highway and into a sandy gully along the road's shoulder.

The wheels of the Thompsons' car turned in place, kicking up a cloud of dust. Emily rounded her head to look behind. The two men in the front seat of the pickup were laughing.

"Let's make a run for it!" Emily yelled out as the truck began to charge toward them. Then, instinctively, with no time to spare, she opened her door. Before she could jump, there came a crunching impact of metal on metal. She was thrown several feet from the car and landed hard on the right side of her body. Her breath knocked out of her. She lay there dazed. She tried to scream but couldn't utter a sound. Paralyzed, with fear and in anguishing pain, she watched as their vehicle rolled on its side, teetered a moment, and then tumbled twice down the embankment with Nicholas in the driver's seat. She covered her eyes with a hand and gasped. The car came to a crashing halt at the bottom of a ditch. Emily's world went dark as she fell into unconsciousness.

"Emme, you okay?" Nicholas pleaded as he struggled to see through the darkness. There was little light so far off the highway. "We need to get out of here." His breathing was labored.

A smell of gas lingered in the air. Nicholas tried to reach out and touch his wife. "Where are you? It sounds like a car has stopped. Maybe...someone saw." Fighting off the excruciating pain coming from his chest, he closed his eyes and gritted his teeth. He reached deep inside for strength and screamed, "Help us!" Then, totally depleted, his head slumped forward into the deployed airbag.

"Is he alive?" came a voice from a shadowy figure, which seemed to have magically appeared alongside the vehicle. Nicholas opened one eye a sliver, just long enough to see the face of a man peering in through the glass. The crouching man turned away from the vehicle, looking at someone behind him. "I can't tell. His face is bloodied."

"Do I have to do everything myself? Get out of the way!" The short, stocky man was pushed aside. Another face was peering in at Nicholas. He recognized the second man's voice.

He opened both of his eyes, glaring back at him was pure evil. Suddenly, a shot rang out, bursting through the already shattered windshield.

"What about her? She landed up the hill," the short, stocky man asked.

"Leave her be. She's gone."

CHAPTER 2

⟪⟨∞⟩⟫

PAIGE THOMPSON GATHERED HER SHOULDER-LENGTH blond hair in both hands, pulling it upward and into a ponytail. It was her favorite time of day, just before the summer heat rose with the sun.

The morning air was cool and crisp. Her ponytail flopped back and forth as her feet pounded the Winding Creek Park trail. She aimlessly ran, her mind preoccupied with the exciting news she had received the day before.

Late in the afternoon, she was called into her boss' office. He advised her she was being promoted to director of the media department at the Williamstown Courier. She had been working toward the promotion for years, dreaming of one day having her own office. It was happening. All her hard work and travel for the last three years were about to pay off. Ever focused on her job and recognition as a professional photographer, Paige had taken every assignment, big and small, to get noticed. It had meant a lot of travel, but to Paige, it had all been worth it. Her travels had taken her across the US, photographing the best and worst of America.

She was humbled as she witnessed earthquake victims who had lost everything only to be thankful for their lives and in awe of the determination of abuse victims who pushed on after having endured the most undesirable of circumstances.

The promotion meant spending more time at home in Williamstown, which would've been great, if she hadn't broken up with her boyfriend of five years, six months earlier. Paige had just returned from a week-long assignment and had planned on spending a quiet, romantic evening at home with Jeremy. Jeremy was distant most of that evening, being more focused on his cell phone than the sexy negligee she was wearing. Not exactly the reception she was hoping for, or expecting.

Jeremy pulled his cell phone out of his pocket, read a text message on the screen, and then abruptly jumped up off the couch and headed to the kitchen.

"Where're you going?" Paige asked.

"It's work. I've been assigned a new client." He took a quick step. "A very needy one."

"Can't you just turn it off? I just got back from California." He ignored her and left the room.

Dumbfounded, Paige stared at the back of Jeremy's head as he walked away. When he returned, she couldn't read the blank expression on his face.

"What? You want me to stop working when all you do is work. You're never here," Jeremy blurted.

"You know my work is important."

"What about me?" He raised his voice.

"What's going on?" Paige walked to meet him halfway. She placed a hand on his arm. "I thought we were on the same page. Concentrating on work so that we can have a better future."

His eyes met hers. "It's been five years. I'm ready for more. I never know from week to week if you'll even be in town. Last week, I had a work dinner that I needed you at. I went alone. Lucky for me, Alexa was alone too."

"Whose Alexa?"

"Whose Alexa?" Jeremy stammered. "She's new. Transferred from the Phoenix office three months ago."

"You never mentioned you had a new coworker." Jeremy looked up and then down. "She's pretty, isn't she?"

"I don't know." He shrugged his shoulders. "Never thought about it." Jeremy's body nervously twitched ever so slightly.

"You like her!"

"No!"

"Yes, you do! I know you!"

"Well, what did you expect? I can't wait around forever."

"Forever? I was gone a week."

"A week this month. A week the month before."

"You should've said something."

"When? During our two-minute conversations every other day? At least Alexa is in town." He looked toward the front door, like a caged animal looking for an escape route.

"You cheating SOB." Paige turned her back to him.

"I can't do this anymore. You always put your job first." Jeremy edged closer.

Paige turned back. "I'm the bad person here?" She pointed to herself. "Why should I have to choose?"

He grasped her arm. "I need you here. Not running around who knows where." Paige stepped back, pulling her arm out of his grip. "She's been here for me. You haven't been."

"Get out! Get the fuck out!" Paige pointed toward the door. *Wow, how could she have been so wrong?*

It had taken months, but finally the sting of the breakup had worn off. Paige supposed the relationship had been convenient for both of them, and Jeremy was not the one for her. But, still, it was a hurtful and unpleasant experience. *I'll never let that happen again,* thought Paige as she stepped on a small tree branch. Her ankle turned outward, and she fell into the dirt.

"Damn it." Forced out of her thoughts and back to reality, she sat on the trail, rubbing her sore ankle. For the first time since she had set out on her run, she paused to take in her surroundings. The sun had fully risen. It was a beautiful summer day, the kind that made one want to play hooky from work. To her right was a small group of lady's slippers, each one with a pillowing, pink flower standing tall among a patch of teaberry plants. She reached over, picked a teaberry leaf, tore it in half, and held it to her nose. Its wintergreen-like fragrance reminded her of learning to make teaberry candy from the plant's steeped leaves at summer camp.

She pushed aside her delightful childhood memory as she realized where she had fallen. It was in the vicinity of where she'd found the shoe of a missing teenager while out on one of her morning runs. It was through her quick thinking the police had said that they were able to recover the young teen's unconscious body before it was too late. Paige had shrugged it off. All in a day's work to her. *Had her job desensitized her to gore and danger?* Anyone would've thought a soiled high heel in the woods was out of place. Especially if they had been paying attention to the news. The missing girl's face had been plastered across the television for the last twenty-four hours after she'd failed to return home from her high school prom. She'd just put one and one together. But it was true, not many would've deviated off the main trail on a gut feeling in search of its owner. Without any thought for her own personal safety and going on sheer instinct, she had wandered into the wooded area, not knowing what she would find. She recalled being frozen in shock at the sight of the missing girl's half-naked body at the edge of the stream.

Once her initial shock wore off, she had sprung into action. The teenager was alive, but barely. Paige called for help and then took off her own tee shirt to cover the girl's nakedness, leaving herself partly exposed in just a flowery running bra. Risk-taking was second nature to Paige. Without taking risks, she never would've been able to capture the award-winning photos that had earned her the promotion to head of the media department. The bigger the risk, the better the photo. That was her motto.

The pain in Paige's ankle subsided. She stood upright. Hesitantly, she put a small amount of pressure on her foot. She continued running down the trail until she emerged out onto the pavement that would take her home to her two-story Tudor-style townhouse. Sprinting past the community clubhouse, she turned left onto her street, Nottingham Lane. All the homes in the neighborhood looked alike. Block after block of brick buildings with white stucco, black trim, and matching black mailboxes.

As Paige put the key in her front-door lock, she heard the house phone ringing inside. She hurried to get in. Just as she picked up the receiver, the ringing stopped. It was her sister, Cate. She never called her on the house phone. Paige pulled her cell phone from her pocket and realized her sister had called three times. *I don't have time for another whine fest,* she thought as she climbed into the shower.

She had just gotten in the shower when the house phone rang again. The ringing stopped, and the answering machine came on. It was her sister again. "Paige, where are you? Mom and Dad have been in an accident." Paige jumped out of the shower, slipping and sliding across the floor, grabbing the phone just before Cate hung up.

"What's happened? Are they okay?"

"It's terrible. Dad is…dead." Cate's voice trailed off. There was silence on the other end of the line. Paige felt like she'd been punched in the gut and the wind knocked out of her.

"Cate! Are you still there?"

Finally, Cate spoke, "You need to come home right away."

"I…can't believe it. It's true? It can't be. How?"

"Their car went off the highway. Mom's in the hospital. Dad… they said he was dead at the scene…" Cate's voice broke for a second time.

"Dad. Dead. And Mom?"

"Mom's unconscious."

"I'm on my way. Did you call Todd?" Paige went into work mode.

"He's catching a plane. Just get here!"

"I'm on my way." Unexpectedly, Paige's knees weakened and buckled. She collapsed to the floor—crumpled, naked, and sobbing uncontrollably. "Dead at the scene" ran through her mind.

When she was finally able to force herself up, she threw herself onto her bed and buried her face in a pillow. As she cried, her chest heaving in and out, her yellow tabby nudged at the top of her head. She lifted her face from the pillow and pulled the purring cat in toward her.

Jeremy had surprised her with Tiger on her last birthday. *Most likely a lame attempt to control and domesticate her,* she'd thought at the time. No matter how she'd come by Tiger, she adored him and was grateful for the comfort he offered.

As the shock faded, Paige began to concentrate on the task at hand, getting home to New Jersey. She telephoned her neighbor. "Becca, can you come over?"

"What's going on? It's early."

"I need to get home to New Jersey today. My parents were in a car accident."

Within five minutes, Becca was at Paige's front door. She was fully dressed for work in a short gray skirt and yellow pastel blouse. She carried two cups of hot coffee. Becca was a petite brunette with a short pixie haircut which accentuated her emerald eyes. So unlike Paige, with her thick dirty-blond mane, light-brown eyes, and broad shoulders.

Becca and Paige shared a bond that went far beyond the common wall in between the two townhouses. Two weeks after Paige had moved into the community, there was a loud thud against her front door and a shrill cry for help. Paige called 911, grabbed the baseball bat from beneath her bed, and ran outside to take a swing at the attacking man. When the police arrived, Becca's assaulting boyfriend was nowhere to be found and Becca was forever grateful to her new neighbor.

"Thanks for coming over so quickly." Paige paused before continuing. "My mom is alive. She may have internal injuries. Dad wasn't as lucky."

Becca set the two cups of coffee on the small kitchen table and hugged Paige. "I'm so sorry. What can I do?"

"Can you watch Tiger for me? I need to leave this morning."

"Of course."

Paige began frantically throwing clothes into her suitcase, a few dresses along with her favorite jeans, sweats, and some tops. "Hospital, funeral, family."

Becca nodded her head in agreement. "Will you be okay to drive?"

"Of course. You know me." She gave Becca a small smile.

"I hate to leave you, but I need to get to work. You'll be okay?"
Paige nodded her head. "Yes."

"You drive careful. Call me if you need anything."

"You're the best."

Once packed, Paige threw her suitcase along with her laptop and camera bag into the rear seat of her white Jeep Cherokee. She drove toward 64 West, which would take her to Highway 95 North. Once on 95, it was a straight beeline to New Jersey. She tried to focus on the road, but images of the accident loomed before her. Her father had taught her how to drive. He was a good driver. How could he have gone off the road? She could hear his words, "Don't ever trust another driver's turn signal until they have committed to the turn." His wise advice had helped her avoid several collisions over the years. *It just doesn't add up.*

It was a six-hour drive from Williamstown, Virginia, to Meadowbrook, New Jersey, and if all went well, Paige would be at the hospital by 3:00 p.m. Paige scanned for radio stations. She paused at WCON Country. Miranda Lambert's "The House That Built Me" piped through the speakers. "This brokenness inside me might start healing…" Paige pulled her vehicle onto the shoulder of the highway. She turned off the Jeep. Tears uncontrollably streamed, like an open faucet, from the corners of her eyes. The song ended. She remained still, in a zombie-like state, staring at nothing. It may've been five minutes. It may've been twenty. Paige didn't know exactly how long she'd been idle when a tandem tractor trailer sped past, rocking her vehicle.

She blinked, dabbed her eyes and blew her nose, and then called Cate. "I should be there in three hours. Any news on Mom?"

"Take the elevator in the ER lobby to the fourth floor. Follow the signs for the OR waiting room. That's where I am," Cate instructed.

"The OR waiting room?"

"The results came back from the CAT scan. The trauma team has taken Mom to the operating room. They need to repair a tear to her aorta. Immediately. Say a prayer."

Paige got back on the road with a new sense of urgency, her mind reeling. *How can this be happening? It must be a bad dream. I can't lose my father and mother in the same day.* She must've been flying along because two and a half hours later, she was pulling into the hospital parking lot.

Paige maneuvered through the hospital halls until she found Cate, sitting alone, in the corner of the OR waiting room. Her eyes were shut with an unopened copy of *Cosmo* in her lap and a navy sweater draped over her shoulders. It had been two years since the sisters had seen one another. As usual, Cate looked trim and well put together. Her short auburn hair was smartly cut and shaped around her face. Paige had always been envious of Cate's high metabolism that kept her slim no matter what she ate. She, on the other hand, had to exercise all the time or risk gaining weight.

Paige tapped Cate on the hand. Her eyes opened wide. "I'm so glad you're here," said Cate as she stood and wrapped her arms around Paige and hung on tight. "I'm worried. The doctor hasn't come out yet." Cate's knees weakened and she fell into Paige. Paige supported her and lowered her down into a chair.

"Are you here alone? Where's Mark?"

"He went to the morgue…to check on Dad's whereabouts…I don't…I couldn't…do it."

"I get it," Paige whispered.

Cate reached into her large designer handbag and pulled out a travel-size pack of tissues. "You can't know." She gently dabbed at the corners of each eye, careful not to smudge her mascara.

"You're right, I can't." *It's just not worth the time or effort.* "Is there a bathroom close by? It was a long drive."

"The restrooms are down the hall. On the left. Just past the elevators."

Paige left the waiting area and headed back the way she'd come in. As she passed the elevators, she noticed a sign that read MORGUE–BASEMENT.

CHAPTER 3

AFTER USING THE RESTROOM, PAIGE headed back to the waiting room. As she passed the elevators, she stopped. She read the sign again: MORGUE–BASEMENT. As if taken over by another being, without conscious thought, she pushed the elevator down button. Just then, the doors opened and there stood Mark. Her brother-in-law was a self-assured, handsome man of 6'3" with brown hair and a splash of gray around the temples. His hazel eyes were open wide with surprise at the sight of her.

"You made it. How was the trip?"

Paige wasn't in the mood. "Did you see his body? Is he down there?"

"No. I didn't see it. They said it might be days before his body's released."

"I'm going down there." Paige was determined.

"I don't think it's the place for you."

"I've seen a dead body or two, *what with photographing victims of storms and riots and all...*you know, for my job?"

"I'm sure you have. But it's different when it's your own father."

"It's unbelievable. A nightmare." Paige softened her tone.

"Something about having to fully examine his body before releasing it to the family."

"It's been hours. They must know something by now," Paige insisted.

"They told me it's not unusual."

"I'll give them till tomorrow. Then I want answers."

"It's not up to us. Why don't we go back and sit with Cate?"

"I need caffeine."

21

"You can go to the café. Or there's a coffee machine down the end of this corridor."

Mark glanced down the hall at his wife. "I'll go sit with Cate."

"She's not doing well."

"Why would she be? Her dad is dead! Your dad!" Paige leveled her gaze. *He doubted her. How dare he?*

"You moved away," he continued.

"So? What does that have to do with this?"

"You never visit. Then something like this happens. Here you are after the fact."

"Who are you kidding? Cate loves playing martyr."

"Go get your coffee." Mark's cold stare grew frigid. He turned and walked away.

Paige went in the opposite direction, shaking her head. *He's probably mad because he's had to put something of his own on hold to deal with his wife.*

Paige found the vending machine and was digging through her satchel for change when a deep masculine voice sounded from behind. "Allow me. This machine is temperamental."

Paige whipped around and found herself staring into the face of a tall, handsome, well-dressed man in a navy suit. His lips were slightly turned upward in a sheepish grin. His blue eyes danced across her face. Her heart skipped a beat. She wasn't sure why; was it because she was startled? Or was it that she was blindsided by his dashing good looks?

"That's not necessary. If I dig deep enough, I'm sure I'll come up with some change," Paige stammered.

"It's my pleasure. What's your poison?" He moved in.

Paige stepped aside. "I was hoping to get a cup of coffee. The stronger, the better."

The stranger reached into his pants' pocket, pulled out four quarters, and proceeded to insert them into the change acceptor. He pushed in one of the tiny red buttons. Immediately, a cup dropped, and hot liquid streamed downward. Once the paper cup was full, the man lifted the cup, turned toward Paige, and handed it to her. When the taste of sweet, luscious chocolate touched Paige's lips, she smiled for the first time all day.

"Much better." He smiled. "The coffee out of this machine is dreadful," he added.

"It's just what I needed. Thank you." Paige turned, taking a step to leave.

"Anything I can help with?"

She turned back around. "I hate to be rude, but I don't even know who you are."

"I'm sorry. I never introduced myself. I'm Michael. Michael Wilson."

"Paige Thompson." She smiled at him again. "I really must go." Paige quickly walked away, glad she had at least tidied herself when she had used the restroom. Back in the waiting room, she sat down quietly alongside Cate and Mark. They waited. *What was taking so long?*

As time dragged on, Paige began to doze off. Cate and Mark whispered back and forth. Abruptly, Mark stood and left.

"What's up with him?" Paige asked.

"Something to do with work. That's all he does." *Well, she had asked.*

"Give the man a break."

Just then, the two doors that led to the operating suite opened wide. "Thompson family," called a doctor wearing surgical green scrubs. Paige and Cate both stood.

"We're her daughters." Cate waved him over.

"Your mother has a strong heart. We put a stent in and repaired the tear in her aorta. She'll be going to the recovery wing shortly."

"And her broken hip?" Cate wrapped her arms around her middle.

"We need to be cautious. Your mother needs to be monitored closely. If all goes as planned, the orthopedic will be able to repair it tomorrow."

"Thank you, Dr. McAllister." Paige let out her breath.

"Once she's settled in recovery, you'll be able to see her. However, I must warn you, she'll still be unconscious."

The color began to return to Cate's face. She looked down to read a message on her cell phone. "Todd's landed. He's coming straight to the hospital."

"I haven't seen Todd in over a year."

"You saw Todd last year?"

"I thought I told you."

"No."

"Oh… It was when I was on assignment in Vegas last April."

"You didn't tell me."

"Thought I did. It was a short trip." Paige shrugged. "Just three days. Todd and I went hiking and camping at the Grand Canyon."

"I've always wanted to see the Grand Canyon."

"You and Mark should take a trip there. I took some spectacular photos of the waterfalls. You need to see them. They're beautiful. They plunge…" Paige moved her arm in a downward motion. "Something like…a hundred feet. Into pools of blue-green water."

"Mark says he can't take time off for a big trip."

"Then go by yourself. Stay with Todd."

"I don't like to travel alone." Sullen, Cate sat back down and opened her magazine.

Paige sat next to her, checked her phone for work messages, and then nodded off. When Cate finished reading the magazine, she picked up another and began to flip through it. Then hastily, she shut it. "What's taking so long?" Paige sat straight up and opened her eyes.

"Todd will be here as soon as he can."

"Not Todd, the doctor," said Cate.

"Don't worry. Soon."

Cate's eyes gravitated to the wall clock. "It's been forty-five minutes. Todd should've been here by now." When Cate looked back, Todd was standing in front of her.

"Did I hear my name?"

"Todd!" Paige jumped up, out of her seat, and gave him a tight hug. "What's this?" She tugged on his facial growth.

"Hey, it keeps me warm in winter." He chuckled. Cate stood up. "Got here quick as I could." Todd gave Cate the comforting hug that she'd needed.

"It's been terrible! Why do you have to live so far away?" Todd and Paige shared a brief look.

"Fill me in. What exactly happened?"

"They were on their way back from Atlantic City," Cate explained. "It was dark. They got off the parkway at their usual exit. Then the car went off the road. It ended up in a ditch."

"Unbelievable," responded Todd.

"It is," added Cate.

"What made them go off the road? It's a straight away. Did they hit a deer?"

"I don't know. I came right to the hospital. Mom was already here. The police said the car was totaled. That Dad was dead. I sent Mark to the accident scene."

"Well, where's Mark? Does he have details?" Todd asked.

"They wouldn't tell him anything! Said he had to stay behind the tape. He tried to see what was going on," explained Cate.

"Someone must know."

"You call the police. Maybe they'll tell you something." Cate looked at Todd, the frustration of the situation clearly showing on her face. "I've other calls to make. It's the least you can do."

"Aye, aye." Todd saluted. Paige giggled.

"You two are so insensitive. This is not a time for jokes."

"You're right." Todd shook his head in agreement. "We're all in shock. It just...doesn't seem real. I'll do what I can."

"Just let me call the relatives," said Cate as she began to walk away.

"She's scared," said Todd. "She means well."

"I know," replied Paige.

Cate pulled out her cell phone and dialed Aunt Dorothy, their mother's sister. She was always the first person you called when you needed the whole family to know something. Cate moved further down the hall and disappeared.

As Paige began to sit down alongside Todd, Michael Wilson entered the OR waiting area. His eyes locked with Paige's as he approached. "I was hoping you'd still be here."

"Are you following me?" Paige asked. Todd stood up.

"No. Well, yes. I guess I am. It occurred to me after you walked away that you must be one of Nicholas and Emily Thompson's children."

"Yes… I am. This is my brother, Todd." Michael extended his hand toward Todd. "Our sister Cate just walked away."

Paige pointed toward the hallway and then turned to look at Todd. "We met at the vending machine." Paige reservedly looked back toward Michael. Her cheeks warmed and flushed.

Suddenly, she felt extremely underdressed in her blue jeans and white cotton tee.

"Our parents are old friends. I heard about the accident. Please accept my deepest condolences on the loss of your father."

"Thank you," said Todd.

"My mother has often spoken of your parents," said Michael.

"Of course, I remember your parents. Don't you?" Paige looked at Todd.

"Right…yeah." Todd nodded.

"I'll let you be. I hope your mother has a quick recovery. If you need anything"—Michael handed Paige his business card—"give me a call."

Once he was out of sight, Todd grabbed the card from Paige's hand. "Let me see that. Michael Wilson, Attorney-At-Law," Todd read out loud.

"What was that all about?"

"I told you. I ran into him at the vending machine."

"Looks like little sister has an admirer." Then in a more serious tone, he added, "I don't like him."

"You just met him."

"So did you! Something about him doesn't feel right. How did he hear about the accident?"

"You're being silly! You know those lawyer types. They have connections. He was just being nice."

"Nice to you." Todd poked her in the arm. "Seriously, I don't like him. The Wilsons have been friends with Mom and Dad all these years, and neither of us has ever met him. Doesn't make sense?"

"You're making too much of it." But Todd was right about one thing, Paige didn't recall ever meeting Michael Wilson before.

"I saw him down in the ER when I came in. He was in a heated conversation with a shady-looking man in a black hoody," Todd went on.

"He's a lawyer. It was probably a client."

"That's how he talks to clients? He was loud. Angry."

"I don't know. I wasn't there!" Paige loudly rebuffed.

"What are you two fighting about?" Cate interrupted. "Who was that?"

"He said he was the Wilsons' son, Michael. We don't remember him. Do you?"

Todd looked up at Cate from his seated position. Her face went pale. "Michael Wilson! Are you serious?"

"What? You know him?" asked Paige.

"I did. We went to school together. Long time ago. You two wouldn't remember."

"Remember what?"

"I don't want to think about it! You were practically babies. At least you were." Cate looked at Paige.

"Yeah, yeah, that's me," said Paige. *Always the baby!*

"What did he want?" Cate asked.

"Gave the family his condolences. Offered his services." Todd handed Michael's business card to Cate. "He's an attorney."

"I don't care what he is. Stay away from him."

"Why?" asked Paige.

"Just stay away."

"He seemed nice." Paige pulled the business card from Cate's fingers.

"Looks can be deceiving!" Cate scowled at Paige. "I've called everyone. Now, funeral homes. I need to see what's available."

"Shouldn't we hold off? We've no idea as to when we can schedule a funeral. We need to think of Mom. She'd want to be there. If she can. Besides, the medical examiner hasn't released Dad's body. Mark said it could be days," reasoned Paige.

"Three days is customary," Cate snapped back.

Paige flinched. *Time to stay out of her way.*

"It was an accident. How long could it take?" Cate went on.

"Maybe he had a medical incident or something. We need to get all the facts," Todd chimed in.

The phone rang at the waiting room desk. "Where's the volunteer?" Cate bellowed.

"She stepped away." Todd pointed toward the doorway.

"The doctor said they'd call the desk with updates. I'm answering it."

"Cate, you just can't..." Paige began.

"OR waiting room," Cate spoke into the receiver.

"I need to speak to a family member of Emily Thompson," the voice on the line said.

"Please hold." Cate pushed the hold button, counted to three, and then pushed the hold button again. "This is Cate Andrews." She listened and then hung up the phone. "She's in recovery. We can see her." Cate pushed back the desk chair. "Let's go. Recovery is down the hall and to the right." Paige and Todd rolled their eyes and then followed Cate down the corridor and into recovery room D. Their mother lay unconscious with an IV in her arm and an oxygen mask covering most of her face. "She looks terrible. Look at the bruises on her arms and forehead." Cate leaned over and fiddled with her mother's hair.

"She's breathing on her own. That's a good sign." Todd moved and took hold of the bed's side railing. Paige hung back a moment, watching as Cate pulled the sheet up further to cover their mother's arms.

Just as Paige stepped up to the bed, a nurse entered. "You need to leave. She needs rest."

"We just got here. I want to stay," Cate replied.

"I suppose it'd be okay for one of you to stay a bit longer. But not all."

"I'm staying," Cate reaffirmed. "You two can go drop your stuff off at Mom and Dad's. While you're there, check on things. And call Mark. Tell him where I am. Tell him to get back here."

"You sure you want to stay?" Todd asked Cate. "You've been here for hours. You look like you could use some rest."

"I'm fine. Just do as I ask."

Paige pulled at Todd's arms. "Let's go. You heard her. She's fine."

CHAPTER 4

WHEN PAIGE PULLED UP TO her parents' cape cod, Todd was waiting at the front door. "How'd you get here so fast?" she yelled across the yard.

"Do you have a key?" he yelled back.

"I have one, but it's from when we were kids," said Paige as she approached the porch. "Who knows if it'll work."

"Might as well try."

The chamber on the door lock clicked. "Yes." Paige turned the knob and swung the door inward. "It feels odd going in the house without Mom and Dad being here," she said as she hesitantly stepped inside. Todd followed. Paige moved slowly from room to room, turning on all the lights as she went.

"Are you still afraid of the dark?" Todd asked as he parted the living room bay window curtains and peered out. "Did you see the dark sedan idling across the street? The man in it was looking at this house."

"Why would anyone be watching this house?"

"Don't know." Todd moved and peeked out the side window blinds. "It's gone. Guess it was nothing." He surveyed the living room as he swung back around. "Wow...nothing has changed since the last time I was home."

"When was that?"

"Must be...almost three years. Time flies by fast. Plus, it's expensive to fly home."

"I'm hoping to get out to Arizona again. I had a great time when I visited. The photos I took of the canyon came out great. I'll have to show you. So much color and depth."

"How long since you've been home?" asked Todd.

"Almost two years. Work has been crazy. But that's no excuse," Paige admitted. "I should've tried harder. I thought they'd be here forever."

"We all did. Where's Jeremy? Didn't he come with you?" Paige gave Todd a scathing glare.

He shrugged his shoulders. "What?"

"We broke up months ago. I told you. He was sleeping with some slut from his office."

"Oh, shit… I'm sorry, sis. You did tell me."

"That's all right. I'm *so* over him."

"He didn't deserve you."

"What about you? Last we talked you were dating that brunette schoolteacher, Diane?"

"She's old news. You know me, on to the next."

Paige gave the room a glance. "You're right. Everything is the same." The living room still had beige walls, white trim, and brown carpeting. The only difference seemed to be that the tiny nine-teen-inch television, which had served as a hub of activity while growing up, had been replaced with a forty-two-inch flat screen.

Paige turned on the light at the top of the staircase that led up to the bedrooms. There hung her high school graduation portrait along with Todd's and Cate's. Cate with her darker hair, light eyes, and delicate features looked out of place next to Todd's and Paige's blond hair, light-brown eyes, and rugged looks. There was no arguing. Cate was beautiful.

"I'm taking my suitcase up to my old room," Paige shouted to Todd, who had disappeared into the kitchen. Once upstairs, Paige placed her suitcase next to her childhood bed.

She walked over to the cork bulletin board that had once held all her pictures, postcards, and treasures as a child and now replaced with dried flowers and various greeting cards her mother had received over the years. She opened the top drawer of a tall bureau and found an old shoebox filled with childhood mementos—her high school softball and field hockey varsity letters, a dried corsage of yellow roses, and silly, candid photos of old friends. She was surrounded by her past.

It was comforting and familiar, and it triggered a deep longing for a stable, steady life. With her job promotion, she hoped it'd allow her to have it.

Flipping through the photos, she realized that most of them had Nathan Edgemont in them. She paused when she came upon her senior prom picture. Her hair was up in a bun with pin curls framing her face. She had spent weeks picking out a full-length tangerine dress. *That was a fun night. The Hilton's largest ballroom filled with silver and purple balloons and a sparkling, psychedelic disco ball pulsing overhead to the music.*

"I thought you wouldn't be coming?" said Samantha to Paige when they were alone in the ladies' room.

"You heard about Jim's grandfather?"

"Yes. How terrible."

"I feel bad for him. Maybe I shouldn't have come."

"Of course you should be here." Samantha leaned over the sink as she applied shiny pink lip gloss. "It's our senior prom. You can't miss it."

Paige shifted her body and adjusted her bodice. "Jim insisted I come. He even dropped off this beautiful corsage." Paige lifted her wrist.

"Yellow roses! Even Jim understands. So stop feeling bad and have some fun."

Samantha offered Paige her lip gloss. "Here, try this."

"I've got my own," said Paige as she opened her silver clutch.

"Did you see Nathan? He's looking cute and he's here alone."

"Where's Amanda?"

"He didn't tell you? I thought you and he were best buds."

"We were...we are."

"You were?"

"Things have been different this year. He's always with Amanda."

"Someone's jealous," said Samantha as they exited the ladies' room.

"No, I'm not. She's just not right for him."

"You don't have to worry anymore. She broke up with him."

"Before the prom. That's heartless," said Paige.

"No one knows why. I bet he'll tell you."

"Maybe," said Paige as they entered the ballroom.

Nathan, looking like James Bond in a tuxedo, was standing near the dance floor, laughing with a group of guys from the baseball team. *He doesn't look heartbroken,* thought Paige as she approached the group and tapped him on the arm. Nathan twisted around. "Hi. I didn't expect to see you," he said.

"You knew I was coming," answered Paige.

"Yeah, but Jim said he wasn't. I just assumed..."

"I wasn't going to. I feel bad his grandfather died, but he said he'd feel worse if I missed the prom because of him."

"He's a nice guy," said Nathan.

"He is. I'm glad you suggested he ask me to prom."

"I'm happy you're here. I won't feel so awkward being the only one stag."

"Sorry about you and Amanda. I just heard."

"Let's not talk about her," said Nathan. "You look great."

"You're looking pretty great yourself."

"Would you like to dance?"

"With you?" Paige snickered. "Remember the last time we tried to dance?"

"I can dance," said Nathan.

"I'll be the judge."

Nathan grabbed Paige's hand and swung her around onto the dance floor. "Impressed?" he said as he pulled her in and placed a hand on her waist.

"Yes."

Nathan smiled. "Amanda made me take lessons. She didn't want me to embarrass her."

"What happened with you two?"

"Long story short."

"Sure."

"She wanted me to be someone I wasn't."

"We don't have to talk about it."

"Good," said Nathan as he spun her out once again and pulled her back in. The music slowed and Nathan placed a hand on each side of Paige's waist. She intertwined her fingers around the back of his neck. Awkwardly, they stepped about the dance floor. Paige kept her eyes straight ahead, trying to avoid direct eye contact. Finally, she glanced up. His eyes were fixated on hers. Her heart fluttered and she dropped her hands down. "Is something wrong?" he asked.

"I'm getting tired." Paige quickly turned away. "I think I'll sit."

He caught her by the arm. "We don't have to dance. How about we get our picture before the line gets too long?"

"Do you think we should?"

"Why not?"

"You're right, let's do this," said Paige, having shaken off her fleeting enchantment with Nathan.

Paige put her memories back, along with the photos in the shoe-box, and headed back downstairs. "Where are you?" she called out.

"In the kitchen," answered Todd.

"You've been in here quite a while," said Paige as she stood in the kitchen doorway.

"The window over the sink was open."

"Dad was fanatical about locking the house."

"I know. He never would've left a window open."

"Maybe he forgot."

"Maybe?"

"I better get some snacks together and head back to the hospital. Cate asked me to bring a small throw blanket too."

"I'll stay here. I'm going to check the rest of the house and then try to locate their wills."

"They're probably in Dad's desk."

"Call me when you get to the hospital," said Todd.

By the time Paige was circling the hospital parking lot, looking for a spot close to the front lobby doors, it was almost 11:00 p.m. It was an extremely dark night with no moon in the sky.

On her second pass through the lot, she noticed a dark sedan idling in a handicap spot with no handicap plates. The scruffy-looking man sitting in the driver's seat was smoking a cigarette and seemed oblivious to her presence.

Paige parked, walked around the illegally parked vehicle, and stepped through the lobby doors. After showing ID to a security guard, she wandered through a maze of hallways to the recovery waiting room where she found Cate and Mark. They looked tired and in need of showers. "Hey, you two. I brought some sandwiches and snacks. How is she?" Mark snatched the lunch bag from Paige.

"The nurse was just here. Mom's being moved to the intensive care unit," said Cate.

"She's going to be okay? Isn't she?"

"She's holding her own. Once she's moved, we can see her again." Cate sounded hopeful.

"Now that I'm back, you two can head home."

Mark jumped up. "Sounds good to me. I've work in the morning."

"I'm not going anywhere," said Cate. Mark gave his wife a hug and a peck on the lips, and left.

"He can be such a selfish ass."

"He can't be that selfish. He stayed here with you all evening." Paige pointed out.

"He was here. But not with me. He spent the whole time on his phone."

"Doing what?"

"Calling the office, his assistant, clients."

"That's called work. Even when terrible things happen, we all have bills to pay."

"You wouldn't understand. You're not married."

"What does that have to do with paying the bills? You're lucky. You don't have to drag yourself out of bed every day. Like the rest of us."

"Boy, have you changed."

"So have you."

"I may not bring home a paycheck, but I work hard around the house every day. Even though no one appreciates it. Maybe you'd understand my life a little if you'd gotten married. You let a good man go when you broke up with Jeremy."

"You don't know anything. Jeremy was a lying, cheating SOB."

"You just don't throw away a five-year relationship on a mistake. If you don't show a little forgiveness and understanding, you'll never be able to keep a man."

"Excuse me. This isn't about forgiveness. This is about betrayal. You sound like you've been talking to Jeremy. You're my *sister*! You're supposed to be on *my* side."

"I *am* on your side."

"It's none of your business."

"Don't you want to get married?"

"If I find the right man. Maybe. Why do you care so much? You want me to happy, like you?" Paige regretted her sarcasm instantly. She was happily saved by a nurse in blue scrubs, emerging through the recovery room doors.

"Your mother has been settled in ICU. Why don't you two follow me. You can see her now," the nurse informed them. Paige and Cate both stood and followed the nurse, who continued to instruct them. "You'll need to put on a gown, mask, and gloves before you enter. There's a cart just outside her room. Make sure you put them on each time you go in to see her."

"That's so that we don't spread our germs. She's very susceptible to infections right now." Cate felt the need to explain as they walked into the ICU wing.

"You have fifteen minutes," the nurse said as she directed them into room 319. Emily Thompson looked helpless—in a deep sleep, doped up on morphine, and hooked up to a heart monitor. Paige fought back tears as she took hold of her mother's hand.

"It's cold in here." Cate pulled their mom's blanket higher up, tucking it under her chin.

"She looks pale. She needs her hair brushed." Cate touched and fixed everything she could until the nurse reappeared fifteen minutes later. "You'll have to leave now. Visiting hours start at 9:00 a.m. for ICU. You can come back then."

"Come on, Cate. Let's go."

"I don't want to leave her...all by herself."

"I know you don't, but we need to leave. The nurse said we can see her again at 9:00 a.m. It's already midnight."

Cate kissed her mother's forehead and then whispered, "Love you, Mom." Paige did the same.

"I don't want to go home. Something could happen. You heard the doctor the next twenty-four hours are critical," said Cate.

"If you're staying, I'm staying," said Paige as they headed down the hall and out the electric ICU doors. Just outside the doors, they found a waiting room with a comfortable couch and television. They huddled together under the one small blanket which Paige had brought back with her. Exhausted, Paige dozed off.

"I can't sleep," Cate announced as she tapped Paige on the arm.

"What? I'm tired. What time is it?" Paige mumbled.

"Almost 6:00 a.m."

"I need sleep."

Cate tugged at Paige's ponytail. "What's this? Are you ever going to cut your hair?"

Paige pushed Cate's hand away. "Stop!"

"You'd look so much prettier if you'd shape this mop. Put on a little more makeup."

"It's been a long day. Leave me alone," said Paige.

"A little cranky, aren't we?"

Paige stood up and threw the blanket on the couch. "Why can't you just leave people alone? You're always picking," she added as she stormed away down the corridor toward the front lobby. Her only thought was to put some distance between herself and Cate. "Pick, pick, pick," she shouted over her shoulder.

CHAPTER 5

PAIGE DROVE OUT OF THE hospital lot and headed east. After driving a good five minutes, she recognized the Broadway Café. She was only a short distance from the beach. The quiet serenity of the waves crashing on the sand and the smell of the salty ocean were exactly what she needed to clear her mind.

She found her favorite bench along the boardwalk, sat down, and took a deep breath in. In a near-comatose trance, she gazed out over the water, trying to make sense of the senselessness of the last twenty-four hours. The orange glow of the sun began to peek up over the horizon. Rays of yellow, orange, and red danced across distant rippling waves. She was mesmerized by nature's colorful display, and here, at last, she found a moment of peace.

The sun rose higher above the water as day broke, and she wondered why it had taken her so many years to come back. This was the place where she'd played in the sand along the shoreline as a small child, building sandcastles and collecting sea glass with Cate, while her father and brother fished off the rocky jetty. She thought of her mother sitting near the water's edge in a rainbow-colored sand chair reading the latest *New York Times* bestseller, looking beautiful with her brown hair pulled back and wearing oversized pink sunglasses.

Paige welcomed the wave of calmness that overcame her as the memories flooded her heart and mind. She turned her face up toward the rising sun. She closed her eyes and inhaled deeply once again, letting the warmth of the sun's rays drape over her body like a blanket. The screeching call of a gull brought her back to reality. Her thoughts flew back to her mother lying in a hospital bed and her father lying on a slab in the morgue. Warm tears seeped from the corners of her eyes and trickled, one by one, down her cheeks.

Paige felt a hand on her shoulder. "Need a tissue?" Startled, she thrashed around. "I knew I'd find you here." It was Nathan Edgemont. Stunned, she stood up and took the crumpled napkin he offered. "I hope this will do. It's all I have."

Immediately, his arms wrapped around her and she collapsed into his hard, muscular chest. "I can't believe he's gone," she whimpered. She was only just now realizing it was true.

She stepped back and took a good look at Nathan through teary eyes. He had turned out quite nicely; the long hair was gone and the thirty pounds he'd put on were in all the right places.

"How'd you know I was home?" Nathan reached in his jeans pocket, pulled out another crumpled napkin, and began to dab the tears gathering in the corners of her eyes.

"He was your father. Nothing would keep you away!"

"But...how did you find me here?"

"I ran into Cate at the hospital. I asked about you. She said you were upset and had left."

"She still gets to me," said Paige.

"You always loved it here. Every time you had a problem or broke up with a boyfriend, I'd find you here." He touched the top of the wooden bench. "Right here. On this bench."

"I was just looking at old pictures of us and now you're here." It'd been many years since Paige had seen Nathan, but he still remembered her secret thinking place. He'd known her like a book when they were children. Apparently, he still did. "What were you doing at the hospital?"

"I was working a case."

"Working a case?"

"I'm with the Meadowbrook Police Department now." Paige tilted her head and raised an eyebrow. "I was there to see the coroner." He paused. "I'm sorry. I shouldn't be...you're already upset over your parents."

"That's only part of it," said Paige.

"Oh..."

"You'd think after all these years I could handle her picking on me. I felt like I was ten all over again."

"Are you talking about Cate?"

"She'll always be the big sister. I'd hoped she'd learn to treat me like an adult by now."

"Things don't always work out the way we want." He looked away from Paige, out at the brilliant sunrise. "It's a good one." Paige nodded her head in agreement. Nathan sat down, put his feet up on the guardrail, and motioned for her to join him. They sat quietly, watching, as the sun rose higher into the sky. "Do you remember coming here to watch the Perseid meteor shower every summer?" Paige nodded. Her lips cracked into the tiniest of smiles. "We'd put a blanket on the sand. Lie there all night. Looking up…counting shooting stars…making wishes. What did you wish for?"

"You know I can't tell you."

"Have any of them come true?"

"Some."

"Some? Like what?"

"College. Job. Others may never come true."

"I guess there's no real science behind wishing on stars." Nathan paused. He twisted his head ever so slightly, just enough to catch Paige's eye. "It's good to see you…really good."

"It's all so crazy. Life is going along just fine. Then *wham*…it smacks you in the face. I wasn't expecting to be planning a funeral for my father. My mom…thank goodness."

Nathan placed his hand on top of Paige's. "I know it's tough right now, but you'll get through this." She always loved Nathan's optimistic outlook on life. No matter what the situation, he always saw the brighter side of things. But it was hard for her to be hopeful at the moment.

"Life sure was simpler when we were kids," said Paige. Nathan stood and pulled Paige up to her feet by one hand.

They walked aimlessly, engrossed in conversation, barely noticing the arcade where they once played pinball, and collected prize tickets playing Skee-Ball. Paige would've given anything for those carefree, youthful days. She stopped and pointed at a dark, gated, glass store front, "Look. It's Sweet Sensations."

"Wow, that brings me back," remarked Nathan.

"I still remember the heavenly smell of chocolate when we entered the shop. I could've spent all day in there…inhaling, getting high on chocolate."

"You always got a caramel apple."

"You loved the walnut fudge."

"I still do!" Nathan bumped his shoulder against hers. "Maybe if you stick around long enough, we can come back when they're open. Inhale some chocolate for old time's sake."

"I don't know how long I'll be in town."

"You just got home."

"I'm back because of my parents."

"Exactly what's so important in Virginia that you can't stay awhile?"

"My job. I just got promoted to director of my department at the *Williamstown Journal*."

"I'm not surprised. You were always so driven. Sounds important."

"And I don't think my family is?"

"Wow… I didn't say that. Relax. Of course, they are."

"Sorry. It's just that I've given up a lot to get where I am. I don't want to risk it." Who *was* Paige trying to convince? "I've spent the last three years traveling to wherever the job sent me. Not everyone understands. You know, it's not just taking photos. They have to tell a story. Anyways, now that I'm director, I won't have to travel as much. I will finally have more time for myself."

"I remember when your dad gave you your first camera on your tenth birthday. You had it with you everywhere we went," said Nathan.

"I still have that camera."

"As I recall, Cate wasn't always happy with your candids." Nathan chuckled, discharging the tension that had built up between them.

"Once she had her hair in curlers and her face covered with a green mud mask looking like the Hulk." Paige laughed. "She chased me all around the house. Needless to say, I never did develop that roll of film."

"You really like your job, don't you?"

"I do," said Paige. "Though, my boyfriend wasn't very happy with my work schedule."

"Boyfriend? Is it serious?"

"Not anymore. We broke up."

"I'm sorry."

"No big deal. It's been over for some time. What about you? I don't see a wedding ring? I'd heard you were serious with Teri Green."

"What? No! Who told you that?"

"Teri. We stayed in touch after high school."

"I did date her. It was casual, never serious."

"Teri made it sound like she was going to be Mrs. Edgemont before she was twenty-five."

"Maybe in her mind, but not mine."

"You mean you've never even come close?"

"I guess I'm holding out for something exceptional." Nathan stopped at a landing of three wooden steps that led down to the sand. "You want to?"

"Race you to the water." Paige kicked off her shoes, took the stairs in one leap, and ran off across the white sandy beach. Nathan chased. She charged ahead and bravely jumped into the surf up to her knees.

"You're still fast," said Nathan as he stopped at the water's edge.

Paige playfully reached down, submerging her hands in the chilly water, and splashed a spray of water in Nathan's direction. He retreated. She swung her leg in the water, sending a surge. She gleefully laughed and the release of all her buried emotions erupted like a volcano and her laughter turned to weeping. Nathan joined her, shoes and all, in the shallows. "We'll get through this," he said as he encircled her in a bear hug. All he wanted to do was to make her feel better, and the only way he knew to make the pain go away, at that very moment, was to hug her.

In between her sniffles, Paige spoke, "I'm sorry I got you all wet."

"No worries. I won't melt."

"It just hit me, you're a cop! After all the laws we broke as kids? Remember the summer before we were seniors?" Paige smiled. "When we went pool hopping."

"Wasn't it 2:00 a.m.?"

"Yes…we'd gone to the midnight showing of the *Rocky Horror Picture Show* that night."

"Boy, did you surprise me when you started peeling off your clothes on our walk home."

Nathan looked at Paige, with an arched eyebrow, a twinkle in his green eyes, a big smile across his dimpled face.

"It was *so* hot that night."

"Next thing I know, you're climbing the chain link fence around the Sun Motel's pool."

"You followed me!" Paige bent over, unable to control her laughter as she tried not to pee her pants.

"I was trying to keep you out of trouble."

Paige looked up from her crouched position. "And I made you climb that fence and jump in?"

"It was fun until the night manager caught us." Nathan took Paige's hand and helped her stand. "When he yelled, you sprinted out ahead of me, over the fence, and down the block. Just like now, except in your bra and panties!"

"You remember what I was wearing."

"Hey, I'm a guy! All I remember is your wet, clingy, see-through underwear."

"You weren't supposed to look. I didn't look at your package in your tidy-whiteys."

"Then how'd you know what I was wearing?" Paige punched his arm. "Do you remember how we jumped in the bushes when that patrol car came by?"

"I thought they were after us. When we finally worked up the nerve to peek, they had pulled over a car."

"I know it's hard to believe, but I've become a law-abiding citizen. I made detective last year."

"That's great." Paige became thoughtful. "I hate to ask. Maybe you could help me find out why the coroner hasn't released my dad's body yet."

"It's been barely twenty-four hours. Sometimes it takes days. Depends on the circumstances."

"It was a car accident."

"It's best to be thorough, no matter what. Just in case there's more to it."

"What department did you say you worked in?"

"I didn't." Nathan hesitated. "I work homicide."

"And you've been assigned to my parents' car accident?"

"I've been assigned to do a follow-up. It's...it's standard protocol."

"Really?"

"I can't disclose the particulars at this time. There was a witness. I'll be interviewing them today."

"A witness to the accident. So there shouldn't be any mystery as to what happened."

Nathan refrained from making eye contact. "Nathan Wayne Edgemont, what aren't you telling me? I have a right to know!" He held his resolve. Paige wanted to jump up and down, to stamp her feet, or to hit a wall. She contained her emotions, refrained from violence, and resorted to pleading. "Please. I need to know, is something else going on?"

"I can't. Please...understand my position."

"But we go way back. You know me."

"I do. And I wish I could say more. I shouldn't have even told you about the witness."

Paige crossed her arms, shook her head side to side, then gave in, at least for the time being. "For now, I understand." *But I'll never give up.*

They walked in silence, back across the sand to the steps leading up to the boardwalk.

Nathan looked on as Paige sat on the top step, wiped the gritty powder off her feet, and put her shoes back on, all without uttering a word. *He wasn't worried about me at all. Just doing his job!* Nathan held out a hand. Paige tentatively took it and stood.

"Come on, we need to head back. I've got to get *you* some answers." Paige, spontaneously, planted a kiss on his cheek, then retreated in embarrassment. *Maybe I was wrong!*

When they reached their vehicles, the sun was high in the sky, the parking lot full, and the beach littered with colorful umbrellas, towels, and blankets. It was still early, an hour before the lifeguards and beach badge attendants were to arrive. "I do wish I could tell you more."

"Promise, as soon as you have details, you'll fill me in."

"I'll do what I can," said Nathan, holding on to her driver's side door as she climbed in.

"No matter what the circumstances, I'm glad you're back."

Before she could respond, her cell phone rang. "It's Todd. I better get it."

"Go ahead." Nathan turned and began to walk away.

"We're staying at my parents'," Paige called after him.

He turned halfway around and nodded. "I know."

CHAPTER 6

PAIGE PULLED HER VEHICLE INTO the drive of her parents' home and beeped the horn. The front door swung open as she stepped out of her Jeep. "Can you give me a hand?" she called out to Todd.

"Where've you been? It's been almost an hour."

"I stopped and picked up a few things at the store."

"A few things?" Todd reached in, grabbing a paper sack in each arm.

"I may've gotten carried away. Did you find the wills?"

"Yes."

"Where'd you find them?"

"In a compartment behind the bookshelf."

"Dad has a secret compartment in his study? How come I never knew?"

"I think I'm the only one who did. I walked in on him putting things in there once when I was about twelve. He told me to never tell anyone about it, that it was a secret. I never did."

"Where'd you put them?"

"On Dad's desk."

"I told Cate I'd bring them to her. She's refusing to leave the hospital." Paige walked in her father's study while Todd took the groceries to the kitchen. She picked up the large manila envelope marked WILLS off her father's desk and walked to the kitchen.

"Did you look at these?" said Paige as she slid the documents out of their envelope.

"Just a glance." Todd closed the refrigerator door and faced Paige. "They were prepared by Frank Wilson's law firm." He bent over and picked up a small white envelope. "Did you drop this?"

Paige waved the manila envelope in her hand. "Must've fallen out of here."

Todd carefully opened the sealed small envelope. "Photos," he announced.

"Let me see." Paige intently studied the top photo. "It's pretty good." A large white bird majestically stood at a water's edge, peering downward, most likely waiting for a small fish to swim by and become its next meal. "Looks like an egret."

Todd peered over Paige's shoulder. "I knew Dad liked taking photos. Didn't know he had a thing for birds."

"Why would he hide these?" Paige asked.

"Just because they were in the compartment doesn't mean he was hiding them."

"Look...here," Paige said as she pointed to a small aluminum boat anchored near the edge of a murky shallow in the photo's background.

Todd leaned in to take a closer look. "Oh, yeah." He took the photo from Paige and held it closer to his eyes. "Is that a shadow? Or a man?"

"Where?"

"There," he pointed, "in the woods."

Paige placed the photos side by side across the kitchen counter. "It's a man. He's in each photo."

"Maybe Dad was taking pictures of him and not the bird," said Todd.

"Your guess is as good as mine. Was that the doorbell?" Paige stepped away from the counter and hurried to the front door. *Must be Nathan.* After all, who else knew they were at the house? Every morning when they were little, Nathan would ring the bell for her so they could walk to school together. As she opened the door, that felt like a million years ago.

Todd emerged from the kitchen. "Sorry for your loss," said Nathan to Todd as he extended his hand. "Long time no see."

"Yeah, it's been a while. Paige mentioned you were with the police department now. Are you here with information about the accident?"

"We've nothing yet."

"I called to get an accident report. I was told it wasn't complete," stated Todd.

"It can take days to gather all the facts and put them into a report. The circumstances surrounding your parents' accident were somewhat unusual."

"Unusual? How? Was it an accident or not?" Paige pressed.

"The department is covering all bases. Speaking with witnesses. Measuring skid marks. I have my best men on this."

"Well, I hope it won't take too long," said Todd. "We'd like to make funeral arrangements and let our Dad rest in peace. Then why are you here?"

"I was in the area. Paige said she was staying here."

"I just made coffee. Care for a cup?" Todd asked Nathan, hoping to take advantage of the opportunity.

"Did you buy eggs? I'm starving," Todd asked Paige.

There was a knock at the front door. Todd gave Paige a puzzled look as he headed to answer it. Paige couldn't image who'd be at her parents' front door, uninvited, at 10:00 a.m. Her father's death and accident hadn't made the papers yet. No one outside of the immediate family and the police would know at this point. But somehow Michael Wilson knew. How was that?

Of course, there's always noisy Mrs. Reilly across the way. She was constantly peering out her curtains, watching the comings and goings of everyone who lived on the block. She might've noticed that she and Todd had shown up instead of her parents.

From the kitchen, Paige heard a male voice. Curious, she walked to the doorway and glanced around the corner. It was Michael Wilson. Dressed to perfection, of course. Not exactly an eye sore. Paige stepped into the living room. But before she could say hello, Todd closed the door, and Michael was gone.

"What did he want?" Paige asked.

"He stopped by to see if there was any news on Mom's condition. Also, if funeral arrangements had been made for Dad. Apparently, his parents have been asking. He offered to help with the arrangements, but I told him we had it under control."

"Why didn't you invite him in?"

"He's a complete stranger. Remember what Cate said, *stay away from him.*"

"He's not exactly a stranger. Our parents and his parents know one another. Besides, Cate has a way of exaggerating."

"Did *you* want me to invite him in? I did sense a little chemistry between you two at the hospital." Todd smirked.

"Ha. Ha. He's not quite my type."

"I saw that look in your eye."

"What look?"

"Oh, you know what look."

"Hush up. Nathan's in the kitchen."

"Do you think you could make breakfast?"

"Do I look like Cate? I don't cook, I eat," said Paige as they walked back into the kitchen to find Nathan searching the refrigerator and cabinets. "Hope you don't mind. Todd said he was starving. I bet you're hungry too." Nathan smiled at Paige as he pulled a loaf of bread from a grocery bag.

"You want to cook. Be my guest." Nathan took eggs, butter, cheese, and tomatoes from the refrigerator. He cracked one egg after another into a glass bowl and then added a small amount of milk.

"Who was at the door?" Nathan asked as he whisked the eggs.

"Michael Wilson. Do you know him? His parents are friends of ours. Paige and I don't remember him," replied Todd.

"I've had a few run-ins with him in court since his return to Meadowbrook."

"Is he a good guy?" Todd asked.

"Depends on which side of the law you're on."

"Cate knows him. She went to school with him," added Paige. Nathan placed the bowl of egg mixture in the microwave and pressed start. "Look at you. So domesticated."

"I picked up a few tricks from an old girlfriend. It's not gourmet, but it's edible."

Nathan looked up momentarily at Paige and then began to dice a tomato and grate the block of the cheddar cheese. The microwave beeped. He removed the hot bowl, which now contained a golden puffy soufflé and set it on the counter. He broke up the soufflé with a fork. "Perfect," he said as he stirred in the diced tomatoes and cheese and then placed the bowl back in the microwave. "Who wants toast? You can handle toast, can't you?" Nathan goaded Paige.

"I believe that might be pushing my limits, but I'll give it a try." Paige reached for the loaf of wheat bread. As soon as she turned her back to make toast, Todd motioned to Nathan to follow him into the living room.

"What's up?"

"It may be nothing…but there was a black sedan parked across from the house last night." Todd moved the curtain and pointed out. "I could swear the man in it was watching this house."

"Did you get a plate number?"

"No. It was dark. The car disappeared right after we got inside."

"Anything else?"

"I took a look around the house. I found a kitchen window partly open. My parents may've forgotten to close it, but…"

"But you're not sure."

"My dad kept this house locked up like Fort Knox. It's just not like him," added Todd.

Nathan nodded. "Did you call 911?"

"No, I…"

"Call 911," Paige asked as she joined them, "about what?"

"About the suspicious car parked out front last night."

Paige eyed Nathan. "I didn't see the car. But I did see a car like he described at the hospital. In the handicap parking area. There was a scruffy blond-haired man in it."

"I didn't get a good look at the driver out front," said Todd.

"Before you two get carried away with some sort of conspiracy theory, let's eat," said Nathan.

"Smells good," Todd said as he filled three coffee mugs. Nathan removed the glass bowl from the microwave, stirred the steaming eggs, and spooned a portion onto each plate that Paige had laid out.

Paige gave Nathan a crooked smile. "Looks edible." Then she dug in. As she shoveled a second heaping spoonful into her mouth, she gave him a big thumbs-up. "It's good. It's really, really good."

Nathan jubilantly bobbed his head. "You doubted me?"

"You haven't told us anything about the investigation," said Todd.

"There's not much to tell," replied Nathan.

"Come on. You must have something," alleged Paige.

"Things are in motion. Believe me, this accident is a top priority."

"It is...then why do I get the feeling you're leaving something out," pushed Paige.

"Have patience. I told you, I've a witness to interview later today. I'm hoping they'll be able to shed some light on how the accident happened. Until your mom is able to answer questions, they may be the only person who knows what happened. Unless, you know something I don't know."

"I'd like to know how they went off the highway," said Todd.

"You're not alone." The conversation stalled and an awkward hush lingered.

"Well... I...better get going. If you come across anything else out of place, let me know," added Nathan.

"It may be nothing, but we found some photos hidden away in Dad's study," Paige volunteered. Todd picked up the five photos and handed them to Nathan.

"Looks like these were taken at the Meadowbrook reservoir."

"Reservoir? What reservoir?"

"Remember Cattail Creek? Where we used to catch frogs and fish for trout."

"Of course," said Todd. "It runs through Cattail Marsh."

"The creek was dammed up to make the reservoir. These could've been taken out there."

"I guess, I've been away too long," said Todd.

Paige turned from the sink with a dish towel in her hand. "So...do you think they're important?

"You said your father had these hidden?"

"Let's just say he had them stashed away in a safe place," said Paige.

"They're nice. The reservoir is a great place for hiking and bird watching. Lots of people love it," added Nathan.

"What about the boat in the photos?"

"They rent boats. Canoes and kayaks too. Well... I've got to get going."

I saw that differently in my head, thought Paige. *Maybe, Dad was just simply taking nature photos.* "The reservoir sounds nice. I'd like to see it before I leave town."

"You should. Call me when you want to go. I'll give you the grand tour," offered Nathan.

"Are you two done planning your play date? We need to get going too."

Paige swung her neck around and gave Todd the stink eye. "Todd, can you put the photos back where you found them?" She then turned to Nathan. "Thank you for making breakfast. It was delicious."

"It was fun," said Nathan as he and Paige stepped out onto the front porch together.

"I'll have a patrol car pass by the house on a regular basis. Just in case."

"Just in case? Just in case of what?"

"You know...to ease Todd's concerns."

"It's not necessary. Save your resources, concentrate on the accident."

"Believe me, I am."

Paige watched as Nathan strolled away. "That was odd," remarked Todd as he joined Paige on the porch. "He never said exactly why he stopped by."

CHAPTER 7

BEADS OF SWEAT POOLED ON Paige's forehead as she frantically paced back and forth. "Where is he? Why did he contact you? He should've called me. You know what this all about, don't you?" Paige pointed a finger at Todd.

"I honestly don't. He just said he had new information." Todd put some distance between himself and Paige, just in case his little sister had a total meltdown. Not that she ever had, but there was always a first time for everything.

"He was an irresponsible child and he still is!" Cate snarled at Paige.

"Calm down you two. I'll get that." Todd ran to the door, happy for the interruption.

"Hope you're wearing a bulletproof vest," remarked Todd as Nathan entered.

"What's going on?"

"They're your problem now."

"We've been waiting two days for answers? You *do* have answers." The words flew out of Paige's mouth without any thought.

"Girls...give the man a break," said Todd as he settled on the couch in between Cate and Paige. "Go ahead. We're listening."

"CIU has concluded their investigation of the accident scene. I've questioned the witness."

"What?" Paige sprang up.

"Hell...there's no easy way to say this. Your parents' car was run off the road."

"It wasn't an accident? I knew there was more." Paige crossed her arms.

Nathan held up his hand as though directing traffic to stop. "Before you ask a hundred questions, let me finish."

Cate sunk back into the softness of the couch. "No... No...it was an accident." She covered her face with her hands. Tears exploded from her eyes and she heaved in and out, gasping for air.

"She's having a panic attack." Paige looked at Nathan. "Help her."

Nathan got on his knees in front of Cate and held her face in between his hands. He spoke in a gentle, calming tone. "Look in my eyes, Cate. Focus on me. Now, take a deep breath in. Slowly. Now breathe out...breathe in...breathe out." Cate listened to Nathan's commands, and with each breath she took, she felt a small degree of relief. The color slowly returned to her cheeks. "Feeling better?" asked Nathan. Cate gave him a small nod.

"You okay?" Paige asked, rubbing Cate's arm. "Good enough for Nate to finish?" Cate nodded again.

Nathan stood upright. "Maybe we should wait."

Cate looked up, her words barely audible. "Tell us."

Not sure if it was the right time or not, he moved forward. He felt a deep obligation not only as a police officer but as a close family friend to convey the department's findings. "The witness confirmed a large black pickup rammed their vehicle several times before bumping it off the road. The witness was a distance away but quite sure. He's the one who called 911."

"Does your witness have a name?" Todd inquired.

"Of course. Once our probe is complete, his name may or may not be released."

"Why would anyone want to run them off the road?" Paige asked.

"Before we get to why, there's more."

"Spit it out. You're scaring us," Paige snapped back.

"I don't have a nice way to tell you this...and I wish I didn't have to. Your father didn't die from the crash. He died from a gunshot wound to the forehead."

Nathan's words echoed throughout Paige's mind. Cate covered her face once again and burst out sobbing. "Is that why they went off the road? He was shot!" Anger kept Paige focused and intent on getting answers.

"It's been determined he was shot after the car rolled down the embankment."

"But that would mean…" Paige slammed her fist on her knee.

Nathan stopped Paige midsentence. "Let's not make suppositions. Not yet. There's more work to be done. It may be as simple as road rage. Road rage carried a bit too far, I must admit. But nonetheless, road rage. I'm sorry I had to tell you this. But I just wanted your family to know the facts before the media got hold of this information."

"Whoever killed my father is a dead man!" Paige fumed.

"Why would someone shoot him? What are we supposed to do now?" Todd asked.

"I know your first instinct is to be angry."

"Angry? Of course, we're angry," said Todd.

"We can't just sit here and wait. I want to help." Paige got in Nathan's face.

"I know you want to help. But your interference will only hinder the investigation. The medical examiner's report will be ready in a day or two. Ballistics will take a little longer. I'm sorry I had to break this news to you."

"Better you than some department flunky," said Todd.

"I'm glad you understand. The chief doesn't know we have a personal connection and I'd I like to keep it that way," added Nathan. "If it comes out, I may be taken off the case. And I really want this case. I really want to help your family."

Nathan started for the door. "I'll walk you out." Todd jumped first, realizing his sisters were still shaken by the horrifically shocking revelation.

"Will they be okay?"

"It's a lot to take in. They just need time. We appreciate that you're on the case."

"One last thing, I'll need to question your mother. I plan on speaking with her doctor tomorrow to see if she's up to it."

"You're welcome to ask, but she tells us she has no memory of the accident."

Soon after Nathan departed, Todd and Cate left for the hospital. Paige stayed behind to make work calls. Not being able to focus on anything, Paige pulled the vacuum out of the hall closet and went to town on the living room rug. The next victim was the hall runner, then the stairs. She hoped that the distraction and exertion of energy would push the image of her father helplessly being shot in the forehead far from mind. But nothing stopped the images and questions looping in her head. The most prominent question: Why? Why her father? Why him?

It must've been a case of mistaken identity. That's it. They weren't after him. He was just in the wrong place at the wrong time. But what if they were after him?

Cate's call was welcomed. "Paige…now that Mom is stable, we need to make plans."

"Plans?"

"For Dad."

"Do we have to?"

"Yes. I made an appointment for 2:00 p.m. today. Todd will be there. You should be there too."

"Of course, I'll be there. Just text me the address."

Paige pulled her SUV into the parking lot of O'Brien's Funeral home and remained stationary, with the engine idling, staring out. Her eyes focused on a small tan rabbit nibbling on a blade of grass along the edge of the lot. She wished life could be that simple, to just be able to sit among the tall green grass and nosh, without a care in the world. Todd gently tapped on her driver's side glass, with a knuckle, causing her to shudder. Seeing it was Todd, she shut off the engine, stepped out onto the pavement, and somberly walked beside him into the two-story brick building with white pillars on each side of the front entrance.

"Where've you two been?" asked Cate.

"Calm down…we're here," said Todd.

They followed Cate into a dark paneled office, where behind a large oak desk stood Mr. O'Brien. "You must be Todd and Paige.

Your sister and I have been going over some details. The next item on the agenda is to pick out a casket." They followed the large balding gentlemen to a closed steel door, which when opened revealed a downward stairwell. Paige grabbed hold of the wooden railing that ran the length of the entire staircase and began her decent. With each step, each breath she took deepened. Her heart rate rapidly increased, step after step, until she was standing on a glossy gray polyurethane cement basement floor.

"You'd think it'd be easy to pick out a casket," remarked Todd.

"I like this one," said Cate.

"The mahogany one! Did you see the price tag?"

"It's beautiful. Feel this satin. Look at the detail on each corner," said Cate.

"Dad wouldn't like it. Too flashy," said Paige.

"He should have the best. What about this one?"

"Brass? No…this is the one." Todd placed his hand on a navy casket with polished steel accents and a white lining. "This he'd like."

"I like it. Especially the seagull embroidered on the inside lid," said Paige. The thought of her father's spirit soaring high in the atmosphere on the wings of a bird up into the heavens gave her a bit of solace.

"It does look like something he'd be happy with," added Cate. "I just wish it didn't need to be a closed casket."

"So…it's settled," said Todd.

"It is. Paige, can you go to the house and collect pictures of Dad. We'll make a collage of his life." Leave it to Cate to think of everything.

"That's a great idea. I'll stop at the craft store. Pick up poster board. A frame too."

"I'll call Father John. I hope he's available to do a Mass," added Cate.

"We also need to make arrangements for a gathering after the service," added Todd.

"Got it covered," said Cate with a tight smile.

It was three days later when the medical examiner's office finally released Nicholas Thompson's body, and due to Cate's exceptional party planning skills, every detail of her father's funeral was choreographed to the most minute detail.

The examiner's report listed the cause of death as trauma to the head from a single gunshot wound. With the examiner's report finally official, the local newspapers started picking up the story. Nicholas and Emily Thompson's faces, along with accident scene photos, graced the front page three days in a row. There was no escaping reality.

CHAPTER 8

ON THE MORNING OF HER father's funeral, Paige awoke to dark, gray skies looking as if they were ready to unleash a deluge at any moment. She felt hollow and wished she could crawl up into a ball under the covers and never emerge. But that was not an option. She remained still, staring out at the swirling clouds, with a blank expression on her face, until pelting rain began to rap against the window, shaking her out of her semi-conscious state.

"Paige, where are you? Are you coming down?" Cate's voice bellowed up the stairwell.

"I'm getting dressed, give me a minute." Paige shouted back down.

"I have Mom in the car. Let's go."

"I'm doing my best. I'll be right down." Paige quickly scampered around, throwing on the one dress she had brought with her.

"Is that what you're wearing?" Cate sized her up as she descended the stairs.

"This is fine. No one is going to be looking at me."

"I guess it'll have to do. We don't have time for you to change."

Welcome to the day from hell, thought Paige.

When the family arrived at O'Brien's Funeral Home, a mustached, robust man posted at the entrance hustled toward the car with an umbrella. Immediately, Mark and Todd jumped out. They helped Emily, her eyes focused downward, out of the car, and into a wheelchair.

Paige's heart ached, but the emptiness and sadness she saw in her mother's eyes could not be matched by her own.

"You're the first to arrive. I placed the memorial cards and guest book in the front hall. If you need anything, please let me know," the director said.

Paige, Cate, and Todd each took a moment to admire their father's portrait in the front hall and sign the guest book. The director then lead them into a large room lined with couches and chairs. Small tables throughout the room were littered with framed photos from the Thompsons' home. How young and handsome Nicholas Thompson looked in his army uniform and how happy was he dressed in a tux holding Emily's hand on their wedding day. At the front and center of the room was the steel blue casket, closed and adorned with red roses and baby's breath. The large room began to fill quickly.

Paige greeted Mrs. Reilly, with memories of selling her pink lemonade on hot summer days in mind. "Thank you for coming. I know Dad would be happy knowing you're here."

"Of course, dear," said Mrs. Reilly.

"I'm sorry I was unable to get home when Mr. Reilly passed."

"How's your mother doing?"

"As expected, she's lost. You understand," said Paige.

"I do. It was hard when I lost Harry." Mrs. Reilly took Paige's hand. "Your father was a wonderful man. I couldn't have asked for a better neighbor."

"Speaking of the neighborhood, have you seen any unusual vehicles or people hanging around?"

"You know me, I'm not the noisy type. But...oh...it's really not my business."

"You can tell me."

"I think Alice Bernard is having an affair. Lately, there's been a black four-door parked in front of her house."

"Don't the Bernards live behind my parents' home."

"Yes."

"Then how..."

"There's a gap in the bushes. I can see through to the other block."

"How long do you think it's been going on?"

"I'm not one to gossip. It's new. Just the last couple of weeks."

Paige leaned in closer to Mrs. Reilly. "I won't say anything. I hope you'll stop in and visit with Mom when she's released from the hospital."

"Of course, dear."

"Will you excuse me? I need to check on a few things. Thank you for coming," added Paige as she stepped away and out into the front hall.

Large, soft arms enveloped Paige. "Baby girl."

Paige turned quickly and gave her Aunt Dorothy a hug. "You made it! Mom will be happy to see you."

"This is such a tragedy. How are you making out?" Aunt Dorothy asked as she held on to Paige's hands.

"Doing the best... I can," said Paige as tears welled up in her eyes.

"Don't cry. It'll be okay, honey." Paige cracked a small smile. "Where's my sister?" Aunt Dorothy asked.

"She's sitting up front. I'll take you to her."

Pity washed over Paige as the barrage of questions from well-wishers mounted about the accident, and the condolences continued. *Yes, it was a tragedy. Yes, his life ended suddenly. Yes, Mom will be lost.* Paige knew they were just trying to give her some comfort and peace, but their words couldn't bring him back or make things right. Instead, they made her only further regret not visiting more often.

At the conclusion of Father John's mass, he invited all those in attendance to join the Thompson family graveside at St. Mary's Cemetery for the interment, followed by a repast at the Old Millhouse Restaurant. Soon, thereafter, the room emptied except for the family. It was hard for Paige to say goodbye to her father. She could only image how hard it was for her mother. *How does anyone say goodbye? Especially after sharing over fifty years, filled of love, laughter, tears, and children.*

The entire Thompson family stood up in unison and then proceeded slowly out the front doorway towards a black limousine. The funeral director stopped Cate in midstride. "I'll make sure all the flowers, pictures, and guest book get sent to you, don't worry," he assured her.

"Thank you for all your help," said Cate as she shook the director's hand with a halfhearted smile on her face. She then continued on, pushing past Mark to the open car door.

Holding on to the skirt of her black dress, Cate slid into the limo. She sat next to her mother and took hold of her hand. Paige grabbed Cate's other hand as the limo pulled away from the curb.

The rain stopped and the gray clouds began to separate just as the limo reached its destination. No one moved to get out. Not one word was spoken. Finally, Todd reached for a door handle. One by one, they all followed his lead and got out, with Emily being the last to emerge.

The whole Thompson family flanked Emily's wheelchair and began a solemn parade down the cement sidewalk that led further into the cemetery. Nicholas's casket had already been placed on wooden planks over a large, deep hole in the earth. Standing next to the casket was an honor guard in full dress. Friends, family, and neighbors began filling the many chairs that were placed in rows under a large green canopy.

Paige scanned the large group of mourners until her eyes found Nathan. He was a sight for sore eyes. She made a beeline to his side. "I haven't heard from you in days. I didn't see you at the funeral home earlier," said Paige.

"I stopped in briefly; but was called away."

"Do you have any updates on the investigation?"

"Nothing since we spoke last."

"Your department has nothing!"

Nathan took a few sideways steps. Paige moved with him. He didn't have the heart to tell her his department hadn't located the truck yet. Or that they were coming up empty when it came to a motive. Nicholas Thompson had led an exemplary life. He'd never had any brush with the law, not even a parking ticket. He had no enemies, no skeletons in the closet, nothing to point them in the right direction. Nathan leaned in closer, so close she could feel his warm breath on her ear. "Your father's murder is *my* top priority. I've every extra man in the department working on it."

"I'm sure you do. But we need answers."

"Let's talk about this later." Paige silently nodded. "From the turnout today, I can see your father had a lot of friends."

"More than I knew," said Paige.

Cate appeared out of nowhere and looked from one to the other. "What are you two talking about over here?"

"I was just saying to Paige that your father had a lot of friends."

"I don't recognize most of them," added Paige.

"If you had made it a point to come home more often, you might know who they are," said Cate.

"You know them all?"

"Pretty much. While you've been off taking pictures, I've been here."

"Well, excuse me. It's called work." Paige held back the rest of her words.

Cate shook her head with an agitated look on her face. "Work, that's all you have."

Wow, did she just say that? Paige knew there was no pleasing Cate. She had given up trying years ago. She looked away and counted to three. She tried, she really tried. Then like hot magma that had simmered too long under a crust of hardened lava, her words cracked through and spilled out. "We can't all be lucky like you. Marry a cash cow and never have to work."

Paige felt a hand on her shoulder. She jerked around. "You two...chill out. This is not the time or place," murmured Todd. Paige stormed off. Stopping at the rear of the canopy, she took a breath and composed herself. Cate was now standing near a tent pole on the other side of the canopy. Paige watched on as Michael Wilson approached Cate, exchanged a few words, and then walked away. Cate, looking annoyed, moved and stood next to her husband, Mark. *Wonder what that's all about.*

Paige directed her attentions back to the guests that were seated under the canopy. Her mother was sitting up front, alone. That's where she needed to be, by her mother's side. She walked toward the front row of chairs, shaking hands and half smiling at all the guests, until she was seated next to her mother. She squeezed her mother's hand. Her mother gave a tight squeeze back as she continued to stare forward with a glazed-over expression on her face. Soon thereafter, they were joined by Cate, Mark, and Todd. Father John stood up before them. "Let us pray," he began.

After the graveside prayer, Cate, Todd, and Paige each stood, placed a red rose on top of their father's coffin, and sat back down. The damp air resonated and ears vibrated as a three-gun salute sounded in Nicholas Thompson's honor. As the bugler played Taps, Paige bit on her bottom lip until she tasted blood. Tears flooded down her face. Taps ended and the silence was unbearable. There was a sudden yet gentle touch on the top of her shoulder. Paige gave a slight turn of the head. "Here, take this." She took the handkerchief Michael Wilson offered and turned back around.

A member of the honor guard approached the seated Thompson family and stopped in front of Emily. She looked up into the soldier's face as he placed a triangular, folded American flag in her lap. She lifted the flag to her chest, cradling it like a small child holding a baby doll. She closed her eyes, hung her head, and silently wept.

Soon, thereafter, guests began milling about. Some left, while others gathered around making conversation among themselves, speculating on how the tragedy had occurred. Emily remained still. Her face was pale, her eyes red, and her body limp. She inhaled and wiped away her tears with a tissue. Then exhaled and opened her eyes. A line of well-wishers had formed.

Paige watched on in awe the miraculous transformation that took place, as her mother pulled herself together and was able to make small talk with each and every one of them.

"Not sure you remember me. I'm Michael. Frank and Sarah's son."

Emily gave him a big smile. "Of course. Your mother mentioned you were back and working at the firm."

"We're all very sorry for your loss. My father and mother are with me." Michael pointed out his parents' whereabouts. Paige's head naturally turned to follow his hand. They were much older than she'd remembered. As Paige scrutinized the Wilsons, she noticed a man standing off in the distance far behind them, almost as if he was hiding among the trees. He was of an average height, wearing blue jeans and navy rain jacket, and had light hair. He seemed fixated on the service. There's something extremely familiar about that man, thought Paige as she watched him throw a cigarette on the ground and stomp on it.

"Thank you for coming. Nicholas would've appreciated it."

Michael stepped aside, turning his attentions to Paige who was standing beside Emily.

He touched her right hand. "Again, I'm sorry for your loss. You have my card. Please call if you or your family need anything."

"That's very kind. I'm sure as soon as my mother is up to it, she'll be contacting your firm."

"You can still call me," he said as he gave her hand a tight squeeze and released it.

Paige gave him a modest smile. "Will you excuse me? There's something I must do. Thank you for coming." She walked away, oblivious to any overture that Michael might have intended. She plopped herself down next to Nathan, who was sitting in the back row of chairs, under the canopy. "Look over to your left, do you see that man? Off in the distance, by the tall pine trees."

"Yes."

"He looks like the man who was sitting in the car at the hospital," Paige whispered.

Nathan nonchalantly glanced to his left and nodded and then looked at Paige. "I can see the gears turning in your mind. I know you like a good mystery, but this time, leave it alone."

"I'm good at solving them. Remember when the Parker twins were blamed for poisoning the Obermeyers' dog? I knew they hadn't done it."

"I remember. You figured it out."

"It wasn't very smart of Mr. Bailey to put a bowl of peanut butter laced with rat poison in his backyard. I know he said the squirrels were eating the peaches off his trees, but that's no excuse. That poor dog. He picked the wrong day to escape his pen."

"That was child's play. This is serious. And you're not exactly objective. Let me handle this."

"Well, you should check that man out. I've seen enough murder mysteries to know the murderer is always close by."

"You've definitely seen too many movies. That's not exactly how it works. Besides, he's one of my men."

"*I've* seen too many movies? You're the one posting a man in the woods. And the hospital?"

"It's just a precaution."

"Admit it. I'm right."

"Your theory has merit. Please, Paige…let me do my job."

She looked Nathan square in the face as she placed a hand on his knee. "I'm counting on you."

He looked down at her hand, then lifted his eyes to meet hers, and whispered softly, "I don't plan on letting you down." Their eyes momentarily locked. He gently touched the curve of her face, letting a finger glaze over her cheek, moving a strand of hair that had strayed. Paige desperately wanted to look away but was unable to move. Her usual self-assurance was gone, and for the first time ever, she seemed vulnerable to him. He couldn't disappoint her. Not now, not when she needed him the most.

"What's going on?" Todd said as he lightly smacked Nathan on the back. Paige quickly pulled her hand from Nathan's knee.

"I better get back to work," Nathan announced as he jumped to his feet.

"You don't have to run off on my account," said Todd.

Nathan glanced in Paige's direction. "I'll catch up with you at the Millhouse."

"What's up with him?" Todd asked once Nathan had scurried off.

"Beats me."

CHAPTER 9

"IT WAS A GOOD IDEA to come here. Your dad would've approved," said Emily as she looked around the elegant room filled with all her husband's friends and family.

"It was all Cate. She knew the Old Millhouse was special to you and Dad," said Paige.

Emily touched Cate's hand. "I appreciate all you did to pull this together." Cate beamed.

"I'll be back." Paige turned and walked across the large ballroom and came to a stop next to Todd. "Have you seen Nate?" she asked.

"Not since the cemetery."

"He said he'd be here."

"He'll be here. Don't worry. I saw that intense look he was giving you earlier."

"What are you talking about?"

Todd began singing. "Paige and Nathan sitting in a tree, K-I-S-S-I-N-G."

"Stop it. It wasn't funny when I was ten and it still isn't."

Todd tried to tickle her with both hands. "You *like* him."

"Cut it out." Paige snapped at Todd, pushing his hands away. Cate darted him a threatening look from across the room. Todd dropped his hands and grinned.

"Sorry, sis. Couldn't help myself." Todd tried to tickle Paige one more time and then held up his hands. "I promise. That's it." Paige had to admit Todd's shenanigans had made her momentarily forget why they were all there.

"Did you know the police had a man posted in the woods at the cemetery?"

"No," Todd said, suddenly sober. "Why?"

"Dad was murdered. That's reason enough," said Paige.

"You're right. Did Nathan say anything else?"

"Just that he won't let us down."

"We need to look around the house again. There's got be more. Maybe more pictures."

"What pictures?" Cate asked from behind them.

Todd turned. "I found some photos at the house," he said.

"Is that all? There are photos everywhere in that house."

"These were hidden in Dad's study," Paige explained.

"You were snooping! In Dad's things."

"No. I was looking for his will and came across them," said Todd.

"I don't believe you. You two are up to something," said Cate.

"You're missing the whole point. They could be important," said Paige.

"Hey, you three." They all turned. "Sorry, I got tied up at the station."

"Any leads yet?" Todd began.

Nathan motioned toward a round table in the corner of the room, far away from the other guests. "Let's go over there to talk."

"What's the big secret?" asked Cate.

"We're working on tracking down another witness. But so far, we've come up empty."

"Another witness," Paige repeated.

"There were two calls to 911 about the accident," answered Nathan.

"You mean they've disappeared?" Cate jumped in.

"I've assigned a detective to track *her* down."

"Only one!" Cate raised her voice.

Nathan ignored her. "The department is also tracking the truck down that ran them off the highway. The witness may be key to finding the truck. We won't let up until we find it."

"I still don't get why this happened," said Paige.

"Your parents may've just been in the wrong place at the wrong time."

"That's what the police always say when they have no answers," said Cate.

"Let me lay out the facts," said Nathan as he gave Cate a hard stare. "Your parents' vehicle was run off the road… Your father was shot… We have no motive. We're working overtime on this case. It's a top priority." Nathan jabbed his index finger into his chest. The smug look on Cate's face disappeared. She looked away.

"Maybe today is not the day for this," said Todd.

"You're right. But I will need to re-question your mother."

"She already told you, she doesn't remember what happened," said Cate.

"Of course, not today." Nathan began to stand. "But soon." He looked at Paige and silently mouthed the words, "I'll call you later." Paige nodded.

"Paige, why don't you come with me. We'll take Mom back to the hospital. Mark…Todd…you take the flowers back home," said Cate.

"I'll walk you out," said Paige to Nathan as he stepped away from the table.

"That didn't go very well," said Nathan. "I should've known better. Today was about your family, not the investigation."

Paige grabbed his elbow. "We pushed you for answers."

"I'm just as frustrated over the facts of this case as you are."

"Mom's tired, let's go," Cate interrupted.

"Just one moment," Paige snapped.

"You heard him. We know everything he knows."

Paige took a calming breath and turned to face Cate. "I need to get my purse."

"Todd and Mark are helping Mom to the car. They'll drop us at the hospital." Paige turned back around. Nathan was gone.

With exhaustion settling in on all of them, it was a quiet trip to the hospital. Paige shut her eyes, rolled her neck, and tried to think of nothing.

Within minutes of getting Emily situated in her hospital bed, Nurse Matthews entered. "How are you feeling? Any aches I need to know of?" she asked as she wrapped a BP cuff around Emily's bicep.

"I'm just tired," Emily muttered. The emotional and physical strain of the day had been showing on Emily's face for hours.

"The medication I gave you will help you sleep."

"That's all I want to do."

"We're going to stay until she dozes off." Cate was firm.

"I know it's been a traumatic day for your family. You're welcome to stay a short while." She looked at Cate. "Not too long." Nurse Matthews left the room.

Cate picked up her mother's chart and perused it. "Just keeping track of things."

"You should've been a nurse," remarked Paige.

"I asked Mark if I could take some classes at the university. He said I didn't need to. Said he was able to support us."

"I didn't know," Paige said surprised.

"It'd be different if we had children. I wish he'd try to understand. I need something for me. Like you have."

"You're always bitching at me for taking my work too seriously."

"Some days I wish I had your life."

"Sometimes I wish I had yours. To not have to worry about money," said Paige.

"I guess neither of our lives is perfect."

"I know we haven't spoken much about it lately, but have you and Mark gone to see a fertility specialist?"

"We've done it all. The specialists. The testing. The praying. It's too late for us."

"There's adoption."

"I've suggested it. Mark won't talk about it. I've given up trying." Cate's voice trailed off.

"I didn't mean to upset you. I know how much you wanted children."

Cate turned away. "It's chilly in here." She walked closer to the bed. "Mom, are you warm enough?" There was no reply. Emily was fast asleep.

"Tea would be nice. I'll get some for us." Deep in her own thoughts, Paige walked out of her mother's room and wandered down the long hall toward the café. She'd really never taken the time to think about Cate's life. She was too busy with her own. But now, she could see. She could feel the pain and the heartache, her sister was holding inside.

Paige pushed in the café glass door. She noticed Michael Wilson sitting in the back corner with a sandwich and a cup of coffee in front of him. He was looking in her direction. She turned around. No one else was there. He motioned for her to join him. Not wanting to be rude, she walked over to his table.

Michael stood. "How nice to see you again."

"We brought Mom back."

"When I saw your mother at the service today, I assumed she'd been released."

"Her doctor allowed her out for the day. She still has issues to overcome. What brings you here?"

"My mother had a fall."

"Is she okay?"

"It may be a broken arm. She's in x-ray right now."

He pointed to an empty chair. "Please sit a minute. I could use a distraction."

"Distraction, that I understand." Michael slide the chair away from the table. "I can only sit a minute. My sister is upstairs waiting. I just stopped in to get us tea."

"Your sister...yes...Cate," said Michael.

"You know her...don't you?"

"I tried to say hello at your father's service, but I think she didn't remember me."

"She mentioned you two were classmates," said Paige.

"She remembers me," Michael sounded surprised. "I got the impression she didn't. Last time I saw her I was...maybe...fourteen, fifteen."

"That's a long time ago. Maybe she didn't recognize you."

"I always liked her," said Michael.

"I better get the tea." Paige pushed back her chair.

"Let me get it."

Paige watched as Michael sauntered up to the front counter with an air of self-assurance that bordered on arrogance. There was something about him that intrigued her. If the circumstances and timing of their meeting had been different, perhaps she would've flirted back.

Although, since her breakup from Jeremy, she doubted her own judgement when it came to men.

"I brought sugar, lemon, and milk. I wasn't sure how you took your tea." Michael set the two cups of hot tea and condiments on the table.

"Your mother, she's getting better?" He sat down across from her.

"She gets stronger every day. But today was a real drain."

"Today must've been hard for your whole family," said Michael. Paige nodded. "I saw you talking to Detective Edgemont at the cemetery. What did he want?"

"You mean Nathan Edgemont?"

"Yes."

"He's an old childhood friend."

"An old boyfriend?"

"No…a friend."

"Was he asking questions?"

"Questions?"

"About your parents. Your father's murder. Are they really attributing it to road rage? I read about it in the paper."

"It was no accident. There are witnesses." Paige regretted her words as soon as they came out.

"Please don't say anything. I shouldn't have said. I don't want to compromise the investigation."

"I get it. But…you can trust me. After all, I'm an attorney."

"But you're not *my* attorney."

"I realize these things are sensitive."

"Please don't say anything."

"I won't…trust me." *Could she? She wasn't certain. What about Cate's warning. He's bad news.* "Do you think you'll be in town long? Perhaps we could have dinner one evening," suggested Michael.

"I can't. I'm in town to help my family." Paige nervously rattled off.

"If you change your mind…"

Paige interrupted him. "It's not a good time."

"You have a boyfriend?"

"No." Paige abruptly stood, picking up the two cups. "Thank you again for the tea. I need to get back upstairs."

Michael jumped up. "I don't give up that easy." He walked with her.

When Paige returned to her mother's room, Cate was sitting in a chair next to the bed.

"Where've you been? I was getting worried."

"I ran into Michael Wilson in the café. He invited me to sit down. He asked about you."

"He did?" stammered Cate.

"What's the story?" Paige asked. "I know there's a story."

"It was a long time ago. Just stay away from him," scolded Cate.

"He seems nice."

"While you've been off flirting, I've been stuck here." Cate stood and moved toward Paige.

"Sorry...you could've come with me."

"I've given up a lot of days and nights to be here to take care of Mom." Cate flailed her arms.

"What are you talking about? It's been your choice. You don't need to be here day and night. It's a hospital...full of doctors and nurses."

"Mom is all I have!"

"What are you talking about?"

"Just forget it," whimpered Cate.

"Have a sip of tea, maybe it'll calm you down," said Paige as she grabbed her purse and left the room. *Where did Sibel come from?*

Chapter 10

PAIGE TOSSED AND TURNED ALL night, reliving her conversation with Cate. Her whole life she had tried to figure Cate out, to live up to her expectations. Then one day, she woke up. She and Cate were just too different to ever agree on anything. But there was a moment, there in her mother's hospital room, when she thought she and Cate were coming to a new understanding of one another. Then, in the blink of an eye, it was gone. Why couldn't it just come easier?

With drooping eyes, Paige went down to the kitchen to start the coffee maker and then went back upstairs to dress. When she returned to the kitchen, Todd was enjoying a steaming mug of coffee and reading the morning paper.

"Thanks for making coffee. Where're you off to?" Todd poured and handed Paige a cup.

"I thought I'd take a run around the old neighborhood. I haven't had any time for exercise the last few days." Paige bent over, touching her toes, stretching out her hamstrings. "I miss it when I don't get it in. It clears my mind."

"There's a little blurb in the paper about Dad's death and burial. It doesn't give much detail, just says the police are still investigating his murder. It's hard to believe it's more than a week and still nothing," said Todd.

"Nothing solid but…think about it. There's the car that was parked out front, the open kitchen window, the gunshot to his head. And let's not forget about the witness they haven't found." Paige was emphatic. "We need to figure out the why, then maybe the pieces will begin to fit."

"Let's hope," said Todd.

"When I get back, we'll go through Dad's things again."

"Exactly what are we looking for?"

"For clues. For motive. For the truth," said Paige.

"You really don't believe Dad was mixed up in something bad. That he had enemies."

"Maybe he did! What about the photos?"

"Maybe we're reaching. There could be a logical reason why they were stashed away. Give it a rest. Go get your run in." Todd picked the paper back up.

"You might be right. But still, something just doesn't feel right." Paige took a sip of coffee.

"Here's a story you might like," commented Todd, "about the new reservoir they built out in the Cattail Marsh. Remember what a great place the marshland was to hang out?"

"Along the creek was fine, but the marsh was eerie, especially at night."

"That's because you and your friends thought it was haunted."

"You're the one who told us all the stories about people disappearing out there."

"And you believed me?"

"Why wouldn't we? And you're not the only one who told us stories. Maybe yours were made up. But I believe there's something supernatural out there. My friends and I experienced it firsthand."

"Sure, you did." Todd nodded his head up and down.

"We did. We went out there on a dare one night. We were trying to find the foundation of the Gatling widow's house."

"Did you find it?"

"We found her. An opaque figure of a woman appeared on the trail. It was spine-chilling."

"Did you have a flashlight with you?"

"Yes."

"It was probably just swamp gas reflecting the light."

"No. It was the shadowy outline of a woman. I know what I saw. She floated up, out of the ground, and came at us. Suddenly, we were surrounded by a high-pitched squeal. It sounded like a wounded animal."

"It was just your imagination."

"Imagination or not, I turned and ran. I got my foot stuck in the mud. Up to my knee practically. I yanked it out and left my shoe behind."

Todd laughed uncontrollably. "You never told me that. You don't have to worry anymore. Most of the marsh is gone."

"I knew you'd make fun."

Todd composed himself. "It says here there's a walking trail around the reservoir with boating and fishing."

"Sounds nice," said Paige.

"Wait a sec. It says a body was discovered during the reservoir's construction. Maybe it's your ghost."

"Do they know who it was? Or how long the body was there?"

"The remains were identified through DNA testing," Todd read. "Ryan Timmons, of Meadowbrook, was fifteen when he disappeared in 1991."

"Does it say how he died?

"His body had juries consistent with being hit by a car," said Todd.

"How did his body end up in the marsh?"

"Doesn't say."

"Must've been dumped there. Can you leave the paper? I want to read that story when I get back," said Paige.

"I may not be here."

"Where're you going?"

"I told Cate I'd be over to see Mom this morning. But first, I need to call work. I can't stay much longer."

"I bet Cate will be upset you're leaving."

"I don't want to leave. I have no choice."

"I get it," Paige said as she stepped out through the kitchen door onto the backyard, redwood deck. The morning sun was brilliant, a welcomed sight after the rain the day before.

Paige set out with a slow-paced jog and then built up to a full-out run until she was rounding the corner to Newton, the street that ran behind her childhood home. Recalling what Mrs. Reilly had said about observing a black four-door vehicle parked in front of the Bernards', she slowed her pace. There was not only a break in the bushes, there was a path that ran through the easement alongside the Bernards' property. Paige sprinted the path and came to the fence that surrounded her parents' backyard. Perhaps, Alice Bernard was having an affair, but Paige doubted it.

However, it was a perfect place to leave a car, if someone was planning on breaking into her family home.

Paige made a mental note and then turned and went back down the dirt path and back out onto Newton Street where she noticed the McAllisters had painted their colonial from white to yellow and had fenced in the yard. Other than these small observances and the path which hadn't existed when she was a child, there hadn't been too many changes to the old neighborhood.

Thirty minutes into her run, Paige suddenly had a recollection of Billy Macintyre, a second-grade classmate who'd disappeared when she was in grammar school. He was never seen again. But it wasn't Billy whose body was found in the marsh. It was a Ryan Timmons.

OMG. Paige stopped dead in her tracks. Billy was seven when he disappeared and Ryan was a teen, but they disappeared around the same time. Could there have been a serial killer on the loose when she was a child? She had always thought of Meadowbrook as a safe place to grow up.

At the time of Billy's disappearance, her parents had told her nothing. They simply said that the Macintyre family had moved away. But there was talk in her class that something more sinister had happened. Her parents never mentioned another boy disappearing. They did, however, start driving her and Nathan to school each morning and picking them up each afternoon. They didn't allow her to play outside in the afternoons either. Paige and her friends had felt like they were being punished for something they hadn't done. She had always supposed there was more to the story. As the years went on and she moved on to junior high, she and her friends forgot about Billy and so did her parents. The neighborhood resumed its complacency. Once again, the laughter and screams of children playing tag, hide-and-seek, and dodge ball filled the afternoons.

Paige looked around. She'd been so lost in thought that she'd missed the turn that would take her back home. She turned around and retraced her steps. Back on track, she began making a mental list of everything she needed to do. First contact work. Then call Becca. Check on the townhouse and Tiger. Call Nathan. Go to the hospital. Check on Mom.

The house was empty and unnervingly quiet when she returned home from her run. Todd had left a note, along with the morning paper on the kitchen table. He was headed to the hospital to sit with Mom and would be back in the afternoon. Paige showered, dressed, and began to work her way down her to do list. First, she spoke with her boss, Steve Johnson. He said to take all the time she needed; her job would be there whenever she got back. That was simpler than she had anticipated. But she still couldn't stop worrying. What if he couldn't wait for her return. Next, she called her neighbor, Becca. Becca was full of questions about her trip home and Paige was more than willing to give her all the details. "I may have to stay on here a little longer than anticipated. My father didn't die from the accident. He died from a gunshot wound to the forehead."

"A gunshot! I thought it was an accident," said Becca.

"The police have been short on answers. They're saying it may've been road rage. Their vehicle was forced off the highway. I don't know what to think. I'm going to stay until I know more."

"Maybe the police know and just aren't saying," said Becca.

"That's always a possibility. But an old friend of mine is running the investigation and I trust him. I think they really don't know."

"That must be hard on you and your family."

"It is...that's why I'm staying. I hope you don't mind watching Tiger a little while longer."

"Tiger's no trouble. He seemed lonely, so I brought him over to stay in my home."

"I owe you."

"No, you don't. I'm just glad I can help. He's good company. So how are you and your sister getting along?"

"Just as expected. Things will never change."

"Is it strange being back home?"

"Yes...and no. It's been nice catching up with Nate."

"Who's Nate?"

"He's the friend I mentioned who's heading up the police investigation. We were friends my whole childhood."

"Is he cute?"

"I guess he is. I never thought of him that way."

"What way is that?"

"As a cute guy."

"He's cute! I hear it in your voice. Have you made out yet?"

"No. We only ran into each other because of the investigation. He's been very kind to me and my whole family. Trying to keep us in the loop and everything."

"What's everything? Maybe…"

"He's like a brother to me."

"Sure…"

"Though when he touched my cheek, I did get butterflies."

"*Ooo*…How long has it been since you last saw him?"

"When I was home on Christmas break my last year at the university."

"That was years ago."

"I did get asked out to dinner, though, by someone else."

"You. On a date."

"Hey, it hasn't been that long."

"Good for you. It's time."

"I'm not going."

"You should go. Who is he?"

"His name is Michael. He's an attorney here in town. His parents and mine are friends."

"So…he's another old friend?"

"I just met him. He's older."

"Nice looking?"

"Yes."

"You should go!"

"I don't know. Besides, Cate says he's bad news."

"I say, there's no harm in having dinner with a good-looking guy. Speaking of good-looking guys, I ran into Jeremy. He asked how you were. I hope you don't mind that I told him that your dad had passed away."

"No worries. We dated a long time and he did know my dad."

"I'm glad you're not upset with me."

"Never! But I do need to get going."

"Okay. You take care. Go to dinner with the man." The call ended.

Paige sank back into the couch and went through her phone contacts. She stopped on Nathan's number. *Should I, or shouldn't I?* She hit send. When he didn't answer, she left a message. "I know you said you'd call when you had something. But I was hoping. Call me. Oh, it's Paige."

With her to-do list almost complete, some free time on her hands, and no one to interfere, she began to search her parents' house for something, for anything, that might lead to a motive, to answers, to the killer's identity. She hesitantly stood in the doorway to her father's study, imagining him sitting tall in his chair, looking handsome and intense, punching numbers into a calculator and scribbling the answers on a scratch pad. With great awareness that she was violating his space, she entered. Dad's study had been a place of mystery as a child; off limits to sticky hands and loud noises, only entered at bedtime to say good night.

Each night as a small child, she would tap on the study door. Her father would look up and say, "Bedtime already?"

"Yes," she'd answer, and he'd motion for her to enter. She recalled meekly walking to the side of his desk. He'd put one hand on the top of her head as he placed a gentle kiss in the center of her forehead. "God bless you. Now off to bed." And with that, she'd head out and up the stairs to her room, feeling truly loved and blessed. Tiny teardrops began to seep from her eyes. She blinked several times and then wiped them away with the back of her hand.

Paige couldn't shake the feeling that her father was watching and going to catch her at any moment.

Sitting in his chair, she pulled the center desk drawer out. "Aha!" *Good thing he was old-school,* she thought as she flipped through the pages of his tiny brown leather address book.

Grabbing her laptop, she began Googling every name in the book. Most were only listed in the white pages. The only names that popped up on various sites were Frank Wilson and Robert Gilbert. She knew of Frank Wilson, he was a prominent Meadowbrook citizen, local attorney, town councilman, and Michael Wilson's father. But who was Robert Gilbert? The entry in the address book looked new, not as faded as the others, and the corner of the page was turned down.

Robert Gilbert, of Layton, Gilbert and Alston Engineering Associates, graduated summa cum laude from Princeton University, she read. Perhaps he was a work colleague of her father's. She read on. Layton, Gilbert and Alston Associates specializes in water supply systems design. The company designed and supervised the Meadowbrook Reservoir project. Well, this explained her father's interest in the reservoir. The first phone number listed next to Robert Gilbert's name was the same as the company website. She grabbed her cell and dialed the number.

The young woman on the other end of the line pleasantly answered her questions. "Robert Gilbert is currently out of the office."

"Will Mr. Gilbert be back in today?"

"He's currently out of town. Can I direct your call to an associate?"

"Yes. Thank you."

"May I ask what your call is in reference to?"

"The Meadowbrook reservoir project."

"Hold one moment."

"Franklin speaking."

"Mr. Franklin. My name is Paige Thompson. I'm not quite sure why I'm calling. I found your company's number in my father's address book. Perhaps you've heard of my father, Nicholas Thompson?"

"Nick Thompson. Of course. I know your father's work. He's been a consultant on several of the firm's projects. I was so sorry to hear of his passing."

"I was actually calling for Robert Gilbert. I was told he was out of town."

"I can tell you he's not in."

"Any idea when he'll be back in?"

"He disappeared without a word to anyone. It's been almost two weeks."

"Disappeared? The receptionist indicated he was out of town."

"I meant…leave of absence."

"Has this happened before?"

"No."

"I must speak with him," said Paige.

"I wish I could be of more help. I'll leave a note for Mr. Gilbert to call you when he resurfaces."

"I appreciate that."

"It was nice speaking with you. Again, I'm very sorry for your loss."

"Thank you." Paige hung up. She paused for a moment to ponder the timing of Robert Gilbert's disappearance. It'd been a little over a week since her father's death. Was it just coincidental that her father was murdered and that Robert Gilbert had pulled a disappearing act?

Paige dialed the second number written next to Robert Gilbert's name. "Gilbert residence."

"May I speak with Mr. Gilbert?"

"Mr. Gilbert is away on business."

"Is Mrs. Gilbert home? May I speak with her?"

"Mrs. Gilbert is out. Is there a message?"

"Will she be home this evening? I need to speak with her. It's urgent."

"I'll leave her a message. Your name."

"Paige Thompson." Paige gave her number. "Please have her call as soon as she gets in."

"What is this about?"

"My father and Mr. Gilbert were work colleagues. My father passed away recently. Please ask her to call me as soon as possible."

"I'll give her the message. Good day." The line went abruptly silent.

Paige flipped back through the pages of the father's address book, stopping on the "W" page. She dialed Frank Wilson's residence.

Expecting an answering machine to come on after the fourth ring, a soft voice said, "Hello?"

"Mrs. Wilson?"

"Yes. Who is this?"

"It's Paige Thompson. Emily and Nicholas's daughter."

"Oh my goodness. You pure dear. How are you? How is Emme?"

"Mom is getting stronger every day."

"I just couldn't believe the news. It's dreadful."

"Thank you for the beautiful arrangement you and your husband sent."

"It was the least we could do. Your parents are wonderful people. Your mother and I go way back. I've been wanting to visit with her. Do you think she's up to it?"

"I know she'd love some company."

"I'll talk with Frank. I don't drive." She paused. "He's a...very busy man." There was a nervous hesitation in her words.

"If you'd like, I could take you to see her."

"That would be lovely, dear. I hate bothering my husband."

"Take my number. You call me when you want to go."

"Thank you, dear. You are definitely Emily's daughter. Your mother has always been one to go out of her way to help others."

"That's kind of you to say. I'll tell Mom you were asking about her. Have a nice day, and please call me when you want to visit with her," said Paige.

There was a sweetness about Sarah Wilson that Paige liked. But the unrest in her voice when speaking of her husband worried Paige. She recognized the tone, having once done a piece on a battered women's shelter in Chicago. There was a deep sadness and tentativeness that emanated from abused women, always fearful that their abusers were close by. And in a way, they were. When your self-esteem, trust, heart, and soul have been damaged by another, it can be a long journey back. Back to who they were before falling under the spell of an abusive, controlling, or manipulative person.

What kind of man was Frank Wilson? What was his association with her father? Were they close? Or just friends through association? Paige dug through her purse. She pulled out the business card Michael Wilson had given her. Rationalizing that she was only accepting his dinner invitation to further her investigation.

Paige's heart raced as she dialed Michael's number. He answered on the second ring.

"Hi," she hesitated, "it's Paige Thompson."

"Paige… I'm happy you called. Have you changed your mind about dinner?"

"Yes."

"Tonight?"

"Tonight?" Paige took a deep breath.

"If it's not good, then tomorrow?"

"Tonight works."

"Great. Where shall I pick you up?"

"At my parents' home. Seven?"

"Perfect." The instant Paige hung up she began to second-guess her decision. But it was too late now.

She spent the next few hours at the mall, looking for something to wear. After picking through racks of dresses, she wandered into the dressing room to try them on. She first tried on a flirty yellow cotton sundress. She twirled around and watched her reflection in the dressing room mirrors. *Too casual. He wears expensive designer suits with silk ties. I'd rather be overdressed than underdressed.* Next, she slipped into a sexy, tight black cocktail dress. She turned her head and looked down, checking out her back side. The dress fit snuggly over her curves, accentuating her derriere. *Maybe it's a little too much. Don't want to give him the wrong idea.* After trying on another three dresses, finally the perfect dress. Paige stared at her reflection in the mirror. She took her blond hair in one hand, pulled it upward, bunched it on top of her head, and pulled a few strands down to frame her face. *Perfect.*

Once Paige's dinner attire was set, it was on to the last item on her to-do list, a visit with Mom and dealing with Cate. It was late afternoon when she wandered into her mother's hospital room.

"Mom is starting to remember," Cate enthusiastically said as she walked into the dimly lit, cool hospital room.

"That's wonderful," said Paige as she turned to look at Cate. "Hi, Mom." She approached the right side of her mother's bed and came to a stop next to Cate. "You look great. You must be feeling better."

"I'm so glad you're here." Emily's voice was low and shallow. She looked from Paige to Todd, then Cate. "Cate has been filling me in on some accident details. I had a memory. I can see your father trying to avoid a big truck. He put his right arm out across my chest. He yelled. 'Hold on.' Then our car went off the road."

"Don't strain yourself," Cate cautioned her.

"Mom, were you and Dad in some kind of trouble?" interjected Paige.

"A pickup was trying to run us off the road."

"The police are investigating. They're looking for the truck. Did you see who shot Daddy?" Paige asked.

"I only saw the truck. Your father wasn't shot. The car rolled down an embankment. Your father was in it." Emily's hands began to quiver along with her voice.

"Look what you've done! You've upset her!" Cate shouted. "Todd, go get a nurse! She needs something to calm her down!"

"I thought she knew." Paige's hand went to her throat. "You said she remembered."

"We were going to tell her. She doesn't remember *that*," said Cate.

"Mom, I thought you knew," apologized Paige.

"Leave it alone." Cate gave Paige a glaring look. Paige opened her mouth to speak again.

Cate yelled, "Stop!"

"I was just going to apologize." *Me and my big mouth.*

Todd returned with a heavyset fiftyish-looking nurse. "You'll need to leave. I can't have you upsetting Mrs. Thompson like this," she ordered sternly.

"We'll be right outside the door," Cate spoke calmly, then leaned over and placed a kiss on her mother's cheek. They all walked out together.

"I can't believe you did that." Cate smacked Paige on the arm with the back of her hand. "She needs to get stronger, not be piled with worry."

"Sorry." Paige took a step backward.

"Let it go, Cate. She didn't know. I need to get back to the house. You two get along," said Todd as he left.

"Why do you always ask so many questions? You might as well go too," Cate snapped at Paige.

"Somebody needs to be asking questions."

"The police have already asked plenty of questions."

"Maybe there are more questions to ask. I'm trying to find out the truth. Don't you want to know what happened?"

"Of course, I do."

"Maybe you know something that could help."

"Me," said Cate.

"Something important about Mom and Dad."

"Like what?"

"Like what Mom and Dad have been up to lately. Any new friends or acquaintances?"

"Mom's life is pretty much the same as always. Walks on the boardwalk in the mornings with the neighbor. Bridge club on Wednesdays."

"Which neighbor?"

"Mrs. Collins."

"I don't know her."

"She moved in next door to Mom and Dad after the Browns sold the house and moved to Florida. Must be two years now."

"What about Dad?" Whomever it was that ran them off the road took the time to get out and shoot him. Not Mom...doesn't that *pique* your curiosity?"

"I've been so worried over Mom that I haven't put much thought into it. Dad...was Dad. You know...he did his own things. Like fishing and golfing."

"Nothing new?"

"He did mention last year that retirement was getting boring. Really…how much fishing and golfing can one man do? I think it was about that time he picked up his camera again."

"When did he start doing consulting work?"

"Before he retired. He was testing the waters to see if after he retired there was a demand for consultants in his field."

"Did you know he was consulting on the Meadowbrook Reservoir?"

"He mentioned it."

"Did he ever mention a man named Robert Gilbert?"

"Not to me."

"I need to ask Mom."

"Not now. You heard the nurse, she needs rest…not be upset by your questions."

"I'm sorry. Really, I am. But she would've remembered eventually," said Paige.

"But it wasn't the right time."

"Okay. You're right, it wasn't." Cate shook her head. "Why don't you go home for a while? Let me sit with Mom. She'll be sleeping most of the afternoon," said Paige as she held up three fingers on her right hand. "Scouts honor, I won't upset her any further with questions."

Cate didn't answer. "Go catch up on things at your home. Come on, Cate. Let me help."

Paige looked out the hallway window. She watched a large gray pigeon teeter on a lower rooftop ledge. Cate approached. "If you promise to call me if she wakes up. It'd be nice to go home for a while."

"Do you think you can come back by six? I have dinner plans."

"I bet Nathan finally asked you out on a real date."

"No. Not him. You know we're just friends."

"Then who?"

"No one special."

"Fine. Don't tell me." Cate sighed, shook her head, and left.

Paige settled in alongside the bed, while her mother peacefully slept. She almost dozed off herself. As the afternoon dragged, Paige became more and more apprehensive about her dinner plans with Michael. But she had to go, she told herself.

As promised, Cate returned promptly at 5:30 p.m. Paige rushed home, and one hour later, she emerged from her bedroom looking refined in a clingy, teal chiffon dress that showed off her curves. Curves she had perfected over the last six months since her breakup with Jeremy.

The endless miles she had run, to let off steam, were paying off. Her hair was half pulled back, which allowed the rest of her hair to hang down in full flowing curls around her face.

"Wow, you look great!" Todd gave a low whistle. "Where're you going?"

"I have a date," said Paige.

"With Nate or the ambulance chaser?"

"If you mean Michael, then yes."

"Are you sure this guy is worth it?"

Paige walked further down the stairs. "It's just dinner!"

"There's something off about him," said Todd.

The doorbell rang. Paige hurried to greet Michael before Todd could get up and embarrass her. She stepped out onto the landing. Michael's eyes lit up at the sight of Paige in her clingy dress and heals. "Wow, aren't you a vision." He placed his hand on the base of her back as they walked down the sidewalk to his black Mercedes SL550 convertible. "I made a reservation at the Scarborough Inn for seven thirty," he said as he opened the passenger side door for her.

"I love that restaurant. My family only went there on special occasions, like birthdays and graduations. My cousin, Theresa, had her wedding reception there in the flower garden."

Paige rambled nervously on as she settled into her seat and fastened her seat belt. "The gardens are beautiful. At night, they become magical with thousands of twinkle lights. It's like an enchanted forest." *Keep it together, Paige.*

CHAPTER 11

IT WAS A THIRTY-MINUTE DRIVE over rolling, winding country roads to the Scarborough Inn, which was in Haddonfield. Paige dreamingly gazed out her window and drank in the scenery. There were acres and acres of tall golden corn stalks and lush green pastures framed with post fencing. The car rounded a curve and an apple orchard appeared. Each row of trees in perfect symmetry with limbs laden with green apples.

Paige was about to ask Michael if there was an issue between himself and Cate when his cell phone rang. He answered it on his Bluetooth. "Wilson here. Yes. Of, course." There was silence in the car as he listened to whomever was on the other end of the line. "No." Michael's tone had changed. "We'll talk later." He looked over at Paige and smiled nonchalantly. "Work." He turned his attentions back to the road.

"Is there a problem?"

"Just the usual." He smiled again. "I'm sorry, it was rude of me to take that call."

"Trust me, I understand."

Paige went back to enjoying the rolling hills with grazing thoroughbreds. It brought to mind the summer she had turned twelve. She'd had her first horseback riding lesson. She'd been so nervous about getting up on the back of Jake, the pinto horse the farm owner had handpicked for her first ride. He had assured her that Jake was a tame and patient animal, accustomed to strange riders. She was petrified and pretended to be brave in front of her two friends. Jake hadn't let her down.

The road dipped, and Paige was jolted back to the present. She turned to look at Michael. He seemed far off and lost in his own thoughts. The call must've been about something very important or disturbing to have changed his demeanor so much. They continued on in silence until Michael slowed the car and turned off the main road. They crossed over an old wooden bridge and the Scarborough Inn appeared in front of them.

"Evening, miss," said an eager young man with a broad grin as he opened the passenger side door of the convertible. Paige stepped out and up onto the sidewalk. The valet jogged around the back of the car and opened Michael's door. Michael placed a folded bill into the palm of the valet.

"Take good care of her," he intimidatingly said. The young man nodded as he tucked the bill into his pocket. Michael joined Paige on the sidewalk and took hold of her hand.

He guided her up the walk and through the glass entrance doors that lead into the restaurant's atrium. Paige wished they hadn't headed straight in. She'd wanted to see all the beautiful flowers and delicate foliage before the sun went down. She smiled at him, not letting her disappointment show. After all, she wasn't there to have a good time. *I'm here for answers.*

A hostess, in a tight-fitting black dress, carrying two menus, approached them. "Welcome back, Mr. Wilson, your table is waiting for you," she said as she motioned for them to follow.

They shadowed the tall brunette into the main dining hall and across the room to an intimate side corner. "I trust everything is to your liking," she added with a beaming smile.

"Thank you, Michelle," he answered her with a twinkle in his eye that lingered a beat too long.

"You come here often?" Paige asked as he pushed in her chair.

"Whenever I win a big case. Victory is better when celebrated."

The waiter appeared, and Michael ordered a bottle of Pinot Noir without consulting with her. Strike two. It didn't matter. Putting up with a little rude behavior was worth it if she was able to get some viable information out of him.

The dining room was dimly lit with a flickering candle in the center of each table. An old stone fireplace that went from the floor to the ceiling in the center of the main dining room glowed with a burning log. Paige suddenly wished she were there with someone special.

"I'm sorry. I've asked you to have dinner with me, and all I've done is conduct business. Please, can we start over?" He seemed genuinely remorseful.

"Yes. Of course. I'm guilty myself of letting my work get in the way a time or two. It's water under the bridge."

"That's gracious of you. How's your mother doing?"

"Better. She had some recollections of the accident today."

"You must be relieved."

"Yes." Paige placed her right hand on the center of her chest. "Soo…relieved."

"I suppose the police will be in to question her?"

"They've already done that."

"But…now that she has her memory, they'll want to question her again."

"The doctors want her to get stronger before reliving the whole experience. It might set back her progress. Can we not talk about this?"

"Sorry, that was insensitive of me."

"A little."

"Wow. I don't intimidate you at all, do I?" Michael looked at her with a mischievous smile.

"No. You don't," Paige lied. "I was hoping to escape the whole nightmare for one evening. Let's start over, have a little fun. Tell me three things about yourself you think I should know." *Playfully done, Paige.*

"Wow. Three things." He paused for a short time. "I'm a lawyer. I moved back to Meadowbrook last year, and I'm thirty-nine."

"I could find out all that if I Googled your name. I mean three things that aren't common knowledge. Three intimate things."

"Intimate, huh! Why don't you start? You tell me three things about yourself."

"Okay. I'm a terrible cook. I love the outdoors, and the name of my first dog was Duke. Now you."

"Your wine," the waiter conveniently interrupted. He expertly opened the bottle and handed Michael the cork as Paige looked on. Michael held the cork to his nose, sniffed it, then gave a nod, and a smile. The waiter poured a small amount. Michael held the glass up, swirled the wine, and took a sip. Paige managed to avoid rolling her eyes. Michael nodded again.

"Why did you leave Meadowbrook?" Michael asked as the waiter filled their wine glasses.

"I went away to the University of Virginia to study media communications. When I graduated, I decided to stay in Virginia. What about you? Why did you leave Meadowbrook?"

"I didn't have a choice. My parents sent me to prep school in Upstate New York when I was fifteen. Then it was on to college and law school in Massachusetts."

"You left home at fifteen? No wonder I don't remember you. Didn't you miss your friends and family?"

"I did what was expected. My father went to prep school, my grandfather went to prep school. It's tradition." His manner was detached, unemotional. She would've never wanted to leave her friends and family at such a young age. What sort of disconnect would that create between a parent and child?

"And you weren't bothered at all?"

"My father and I didn't exactly see eye to eye. I did hate to leave my mother. She was always so fragile, and he…"

"He what?"

"My father wasn't a very loving man. Let's leave it at that."

"But you're working with him now."

"It was time to come home and settle some things. But sometimes I wish I'd never come back."

"Wow."

"It is what it is."

"Why don't you go out on your own?"

"It's not an option right now."

"There are always options."

"I see the garden is lit up." Paige looked out the large pane glass window that overlooked the deck. "Why don't we have coffee outside after dinner?"

"I'd like that." Despite her mission, Paige found herself being pulled in.

"And a walk through the gardens afterward?"

Paige nodded. "You read my mind."

"I must admit, I was surprised by your call today," said Michael.

"I surprised myself."

"Why the change of heart?"

"I needed to get away."

"So you're using me?" He chuckled. A flicker of candle light caught his eyes. Paige kept her hands in her lap. She dug a fingernail into her wrist and gave him a tight-lipped smile. *It's working. Keep focus*, thought Paige as the waiter placed a luscious, colorful salad in front of each of them.

"Looks delicious," said Paige as she picked up her salad fork.

"Would you like some?" Michael asked as he lifted the bread basket up off the table and moved it toward Paige.

"Thank you." She took a warm roll and placed it on her dish.

There was quiet as they ate. Soon, a bus boy appeared and removed their empty salad plates.

"More wine?" Michael asked.

"Yes."

He poured a generous amount of red wine in Paige's glass, then his own. "A toast," he said as he lifted his glass.

"To what?"

"To new friends."

"And old friends," added Paige. "Speaking of old friends, you and my sister, Cate? You were classmates? Friends?"

"We were classmates...and friends," said Michael.

"But not anymore?"

"I guess not." Michael shrugged.

"Did something happen?"

"I went away to prep school."

"That's all?"

"It was a long time ago. I try not to think about it."

"About what?"

Michael looked away, then back to Paige. "A friend of ours went missing."

"Do you mean Ryan Timmons?"

"I guess Cate told you."

"Yes. But why don't you tell me your version," said Paige. *Maybe now I'll have a clue.*

"Ryan came over to my house after school the day he went missing. I may've been the last one to see him alive." He sighed, looked up at the ceiling, and took a deep breath. "I haven't talked about this is years."

"You must've been horrified when they dug up Ryan's body."

"I hadn't returned yet, but yes. I never knew what happened. He left my house that afternoon and I never saw him again." There was irrefutable sadness in his words as he spoke.

"If I had known…"

"Known what?"

"Your lobster?" Paige turned and looked up into the server's face. She smiled as he placed the beautiful plate of food in front of her.

"Thank you," said Paige.

"A bib?" asked the server. Paige hesitated. She looked at Michael, then back to the server, and nodded. *Maybe the lobster wasn't the best choice.*

The server turned and set the other plate with a filet mignon wrapped in bacon with blue cheese crumbles in front of Michael and then disappeared. He quickly returned with a lobster bib in hand, "you don't have to use it."

Paige shrugged. "It's all part of the fun." She gave Michael a wide grin as the young man tied the bib behind her neck.

"Anything else?"

"I don't believe so," said Michael.

"I recently read an article about Ryan's body being discovered," said Paige not wanting to lose the momentum of the conversation.

"Your dinner…you're happy with it?"

Paige looked down for the first time at the plate of food in front of her. "It looks delicious."

Michael picked up his knife and fork and sliced his filet. "Nice and rare, just the way I like it."

"So what do you think happened?" Paige pushed on.

"I'd rather not talk about it." Michael raised his voice ever so slightly.

"Forgive me…sometimes I forget," remarked Paige.

"You ask a lot of questions," said Michael.

"I've been told that."

Paige picked up the claw crackers from a side bowl and began to break apart her lobster. Water squirted out and she flinched in surprise. She shrugged it off and dug back in.

When their plates were nearly empty, Paige sat back and pushed her plate aside. The waiter appeared and asked, "May I take this?" Paige nodded.

He looked at Michael. "Coffee? Dessert?"

"We're going to have our coffee out on the deck," said Michael.

"Very good, sir."

Michael and Paige headed out through glass doors to the deck. They sat down at a small table near the deck's edge with a good view of the gardens. Paige was mesmerized by the haloing glow given off by the thousands of tiny lights. The evening air was cool and the coffee hot.

"Excuse me," said Michael as he leaned forward. "I didn't mean to snap at you inside."

Paige looked away from the gardens. "I was being noisy." She lifted the delicate china cup to her lips and took a sip. "I remember the last time I was here."

"When was that?"

"I think I was thirteen. It's as beautiful as I remember."

"How about a walk?" Michael held out his hand. Paige took it and stood. "Chilly?" he asked.

"A little."

In true gentlemanly fashion, Michael took off his suit jacket and placed it around her shoulders. His hands lingered just a moment.

Delicately, she reached up to adjust the coat and bumped his hand aside. Though arrogant and pompous, she had to admit, Michael had been a gentleman all evening. He hadn't missed a beat at holding a chair or door. But it seemed like he was on autopilot like he'd done it a hundred times before and he did what was expected, a learned behavior, which made it difficult to gauge his interest in her or anything. *He must be good at poker,* she mused. *But there was a moment when he was talking about Ryan.*

As they walked the winding path through the gardens, thousands of twinkling white-and-blue crystal lights illuminated their way. Paige could not think of anything more beautiful. At the center of the garden was a colorful fountain with stone benches set all around. Two couples snuggled together, listening to the piped-in music. Paige suddenly felt sad. They walked quickly around the fountain as to not disturb the couples and then headed back toward the inn. Just before reaching the deck where they had begun their walk, Paige heard a rustling in the bushes. She turned quickly. There was something moving in the underbrush.

"Did you hear that?"

"Hear what?"

"I thought I heard a noise over there, in that clump of bushes," said Paige as she pointed to an unlit area of the garden.

"I didn't hear anything."

Paige stood still, listening. She bent forward to get a closer look. "There it is again," she said as she gave Michael an upward side glance.

"Probably an animal or maybe one of those couples back there is getting carried away," he said as he grabbed her elbow and steered her in the direction of the wooden steps that led up to the top of the deck. When they reached the top step, Michael's cell phone pinged. He pulled it out of his pocket and read the text. He took a quick look back down the steps and then returned the phone to his pocket. "Work again," he said as he gave Paige a side glance. His face was strained. He turned again and looked behind. Paige had a nagging feeling that something more was going on. She couldn't pinpoint what, but she knew she was right. She excused herself and went to the ladies' room to collect her thoughts.

When Paige returned, Michael had disappeared. *He must be inside, getting the drinks he'd promised,* she thought. She stood atop the deck and scanned the gardens. A shadowy figure moved in the darkened section of bushes where Paige had heard rustling earlier. She descended the steps and followed the shadow as it moved. As she crept through the bushes in her chiffon dress and three-inch heels, she was careful not to make a sound. When the shadowy silhouette stopped, she stopped. Hopefully, whomever it was, hadn't realized she was trailing them. She remained still and watched as the figure of a man emerged from the bushes in front of her and stepped out onto the parking lot blacktop. Another man stepped out from behind a large dark SUV. She strained to see through the bushes and the darkness. Her heart raced. She gasped and covered her mouth with her hand. *Oh my god. What is going on here?*

"Why are you here?" Paige recognized Michael's voice.

"You wouldn't talk to me. The police are asking questions." It was the man who had crawled out of the bushes. He stood in the shadows of a large fir tree, making it difficult for her see who he was. She squinted. She couldn't make out much of the tall, sticklike figure.

"Keep your cool. No one knows anything. Get yourself out of Meadowbrook for a while." Michael began to walk away and then turned back and said, "Don't bother me again."

Paige quickly backed herself out of the bushes and onto the cobblestone path. Just as she stepped out onto the pathway, Michael appeared at the top of the deck. "I thought I'd lost you." He called down to her.

"Were you looking for me? I couldn't find you, so I thought I'd take one last look at the gardens." If he'd seen her near the bushes, he didn't let on. Perhaps the man in the parking lot was just a nervous client. Perhaps not. Perhaps there was a lot more to Michael Wilson then what was on the surface. Whatever it was, she needed to know more.

"Do you think you could drop me at the hospital when we get back to town? I promised my sister I'd stop in for a while," said Paige.

"Your family, you're very close?"

"I'd like to think so. Like all families, we have disagreements from time to time. But, at the end of the day, we're family."

"I wouldn't know. I never had that." Michael took her hand. They walked out the glass entrance doors toward the valet station.

"I'm not letting you off the hook," Paige enticed him. "You still haven't told me three things about yourself. I told *you* three." Paige reminded as they waited for the car.

"You got me. Okay. I hate dogs. I've never been in love. And meeting you is the best thing that's happened to me since I've come back to town."

"Wow. You hate dogs? Some horrid dog-biting incident in your youth?"

Michael laughed. "No. I just never understood why anyone would want to trouble themselves with having to tend to a filthy animal."

"They're not filthy, if taken care of. And their loyal."

"To each their own, I say," he countered. "You're not focusing on the right piece of information." He raised an eyebrow and smiled dangerously.

The valet pulled Michael's car alongside the curb. He jumped out and opened the door for Paige. "Hope you had a nice time, miss." Paige smiled. Michael handed the valet a bill, got in, and put the car in gear. He was quiet the entire half-hour trip back to Meadowbrook. *This silence is annoying. Did I hit a nerve or was it the man in the parking lot?*

Michael pulled into the first open space and put the car in park alongside the hospital. He turned to Paige.

"Is something bothering you?" Paige asked.

"No." He shook his head and smiled. "I hope we can do this again."

"You do! You were awful quiet on the ride back to town," said Paige.

"Was I?"

"You were."

"I'm sorry. I've a habit of not letting go of work," said Michael.

"Speaking of work…" Paige hesitated.

"What?" Michael arched his neck and gave her his full attention.

"Nothing…it was a nice evening. Thank you for dinner." Paige pulled on the door handle and stepped out.

Michael hurriedly jumped out and came to stand next to her. "You're welcome." He leaned in. Paige turned her head. The kiss he intended for her lips landed on her cheek. He pulled back.

"Guess things didn't go as well as I thought."

"I'm just tired."

He looked her straight in the eye. "As long as I can hope," he said as he opened the lobby door. Paige walked through. She could feel his eyes following her every movement until she disappeared into the elevator.

CHAPTER 12

As PAIGE PUSHED THE ELEVATOR button for the third floor, her mind wandered back to the almost kiss from Michael. A good-night kiss was the last thing she'd been expecting when she accepted his dinner invitation. But it wouldn't have been the worst thing that could've happened, and besides, she needed him to stay interested. He was up to something and she was going to figure it out. Why had he kept showing up everywhere she was? And why all the questions? *I love a good challenge. I hope he didn't think I wasn't interested.*

Paige was still thinking about the events of the evening as she approached her mother's hospital room. She opened the door slightly, removed her strappy heals, and tiptoed in. She walked right past Cate, who was sound asleep, with her forehead on the edge of the bed. Paige sighed with relief and then settled into an uncomfortable chair in the far corner of the room.

The quiet in the room was disrupted by the squeaking of rubber soles as a nurse entered.

Cate lifted her head.

"I didn't realize you were still here," said Nurse Holly.

"I must've fallen asleep," said Cate. "I'm waiting for my sister."

The nurse pointed toward the far corner. "Isn't that her in the corner?"

Cate looked behind. Paige grinned. "When did you get here?"

"A short while ago. You looked so peaceful. I didn't want to wake you."

"I just dozed off for a minute." Cate was defensive.

"You're allowed," said Paige.

"I'll be back shortly with your mom's meds," said Holly after checking Emily's blood pressure and oxygen level. Paige stood and walked over to her sister's side.

"I'm sorry I was so short with you earlier. I was tired and overwhelmed," said Cate.

And in need of Xanax, thought Paige. "How's she doing? Has she been sleeping long?"

"She wakes up every once in a while. When she does, she's groggy."

"It's been a long night for you. You go home. I'll stay a while."

"I will…in a bit," said Cate. The sisters moved away from the bed toward the windows and out of their mother's ear shot. "I really am sorry. How was your date?"

"It was…fine," said Paige.

"You don't sound too enthused."

"The food was good."

"You look great in that dress."

"Thanks. I'm sorry you were here alone."

"I wasn't alone the whole while. Mark stopped by with dinner. Where did you eat?"

"The Scarborough Inn."

"Fancy. Who did you have dinner with?"

"Michael Wilson."

"Are you crazy? Why would you do that? You're trying to get at me."

"No… I'm not. He said you and he were friends."

"Is that what he said?"

"You weren't?"

"I guess we were. He moved away a long time ago. Frankly, if you hadn't told me who he was, I wouldn't have recognized him," Cate said.

"If you were friends, why the ominous warning about him?" Cate looked away and mumbled something. "Did you say something?" Paige asked.

"No."

"Why do you keep avoiding this conversation?"

"Maybe it's better not to dreg up the past," said Cate.

"I'll keep asking till you tell me," said Paige.

"Well, it's not going to be tonight." Cate kissed her mother's cheek, picked up her purse, and left. Paige watched as the door closed behind her. *There's a story there.*

Paige sat down next to her mother's bed. She sighed and then took her mother's hand.

"Mom, I miss our talks. You've always given me great advice. I sure could use some right now." Paige shuddered with a chill. She placed the small green throw Cate had left behind, over her legs and squirmed in the uncomfortable, pleather chair. "Remember, what you said when I asked you about going away to the university?" Paige smiled. "You don't? I do. And you were right." Paige squeezed her mom's hand tight. "You said I would make mistakes. And...and... I have. But you also said you trusted me to make good decisions. You said I was smart and strong of character and that I could never disappoint you. I try harder every day because I don't want to disappoint you." *Your words are always in my head.* Emily stirred. "I didn't mean to disturb you," said Paige. Emily remained asleep.

Paige moved and settled back in the dimly lit, far corner of the room once again. There she stayed several hours, with her feet up, dozing off and on. Then, in the still of the darkness, there was a noise. A slight squeak, just enough to make one sit up straight. The noise was coming from near Emily's bed. As Paige's eyes focused, she saw a shadowy figure near the IV setup and a gloved hand on its pole. Paige strained to see. She was expecting to see Nurse Holly, but instead, a large man stood alongside her mother's bed. He wore a dark sweatshirt with the hood half pulled up over his head. Paige jumped up. The man looked away from the pole. He was now looking in her direction. "Hey, who are you?" He turned and quickly made for the door. "Get back here." Paige called after him. He moved faster. Paige chased after him in her stockinged feet. She slowed herself when she began to slip on the newly polished floors. "Stop," she yelled as he rounded the far hall corner.

"What's going on?" Nurse Holly emerged from another patient's room.

"There was a man in my mom's room. He was fiddling with the IV. I don't think he works here. Please check it."

The two women swiftly entered the room. Holly flicked on the bright overhead lights.

Paige squinted her eyes as her mother woke up. "Paige." Her mother's voice was hauntingly low, a mumble. "What's going on?"

"How are you feeling?" Paige moved to the bedside as Holly checked the IV and its lines.

"Everything seems to be intact. Just in case, I've stopped the IV. I'm going to replace the fluid bag. You stay with her. I need to make a call." Holly stepped out into the hall, picked up the floor telephone, and called hospital security. When she returned, she had new IV lines and a fluid bag in hand.

"Emily, I'm Nurse Holly. You remember me, don't you? I need to check your blood pressure and draw some blood."

A hospital security guard, who looked to be about sixty and wearing a crumpled uniform, appeared in the doorway and waved at Paige to join him in the hall. "I'm Officer Stanley. The nurse said you were surprised by a strange man in your mother's room. Are you sure it wasn't a staff member?"

"If he worked here, he wouldn't have taken off when I asked who he was. He ran, and I chased him. That's when Holly stopped me."

"You have no idea who it was?"

"None. You need to check your surveillance tapes!"

"I hardly think that's necessary. It was probably someone who wandered into the wrong room."

"My father was murdered and now someone is trying to kill my mother!" Paige shouted, panicked.

Holly joined them in the hall. "Did you see anyone?" the security guard asked her.

"I was in room 311. I came out when I heard shouting."

"The patient good? Everything in order?"

"I found nothing out of place. Her vitals are good. Maybe you've over reacted," Holly added as she looked at Paige. "It's very late, and you shouldn't even be here. Out of respect for your sister I've been looking the other way. But maybe..."

"That's kind of you." Paige fought to hold her tongue so as not to upset the situation further.

"But what would've happened if I wasn't here?" Paige looked from Holly to Officer Stanley. "I thought everyone had to be buzzed in on this floor."

"Visitors do. Employees have keycards," he answered.

"Why don't you go sit with your mother. She's awake and asking for you," said Holly.

"I'll be going now." Officer Stanley started to walk away.

Maybe we shouldn't have woken him from his nap, thought Paige angrily. If he wasn't going to do anything, then she was.

"Really? That's it." He turned back. "Someone comes into my mother's room, touches her IV, and that's it?" Paige was at her wit's end. "I'm calling the police. Better than that, I've got connections."

"I'm going to check the halls. See if anyone else saw your man. If you think of anything else, don't hesitate to call me back." Officer Stanley walked away. Paige watched as he shuffled down the hall. When she turned back around, Holly was gone. She was left standing, alone, in the hallway.

Paige stormed to the door of her mother's room. She stopped, took a deep breath, and calmly pushed the door in. Her mother was fast asleep, oblivious to the commotion that had just occurred. She was thankful for that. Her mother had enough to deal with. Paige rummaged through her purse, pulled out her cell phone, and dialed Nathan.

Chapter 13

PAIGE COUNTED TO HERSELF AS the phone on the other end rang—
one, two, three, finally, Nathan answered, "Edgemont. This better
be good."

"Nate, it's me. Paige."

"What's wrong?"

"I know it's late. Or early. I need you to come to the hospital."

"Now? Is it your mother?"

"There was a strange man in her room."

"Are you sure?"

"Yes, I chased him out. He got away. I don't think security
believed me."

"I'll be there in ten."

"My mother's room, three-nineteen. Please hurry."

Not able to sit still, Paige paced back and forth between the
closed door and the windows, fiddling with her cell phone, hoping
her mother would remain asleep and not see how panicked she was.
What was going on? *This has to have something to do with the accident...Dad's murder.* Realizing she was in her stocking feet, Paige sat
to put her shoes back on. Just as she was fastening the clip on the
second heel, the door swung inward. Her head snapped up from its
bent position, straight up into Nathan's face. Paige sprang to her feet
as he moved toward her.

"You didn't need to get all dressed up for me." His eyes lingered
a moment.

Paige could feel her cheeks flush. She was thankful for the dim
lighting. "I was out to dinner."

"Let's go in the hall." They stepped out of the room and Paige closed the door gently behind them. "Tell me what happened," said Nathan.

"I was sitting in a chair near the windows. I'd dozed off. There was a squeaking noise. When I opened my eyes, there was a large man in a dark sweatshirt near the IV setup."

"Think hard, do you remember anything else besides his size? How tall?"

"Very tall, at least six four, I'd say. His hand was on the IV pole. It looked like he was wearing a white surgical glove. His hair was on the dark side." She shaped her hands around her face. "And not too long. About here."

Nathan looked down at her feet. "You chased him, in those shoes?"

"I had them off at the time." She pointed to the left. "He went that way, then rounded the corner. The nurse on call stopped me. I wish I'd kept on him."

"I'm glad you didn't. You could've been hurt."

"You believe me?" Paige was surprised. Just then, two uniformed police officers walked through the double doors and straight toward them.

"Where do you want us?" one of the officers asked.

"Officer Taylor, I need you to stand guard outside room 319. Montgomery, check the halls for a large man of six feet four with dark hair, wearing a dark hooded sweatshirt. If you find him, hold him for questioning."

"Why would I doubt you?" Nathan said turning back to Paige. "You stay in your mom's room. I need to interview the floor nurses and check with security." He put his hand on her arm.

"Everything will be okay." She gazed up at him, gave him a nod, and a thin-lipped smile. He suddenly released her arm and added, "Not that I noticed, but you look really nice." He left her no time to react before he walked off toward the nurses' station.

Paige smiled at Officer Taylor as he opened the door to room 319 for her. She lowered herself into a chair. She tapped her foot—heal, toe, heal, toe. She shook her knee and then shook her head, as her mind imagined what might've happened, if she hadn't run the man off.

After a time, she went back to the doorway and peered out toward the nurses' desk. Nathan was still there. He was in an intense conversation with a 5'7" brunette with large brown eyes. Her hair was perfectly pulled back with small side curls. *Where did she come from?* She didn't recall seeing her earlier. She watched as the nurse smiled up at Nathan, flirtatiously touched his foreman and sheepishly giggled as he made notes in a small book. Nathan closed his notebook and turned. He was walking in her direction. Paige quickly pulled her head back inside and scampered back to her chair. Nathan slowly and quietly opened the door. "No one else saw the man you described." Paige looked up in surprise as she tried to catch her breath.

"I'm headed down to security. Maybe he was caught on the hospital's cameras," said Nathan from the doorway.

"I'm going with you," said Paige as she approached Nathan.

"You stay here."

"No. You need me, I can identify him," Paige insisted.

"Your mother needs you here."

"She's sound asleep. Besides, you have an officer posted at the door." Paige tugged at Nathan's arm. "I'm of much better use with you."

"Okay, okay. You can come with me." Nathan reluctantly gave in. The two of them left room 319 and headed down to the first floor, where the main security office was located. Just as they passed through the double doors, out to the main hall, Nathan's portable radio went off. "Montgomery reporting. I have an unconscious, injured man in the second-floor utility room."

Nathan pushed the small red button on the side of his portable. "This Is Edgemont. Hold your position. On my way." He quickly moved through the empty corridors with Paige in tow.

When he came to a sudden stop in front of a steel door, Paige found her nose planted in his back.

Nathan pulled open the heavy utility room door. Officer Montgomery was kneeling next to a body in gray maintenance overalls. The lifeless man looked to be in his mid-forties and surrounded by a halo of a dark red liquid, thick as syrup.

"Looks like he was hit over the head several times. I can't get a pulse," Officer Montgomery reported.

There was a gasp behind them. Paige turned to look. It was the floor nurse who had followed them into the utility room. She swallowed hard, trying not to gag. "Charlie," she shouted as she turned and ran out. Paige stepped backward, opened the photo app on her cell phone, and began to snap away.

Nathan looked up at her. "Really?"

"Sorry. Professional hazard," she looked away. The walls and shelves of the small room were dotted with blood. She flinched.

Nathan placed two fingers on Charlie's neck before gently lifting his head. There was a three-inch gash, still oozing, on the side of it. Nathan grabbed a rag and applied pressure to the wound.

"In there," said the floor nurse.

The doctor's white coat opened as he rushed in and knelt next to the body. He pulled a penlight from his top pocket and checked Charlie's eyes. He felt for a pulse. The nurse unbuckled Charlie's overall bibs. With a tug, she yanked up his shirt and held it as the doctor listened with a stethoscope. The doctor began compressions on Charlie's chest. Nathan assisted by tilting Charlie's head back and pinching his nose. He then placed his mouth over Charlie's and began to blow, while Montgomery counted.

"Hand me the AED," ordered the doctor. An electric shock raced through Charlie's body. The doctor listened to Charlie's chest. "Charge it again," he said. Another electrical shock ran through Charlie.

"Come on, Charlie," chanted the nurse.

"I'm calling it. Time of death, 4:32 a.m.," said Doctor Turner.

"We need to close this room off till the investigation unit gets here," Paige remained quiet. "Cordon off the entire floor. No one goes in or out without proper ID," said Nathan. He turned to Paige.

"Paige, Officer Montgomery will take you back upstairs. Wait there." There was no arguing with him.

"We'll keep looking for your intruder…but right now we need to find out why this man is dead." Normally, Paige would've tried to convince Nathan she needed to stay, but this time she didn't. And it was fine. She silently nodded and upon second thought, was only too happy to get away from the bloody, lifeless body.

Paige followed Officer Montgomery back to her mother's room. "I'll be right outside," he said as Paige pushed in the door. She sat herself down on the chair next to the bed and took her mother's hand. She held on tight. With her eyes closed, she said a silent prayer, desperately trying to forget what she'd just seen.

Paige remained still until she uncontrollably yawned. She yawned once more, this time bigger than the first. She took a deep breath and sighed as she released it. She'd been going on sheer adrenaline from last evening till now and this tranquil moment was a welcomed reprieve.

"You don't always have to be so strong." Stunned, Paige twisted her neck and looked up at Nathan with her red, tired eyes.

"You need sleep."

Paige rose to stand face to face with him. "I can't leave her. Not now."

He placed his hands on her shoulders and looked her straight in the eyes. "Your mother is safe," he whispered. He dropped his hands down. Holding onto her wrists, he guided her away from the bed. "There's an officer at the door. Go home, get changed…get some rest."

"I won't leave. There's too much going on."

"You're impossible."

"I bet the maintenance worker's key card was missing," said Paige with a renewed strength.

"Slow your roll. I've a murder to investigate, not you."

Paige pouted her lips. "I know you do! But, don't you see… there's a connection!"

"Yes. Maybe. But at this point, it's only conjecture. I need to get back downstairs. Text me when you're leaving. I'll have an officer escort you home."

"It's not necessary," said Paige.

"Oh, yes, it is." Nathan was stern, his voice commanding.

Paige remained in place, watching, as the door closed behind him. *He's crazy if he thinks I'm going anywhere.*

CHAPTER 14

A GENTLE TAPPING SOUND BROKE the silence in Emily Thompson's room. Paige snapped her attention to the door. A sliver of light appeared and danced across the floor, cutting the room in half, as the door opened.

"Ms. Thompson." Officer Taylor waved Paige toward the door. She stood, tiptoed past her mother, and stepped out into the hall.

"Todd! You're finally here," said Paige.

"The police wouldn't let me in. I tried to reach you."

"My cell must've died."

"Is Mom okay?"

"Yes."

"Is she upset?"

"She doesn't know anything yet." Paige took a few sideways steps. "Mom only woke up when the nurse checked her out." Todd moved with her until they were far away from the door.

"Good. Why so many cops?"

"A maintenance worker was found dead on the second floor," said Paige waving her hands. "It was awful. Blood everywhere."

"What? You were there?"

"Not when he was killed. But after," said Paige.

"Are you okay?"

"Yes. Nathan and I were going down to the security office when the call came in."

"I'm confused. Was the dead man the man you saw in Mom's room?"

"No. But it's connected," said Paige as she looked past Todd.

Todd whipped around. Nathan was walking toward them. "Nate. Is my mom safe here?"

"Yes," replied Nathan.

"Are you sure? What about the dead man?"

"There's an officer at your mom's room and he'll be there for as long as it takes."

The young brunette nurse Nathan had spoken to earlier stepped out from the nurses' station and made her way to his side. "I was told you needed my assistance." She radiated.

Nathan smiled.

"How can I help?" she asked.

"Can the patient in room 319 be moved?"

"Moved? Where?" Paige stepped in between them.

Nathan held up a hand. "Temporarily. The crime unit needs to get in your mom's room."

"Right now?" Paige gave Nathan a look.

"When CIU is done downstairs," said Nathan.

The pretty nurse touched Nathan's arm and pointed. "There's an empty room, end of the hall. I'll have it set up."

"Thank you, Jane," said Nathan.

Paige looked from Nathan to Jane. "I'll tell my mom." She pointed at herself. "I'd like to be the one who explains what's happened." Paige's tone softened.

Nathan gave Paige a tight smile. "I need to get back downstairs." He looked at Jane. "I'll let you know when the team is ready." Nathan turned and headed toward the elevator.

Jane hurried after him. Paige looked on as they walked away, down the long, brightly lit corridor, and disappeared. She shook her head from left to right and shrugged. *Whatever.*

"You okay," said Todd as he touched her arm.

Paige jumped. "What?" She turned. "Let's get this over."

Paige watched her mother peacefully breathe in and out. *I have no choice. I'm sorry,* she thought as she pulled on a long white string hanging alongside the bed. The wall light above the bed illuminated.

"Mom." Paige placed a hand on her mother's arm. "Mom."

Emily partially opened her eyes. "Paige…what time is it?"

Paige leaned in closer. "It's a little after six."

"Is it morning? Or night?" Emily opened her eyes wider. "Water," she said as she placed a hand on her throat.

Paige poured some water from a small blue pitcher into a plastic cup. She placed a red-and-white straw in the cup and handed it to her mom. Todd picked up for the bed controller and untangled the cord from the bed sheets. "Let's sit you up," he said.

Emily turned her head, "You're here too."

"It's morning," said Paige as she adjusted the pillow behind her mother's head.

"So early. Why are you here?"

"I never left. We need to tell you something," said Paige.

"What's wrong?" Emily sat straight up. "Is it Cate?"

"No. It's not Cate." Paige took hold of her mother's hand. "Do you remember being woken up last night?"

Emily looked from Paige to Todd. "I remember Holly was in."

"Anyone else?" Todd asked.

"No. Why?"

"I chased a strange man out of your room last night," said Paige.

"You did." Emily gasped. "I don't remember."

"Don't worry. The police are here," said Todd.

"They also found a maintenance worker…dead on the second floor," said Paige as she took the plastic cup from her mother's trembling hand. Emily held on to the edge of the bedsheet. "You're going to be moved to another room."

Emily tightened her grip. "The man in my room, you think he wanted to hurt me?"

"Maybe," said Paige. Emily released the sheet. She placed a hand on each side rail of the bed. Todd placed his hand on top of her left hand and Paige her right.

"Yes," said Todd as he rubbed his mother's arm. "The move is for your protection."

Emily remained quiet. "You understand?" Emily took a deep breath and nodded.

The door opened. Jane and a tall lanky orderly, in white cotton scrubs, pushing a wheelchair, entered. "It's time," she said. Todd and Paige stepped back and then left the room.

"It'll take fifteen, twenty minutes to settle her in," said Jane as they passed Todd and Paige in the hall. Paige gave Jane a small smile. *Pretty and efficient.*

"Here you are!" Cate announced as she joined Paige and Todd in the hallway near room 327. "Why did they move Mom?"

"Didn't you get my message?" Todd asked.

"No. What's going on?"

"A strange man slipped into Mom's room last night," said Paige. Cate covered her mouth with a hand. "Mom?"

"She's fine," said Todd.

"Why?"

Paige tilted her head and gave Cate a look. "Isn't it obvious?"

"What?"

"Someone thinks Mom knows something," said Todd.

"You think it has something to do with Dad's murder," said Cate.

"Of course, it does," said Paige.

"What are the police doing?" Cate put a hand on her hip.

"Nathan's here. He had Mom moved to protect her," said Paige.

"I should've never left," said Cate.

"I was here," said Paige.

"You should've called me right away!"

"You were exhausted when you left last night," said Paige.

"You should've called anyways," said Cate.

"Calm down. Mom is okay. A police officer has been assigned to protect her," said Todd. Just then, the door to Emily's new room opened.

Nurse Jane stepped out and walked over to the siblings. "Your mom is all set. You can go in. She's asking for you."

"Thank you," said Cate as she stepped away. Paige and Todd followed her past Officer Taylor and through the doorway into Emily's new room.

"Mom! I won't leave you again. I promise," said Cate.

"I'm okay. Just hungry," said Emily. "Jane said she'd be back with my breakfast."

"It's nice to see you sitting up in a chair," said Todd.

"It feels good to sit up. I'm tired of lying in bed," said Emily.

Cate brushed a hair from her mother's forehead. "You look good."

"She looks better than I feel. I'd like to go home and change," said Paige.

"Todd, can you take her home? I'm staying with Mom." Cate stared at Paige.

Paige turned to Todd. "Do you mind?"

"That's why Nathan called me," he replied.

On the ride home, Paige leaned her head against the car window and closed her eyes. The coolness of the glass against her forehead was refreshing. *Damn that Nathan, he knows me like a book.*

"Now that we're alone, give me some details," said Todd.

Paige slightly lifted her head. "Can we talk later? I'm exhausted. Last night was…insane."

"Nathan told me a little, but…"

"I promise to tell you all the gory details once I get cleaned up and changed."

Chapter 15

PAIGE ALLOWED HER BODY TO sink down into the tub until her head was totally submerged. She counted to five, ran her fingers through her wet silky hair to its ends, and resurfaced. She dunked into the bath water again and again. But no matter how hard she tried, she couldn't get clean; she couldn't erase the image of Charlie Reynold's bludgeoned body from her mind.

After her long soak in the tub, Paige dressed in her most comfy gray sweats and settled herself on the couch. "I feel much better," she said to Todd as he plopped himself down in the recliner alongside her.

"I've been thinking," said Todd as he popped up the foot rest of his chair. "If the man you chased is tied to Dad's murder, then we're all lucky you were there."

"I just reacted. If I'd stopped to think, I'd probably have screamed," said Paige.

"Why Mom? Why now?" Todd asked.

"The police said she was found unconscious at the accident scene. The killer must've thought she was dead," said Paige. "And now they know she's not." A haunting silence fell over the room.

"That's a scary thought," said Todd.

"It's the only explanation. And now...that poor maintenance man. The room was splattered everywhere with blood, like a spin art project out of control. His body...in a puddle of his own blood. It was gross...so much." Paige drew in a deep breath. "I wonder how long he lay there, bleeding out..."

"What was Dad mixed *up* in?"

"Something dangerous!" said Paige.

"Dad? Come on," said Todd.

"What else?"

"You don't really think that…"

"I thought it was a crazy idea. After this, I've changed my mind," said Paige.

"Maybe you're right. Wonder how they knew where to find Mom?"

"Someone's been watching us."

"Did you talk to anyone about Mom?"

"Michael asked a few questions at dinner last night."

"Like what?" Todd raised an eyebrow.

"He asked how she was feeling." Paige hesitated. "He did ask if the police had been in to question her."

"What did you tell him?"

"That…they had," said Paige.

"Anything else?"

"I may've mentioned Mom's memory was coming back."

"You tell him Mom remembers… Now a man sneaks into her room."

"It wasn't Michael." Paige pulled her legs up and in to sit Indian style. "No… Michael dropped me at the hospital. He knew I'd be there. It doesn't make sense. The man I saw was surprised. He ran when he saw me."

"Guys like that don't do their own dirty work. I don't trust him."

"Not sure I do either," said Paige.

"Then why did you go out with him?"

"He's been nosing around our family. And it's not just because our parents are friends."

Paige paused. "But mostly, I was curious. Don't you want to know why Cate said he was bad news?"

"Leave me out of it. That's between you and Cate," said Todd.

"Now that I've said it out loud, it does sound childish," said Paige.

"You think," said Todd. Paige shrugged. "We need to start taking a good look at Mom and Dad's recent activities," Todd continued. "We should ask Cate."

"You call her," said Paige as she jumped up and headed to the study. "Ask her if she knows where Mom's date book is."

Todd followed and stood in the study doorway, watching Paige. "We've already looked in here," he said.

"We must've overlooked something," said Paige as she slid open a side drawer of the desk. Pulling everything out, piece by piece, she set the contents on top of the desk. "Better us than the police. After last night, they'll be dissecting all our lives. We need to know if there are secrets." Paige struggled with the thought that her parents had secrets. Secrets that may've gotten her father killed, secrets that were putting her mother's life in jeopardy, the evidence was piling up. *I'm not going to just stand by and let another person I love be murdered.*

"You make it sound like our parents were mastermind criminals," said Todd.

"Of course, they weren't. But something was going on. We need to be certain," said Paige.

"You're right." Todd picked up the small, brown, address book from the desktop.

"I already went through that."

"When'd you do that?"

"Yesterday afternoon. I checked out the names online. Then called some of the numbers. I left a message for one of Dad's work colleagues," said Paige.

"But he was retired."

"He did some consulting with a local engineering firm recently," remarked Paige as she continued to rummage through her dad's desk. Nothing seemed to jump out at her, just the usual pens, pads, paperclips, and a stack of business cards. She quickly sifted through the cards—an electrician, plumber, hardware store, cardiologist, attorney, and accountant. She separated them into two piles on top of the desk. Todd began removing books from the shelves. One by one, he took them down, flipped them over, then flipped through the pages.

"What are you doing?" Paige asked.

"I'm looking for Dad's journal," said Todd.

"Hey, look! Newspaper clippings." Paige held up a manila folder. She placed the folder on the desk blotter, seated herself, and began to read. "They're all from local papers and they're all about the new reservoir. This one's about the body that was found during its construction."

Human Remains Found during Meadowbrook Reservoir Construction
June 15, 2012

The remains of what appear to be a human body were found Thursday during the construction of the new Meadowbrook Reservoir. Authorities have reported that the backhoe operator, who unearthed the remains, was surprised and shaken by the discovery. "I was just doing my job," said Mark Phillips. "Nothing like this has ever happened to me before."

The Meadowbrook Police Department was quick to respond to the scene and have cordoned off the area to the public. The remains were removed by the medical examiner's office and have been sent to the state university for forensic testing to determine how long the body has been concealed in the area. University personnel will be working on identifying the victim; test results may take months.

When asked if construction would continue, Meadowbrook Mayor William Jacobs stated, "Until the results are back from the state lab, the reservoir project is indefinitely on hold."

Paige swiveled the desk chair around till she was facing Todd. "Look, another article. Eight months later." As Paige read aloud, Todd stopped and turned his attentions to her.

Construction Resumes on Meadowbrook Reservoir Project
February 15, 2013

After being halted eight months ago, when human remains were unearthed during phase II of the project, construction of the Meadowbrook Reservoir is back on starting Monday, February 18, 2013. The State Medical Examiner's office has completed its investigation and released the site. Once restarted, and with no further delays, the reservoir should be up and running by July of 2014.

It has been determined that the human remains found while grading the construction site near Cattail Creek are the remains of an adolescent male approximately 12 to 16 years of age.

After months of forensic testing the lab has ascertained that the remains were buried for a period of at least 20 to 26 years. Injuries to the body are consistent with those of being hit by a vehicle.

Cause of death has been listed as vehicular homicide. Police believe the body was moved and dumped in the Cattail Creek Marsh. Officials are reviewing all open missing children cases from the '80s and '90s in an effort to determine the adolescence's identity.

Remains Found during Reservoir Construction Identified
September 12, 2013

The remains of a teenaged boy found in June of 2012 during the construction of the Meadowbrook Reservoir were identified yesterday as Ryan Timmons of Meadowbrook. He was 14 years old and a freshman at Meadowbrook High School when he disappeared in 1991. At the time of his disappearance, the whole town of Meadowbrook searched for weeks to no avail. The Timmons family moved from Meadowbrook in

1995, making a DNA sample difficult to obtain and delaying the identification of the remains.

Ryan Timmons was not the only child from Meadowbrook to go missing during 1991.

William McIntyre, seven years old, disappeared in January of 1991. His body was recovered in Echo Pond in March of 1991. Police records list his death as an accident.

Paige looked up from the article, "I thought they never found Billy McIntyre."

"I thought his family moved," said Todd. "It was a long time ago. What does it matter? None of this has anything to do with Dad's death."

"Probably not. But if Dad saved them, they must've meant something to him."

Paige held up another newspaper cutting, "this is the last one." She read it aloud:

Meadowbrook Reservoir Recreation Area Opens
July 2, 2014

Just in time for the Fourth of July holiday weekend, the long-anticipated opening of the Meadowbrook Reservoir Recreation area occurred on Tuesday, July 1, 2014. Mayor Jacobs was on hand to cut the ribbon and allow the first visitors into the area. The park will be open seven days a week, Sunday through Saturday, from dawn to dusk.

Special activities are planned for the holiday weekend, which include a fishing tournament for 4—to 14-year old youths, free pontoon sightseeing boat rides, children pony rides, and a petting zoo. For a complete list of all events, go to www.meadowbrookrecreation.com.

"Everyone likes a good mystery. Especially, Dad," said Todd. "That's probably why he saved those articles."

"Maybe…but he was consulting on the project."

"He was?"

"When I spoke with an associate at Layton, Gilbert and Alston Engineering yesterday, he mentioned it."

"Then…that explains it."

"Maybe…I just think there's more here than meets the eye. Put this information together with the pictures. Where *are* the pictures?"

"I put them in a book." Todd removed Mark Twain's *The Adventures of Huckleberry Finn* from the top shelf and opened it. "Here they are." He handed the photos to Paige.

"Can they be enlarged?" asked Todd.

"I'd need a scanner. Or the memory card. Have you seen a camera anywhere?"

"Not in here. Check the basement."

"Did you speak to Cate yet?"

"She didn't answer," said Todd.

"Can you call her again. Ask her about Dad's camera." Paige handed the envelope back to Todd and left the room.

As she pulled open the basement door, she called out, "Don't forget to ask Cate about Mom's date book." Holding on to the stairwell railing, she felt along the wall for the light switch and then mindfully took a downward step. *It's just a basement.* She continued until she was standing on the cold, cement, basement floor with her bare feet. It still had the same dampness and musty smell, as when she was a child. Her parents had always planned on finishing the basement, but time and money had gotten away from them. Instead, it became her father's would-be workshop. She reached up and pulled on a short string dangling in the middle of the room. A single overhead light bulb came on.

A stack of gray plastic utility boxes stood alongside her father's wooden workbench. Paige walked over to the bench, picked up her father's red-handled screwdriver, and held on to it firmly. He had spent endless hours in the basement putting things together, fixing broken toys, and fiddling with an old ham, radio. She remained stationary picturing her father using that very same screwdriver to remove the training wheels on her bike when she was six.

"Yes, Paige, tell your mother I'll be up for supper in a minute."

Startled, Paige spun around. "Dad?" A chill ran through her. *It's just your imagination.*

The front doorbell chimed, breaking the spell of the unsettling occurrence. She shook it off and returned back up the steps to the first floor.

Chapter 16

TODD WAS JUST OPENING THE front door as Paige entered the living room. Much to her surprise, it was Nathan along with another plain clothed officer. Nathan asked the officer to wait outside on the front porch and then stepped inside. He looked as tired as Paige felt; his clothes were unkempt, and he had dark circles under his eyes. What had she expected, she *had* roused him out of bed, before dawn! "Todd, pour him a cup of coffee. I'll be back in a moment," said Paige as she ran upstairs to her bedroom. Paige saw her reflection in the mirror. Horrified at what see saw, she ran a hairbrush through her damp hair, quickly applied some makeup, and threw on a pair of jeans and a navy tee. *What am I doing?*

Paige ran back down to the living room. Todd and Nathan had disappeared into the kitchen. She stood outside the door and listened. "CIU has finished going over your mom's hospital room," said Nathan. "We're not going to move her back. She'll be safer in the new room. Don't worry…there'll be a uniformed officer outside the door at all times."

"Did the crime unit find anything?" asked Paige as she entered the room.

"There were no fingerprints on the IV pole," added Nathan.

"Why would there be, I told you he was wearing gloves."

"And you were right. We found a surgical glove in the trash just outside the door of ICU. It's been sent to the lab."

"Have you looked at the security footage from last night?"

Nathan looked directly at Paige. "Who's running this investigation?"

"You are," replied Paige.

"My team is reviewing the footage."

"Sorry." Paige looked like she was about to break. "I just want this over."

"It will be...soon."

"How soon?"

"I don't know." Nathan held up his index finger, with a determined look in his eyes. "I will wrap this up as soon as possible... You have *my* word."

"What about the maintenance man?" Paige continued.

"There's still more work to do on that crime scene. I'd appreciate you not disclosing to anyone what you saw."

"I already told Todd."

"No one else."

"Okay."

"This is the kind of thing the newspapers like to get a hold of and blow out of proportion. The department will make a statement shortly."

"We appreciate you keeping us in the loop," said Todd.

"Of course, you two are like family to me," said Nathan. "But that's not the only reason I'm here."

Paige tilted her head and gave Nathan a sideways look. "Oh..."

"I'm here to get you."

"Me," said Paige.

"You need to come downtown and make an official statement about last night."

"I already told you everything I saw."

"This is for the record. We are taking statements from everyone who was present last night...and that includes you."

Paige stood. "Okay. But I need to put on shoes."

"I'll wait for you outside."

As Nathan opened the back door of his dark gray unmarked cruiser, Paige gave him a puzzled look. "It's department policy. Sorry," he said.

"What about your friend?" Paige asked.

"You mean Detective Boyd?" Nathan held on to the open door. "You were upstairs. Todd knows."

"Knows what?"

"Boyd's been assigned to stay in the neighborhood…watch the house." Nathan looked Paige in the eye and took her hand. "I'm not taking any chances."

Paige looked down at his hand then back up. There was a glint of sunlight reflecting in his eyes. She gave him a half smirk of a smile. "Is there something you're not telling me?"

"No," he replied as he quickly let go of her hand.

Paige sat sideways on the back seat, swung her legs around, and got in the car. Nathan closed the door behind her and then settled into the driver's seat. Paige leaned forward to speak through the steel bars that divided the front of the vehicle from the back.

"This is awkward," she said as she leaned forward and held onto the bars.

"Can't be helped."

"Hey, I never thanked you for rushing to the hospital this morning."

Nathan slightly turned his head. "No worries."

"I really am grateful."

"It's my job. If you hadn't called, it would've been dispatch." He turned his attentions back to the task at hand and started the cruiser.

"I'm sorry I didn't keep in touch over the years," said Paige breaking the awkward silence. "Don't be, life happens." He pulled at the collar of his shirt. He took a deep breath, adjusted his shoulders, and moved forward, away from the metal bars. Away from Paige's warm breath curling the hair on the back of his neck, making his heart pound wildly.

"Please sit back and put your seat belt on," Nathan calmly but abruptly said.

Paige sat back, clipped her seat belt, and continued, "Back in the day, if someone had said this would be happening, I wouldn't have believed them."

"Believed what? You in the back seat of a cop car?" chuckled Nathan.

"Funny," said Paige as she settled in for the ten-minute ride to the police headquarters.

CHAPTER 17

IT WAS LATE AFTERNOON WHEN Nathan returned Paige to her parents' home. He quickly jumped out and opened the cruiser's door for her. As he took her hand and helped her out, she yawned.

"You need sleep," he said as he yawned.

She laughed. "It's contagious."

He yawned again. "You're right."

"We both need rest," said Paige. She looked up at him. "I'm glad you're lead detective on this."

"I'd have it no other way," said Nathan as he looked both ways, up and down the street.

An unmarked SUV was parked two doors away. "The white one." Paige turned to look.

"That's Boyd's vehicle. If he's not here, he's in the neighborhood. When he's off duty, someone else will be there." They stopped just short of the front porch. The door opened and Todd waved them in. "You're in good hands. This is where I leave you. Get some rest," said Nathan.

"I will."

"You get some rest too," said Paige. Halfway down the sidewalk, he turned back, smiled, and gave a small wave.

"You and Nathan…looking friendly," said Todd.

"Please…let it go…" Paige threw her hands up and walked into the house. Her mind was already clouded. She didn't need to be explaining herself to Todd. Especially, when she wasn't sure, what she was thinking…let alone feeling.

"While you were at the station, I did some more digging. I found some more newspaper clippings. Frank Wilson is off his rocker, if you ask me."

"What?"

"He was against the town building the reservoir."

"I'm sure he wasn't alone," said Paige as she followed Todd into the study.

"Read the top story, you'll see," said Todd.

Local Attorney Organizes against Meadowbrook Reservoir
April 10, 2010

Frank Wilson, local attorney, and town councilman, has organized the group "Save the Tree Frog" to help preserve the farmland and wooded areas along Cattail Creek which lie southwest of Meadowbrook. The group states that the area being surveyed for the Meadowbrook reservoir, is home to the endangered Southern Gray Tree Frog, which rely on the freshwater creek, farm fields, and oak and pine forest throughout the area for their survival.

A spokesman from Layton, Gilbert, and Alston Engineering, which is designing and engineering the reservoir, has stated that an ecological survey of the area was done by the township and his firm. No evidence exists to substantiate Frank Wilson's claim that the Southern Gray Tree Frog is living in the area. The Southern Gray Tree Frog, which does habitat in New Jersey is not a native of the county and only lives and breeds in the southern counties of the state.

"We ask that all the friends of the Southern Gray Tree Frog come out this Saturday and support our cause. Our group wants to conserve not only the Tree Frog, but all the vegetation and wildlife in the Cattail Creek area. We hope to educate the public with our rally. We can only stop the destruction of the marsh lands around Cattail Creek with the help of all concerned Meadowbrook citizens. We need to halt this travesty," said Frank Wilson when interviewed at his law office. A permit for a rally has been granted to the group and will be held on Saturday, May 15, 2010, at the Meadowbrook Fair Grounds.

"Look at the picture attached to this other article dated, May 16." Todd pointed. "Isn't that Dad standing in the background?"

Paige leaned in closer. "It does look like Dad. Why would he be there?"

"You said he worked on the project."

"I guess that's it," said Paige.

"Any word from Cate?" Paige asked as she set the remaining articles aside and picked up the photos of the white egret.

"Yes."

"And?"

"Mom is doing well," said Todd.

Paige shot Todd a look. "What about Mom's date book and Dad's camera?"

"The date book is in Mom's purse, which is at her house."

"What about the camera?"

"She didn't know."

Looking down at the photos in her hand, Paige added, "After I nap, I'll go over to the library. They might have a scanner I can use to enlarge these."

"Good idea. You take a nap. I'll finish up here."

Paige buried her face in a large bed pillow and closed her eyes. Her aching body began to relax, but as tired as she was, adrenaline kept pumping through her veins. She flipped over the pillow, punched it, and then fluffed it until it conformed to her head. She rolled her body from the left side to the right then back again. She wiggled her feet and ankles and stretched her body. Finally, after endlessly staring at the ceiling fan spinning round and round above, she fell asleep.

CHAPTER 18

A CLAP OF THUNDER RADIATED through the house, shaking Paige awake. Without opening her eyes, she instinctively reached to turn on the table lamp next to the bed. Nothing. She clicked the lamp switch again. Nothing. She pried her eyes open. The digital clock wasn't illuminated.

The room was pitch dark. How long had she been napping? She sat on the edge of the bed, watching out the window as the sky lit up and thunder rattled the house. There was something exciting and extremely beautiful about nature out of control. The thrill of it stirred her. A smile formed on her lips as she thought of her and Jeremy rolling in the sheets during a thunderstorm. Would she ever be able to let herself go again? Let go enough to the point where she could unreservedly give her heart, soul, and body to another? Would she ever trust again? She was so involved in her own thoughts that she didn't hear Todd banging on the bedroom door.

"Are you up?"

Stunned, she jumped up and off the bed, and with a racing heart, she yelled, "Yes." Then she yanked open the door. Todd stood there with a large baton flashlight.

"Hey!" She placed her hands over her face to cut the streaming light from blinding her.

"Looks like the power's out."

"Any idea what time it is?"

"It was close to 3:00 a.m. last time I checked."

"I can't believe I slept that long."

"You were tired. I found Dad's camera in his toolbox in the basement."

"His toolbox...that's a strange place. Where is it?"

"I left it on the kitchen counter."

Paige grabbed her fully charged laptop from the nightstand and walked past Todd. "Are you coming?" Todd followed her with the flashlight guiding their steps.

"It's chilly down here. Did you leave a door open?"

"No. I locked up everything before I went to bed. Stay here." Todd pushed past her and entered the kitchen, flashlight first. The kitchen door was swinging in and out with the wind. The floor was sopped with rain water.

"The wind…it blew the door off its hinges." Todd tried to close the door. "This wasn't the wind! There's a muddy footprint on the outside of this. This door was kicked in!" He looked from the door to Paige.

"What the hell…is going on?" Paige grabbed a dish towel and threw it on the floor. "I better get some bigger towels from the bathroom."

"Don't go anywhere. Someone could be in the house," said Todd.

"I think we ran them off when we came downstairs."

"Maybe…but we better check," added Todd.

Todd led the way as they carefully and methodically checked all the rooms and windows on the first floor. Right behind him, Paige carried a ten-pound fire extinguisher, checking their six all the while. Once they were convinced the house was empty, Paige grabbed an armful of towels from the linen closet and went back to the kitchen. As she placed the towels on the table, the lights came back on.

"This is a muddy mess!"

"We need to call the police," said Todd.

"We will." Paige hesitated. "Where's the camera?"

"I put it on the counter…by the canisters."

"It's not here…"

"Check by the outlet, I was charging its battery."

Todd picked up the house phone and held the receiver to his ear. He tapped it in the palm of his hand and then banged it on the wall. He held it out toward Paige. "No dial tone."

"Use your cell."

Paige double-checked the counter. "I can't find it."

Todd walked over and smacked the counter. "It was right here. Damn it! They took it."

"I'm going to check outside," said Paige as she went out the front door. She walked the outside perimeter of the yard, checking for any evidence of the intruder. She desperately hoped that in the thief's haste to escape, they may've dropped the camera.

"What are doing out here?" asked Nathan. "You're drenched."

"Just looking," said Paige. "Unfortunately, the rain has washed away any footprints. But there's a path of mud to and from the deck. It leads to the side gate. The gate is open. It's always closed."

"Please get inside. We'll take it from here," said Nathan.

"What happened to your man? Boyd."

"There was a hit-and-run a short distance from here. He was called away. I'll deal with that when we're done here."

"We're safe. Don't be too hard on him."

"He was assigned here. He should've stayed here." Nathan was firm. "And if the higher-ups changed his assignment, I should've been advised."

They stepped up onto the deck and waited under the overhang of the roof while an officer took pictures of the damage to the lock and muddy footprint on the door. "Once the sun comes up, we'll take another look around the property." Nathan moved a strand of Paige's tousled, wet hair from her face and gently tucked it behind her ear. "You're going to get yourself sick."

"I'll be fine." A chill ran through Paige and her body shook. He placed an arm around her shoulders and drew her closer.

"It looks like they never got past the kitchen. Though to be sure, we'll need to search the house," said Nathan.

"We already did. But you're welcome to it," said Paige.

"Maybe you two shouldn't be staying here," said Nathan.

"No...we're staying," insisted Paige.

"I don't need you getting hurt...or worse..."

"What aren't you telling us?"

Nathan blinked and then closed his eyes. He ran his fingers across his brow and down his face, sighed, and took a deep breath.

"I believe…I know…someone is looking for something. I've put in a request to the department chief for round-the-clock protection for your whole family."

"What does that mean?" Paige asked.

"If approved, they'll be a man with you at all times."

"Like a bodyguard!" Paige waved her arms. "Oh, no."

"Exactly. Until then, they'll be a man out front. A perimeter check will be run every half hour."

"I don't need a bodyguard. It was a break-in," said Paige.

"Let's see what Burglary comes up with. They'll be writing up the report on this. I'll get a copy when it's complete." Nathan took a few steps away from Paige.

"Are you leaving?"

"I've a lot of work to do on the Reynolds' murder…and your father's."

"Any new leads?" Paige asked as they moved back into the house.

"Progress."

"What kind of answer is that?"

"The only kind I can give you."

"Come on, it's me. You can tell me," said Paige as they walked from the back door to the front.

"You know I can't." Nathan left, leaving Paige standing in the open doorway pondering all the possibilities.

CHAPTER 19

PAIGE PULLED HER JEEP INTO the first parking spot she found in the downtown lot, jumped out onto the asphalt, and made her way through a narrow alley that lead out to Main Street. The hurry in her step halted the moment her feet hit the maple-lined sidewalk, and in an instant, she was transported back to a simpler time in her life. A time when all she cared about were childish games. She walked a short distance before coming to a complete stop in front of Dobb's Hobby Shop, where every Saturday, she and Nathan would meet.

They'd rush to finish their chores, get their weekly allowances, pool their funds, buy the latest toy on the market, and then giggle with delight as they biked to Deer Hollow Park to play. She was lost in the vivid memory of a rocket mishap, when fingers wrapped around her right arm.

"I thought that was you."

Paige whipped around, looked down at her right bicep, and straight up into Michael's face. "Do you often accost women on the street?"

"I was just thinking about you, and here you are. What're you doing in town?" He eased his tight grip, slowly slid his fingers down her arm, and gently squeezed her hand as he released it.

"I'm on my way to the library."

"Work research? Can I walk with you?"

"If you'd like." Annoyed that her pleasant memory had been interrupted, Paige took a step and Michael moved with her. "I'm sorry... I was so distracted the other night. I want you to know, I did enjoy our evening."

The other night, thought Paige. Had it only been two days since they'd had dinner? So much had happened in the last forty-eight hours that it didn't seem possible. "Yes, *it was* nice," Paige tentatively replied.

"Now *you* seem distracted?"

"Just tired." Paige continued to walk. "So much going on."

"Is your mother all right?"

"She's good."

"Then what is it?" He touched her arm again.

Paige stopped. "It's a long story. Right now, I need to get to the library before it closes."

"You have a deadline."

She didn't answer. In a way, she did have a deadline. A deadline to figure out who, what, and why her parents had been targeted.

"Why don't you come by my office after you're done? It's at the corner of Third and Main. Just two blocks up."

"I really don't have time," Paige finally answered.

"We can go to Mahoney's for a drink. You can explain it all to me." He seemed genuinely interested. And she did have questions…about his father's campaign against the development of the Meadowbrook Reservoir.

"That'd be nice. Maybe tomorrow?"

"Are you sure…you can't today?" His blue eyes danced across her face. On any other day, she might've been easily enticed by his sweet smile and gorgeous eyes, but today, she was just too preoccupied.

"I'm sure."

"Okay, then…tomorrow. Meet me at Mahoney's tomorrow evening. Six p.m."

"I'll call you tomorrow, if I can make it. I must go now." Paige briskly walked away, leaving him dazed. He was not used to indifference.

Paige took the library steps two at a time until she pushed through the front glass doors.

She read aloud from a large sign in the lobby. "Summer hours, Monday–Thursday, 3:00 p.m. closing." *Crap…it's almost two.*

Well, it couldn't have been helped. She'd never have forgiven herself, if she hadn't stopped by the hospital first to check on her mother. It'd been a relief to find her awake and talking with Cate.

Cate was carefully running a small pink brush through her mother's auburn hair. Paige remembered her sister brushing her own hair when she was young. Of course, she wasn't as gentle with her. "Look, sis, doesn't she look wonderful," Cate had said with a big smile as Paige entered Emily's room.

"She does," replied Paige as she approached them and took hold of her mother's hand.

"Mom, you *do* look great." The color had returned to Emily's cheeks and there was some resemblance to the vibrant women she had been before the accident. "How are you feeling?"

"Physically, I feel quite well. But I'm still trying to comprehend... Cate has been telling me about the commotion the other night. I still don't remember any of it. I feel like I've just woken up from a nightmare."

"Let's not overdo it. We can talk more later," interrupted Cate as she gently swiped a makeup brush in an upward motion over her mother's cheek. "How about a little lip gloss?"

"Stop fussing over me," Emily said, pushing Cate's hand away from her face.

"Your lips are dry and cracking. You need this."

"I don't care what I need. I want to know what's been going on."

"If you stop moving around and let me do your lips," Cate spoke to her mother as if speaking to a child, "we'll tell you the rest." Paige rolled her eyes as she shook her head ever so slightly with a snicker on her face. "Maybe Paige should be telling you. She was here."

"It's over. The most important thing is...you're safe here," said Paige.

"Here...I'd rather be home," said Emily.

"You will be...soon. Nathan and his whole department are working overtime. Once he has answers...he'll fill us in. Right now, I need to get to the library."

"Do you have to?" Cate asked.

"I've some research to do...you know...the project I've been working on," said Paige.

"That's right...I forgot...go ahead. I'll stay with Mom," said Cate with a knowing look.

With no time to waste, Paige headed straight to the front desk of the library. An elderly gentleman behind a large desk, dressed in tan khakis and a green plaid button-down, asked if he could be of service. He pointed her in the direction of the copier. He must've misunderstood when she'd asked if they had a scanner. But Paige figured, it wouldn't hurt her cause to try and enlarge the photos on the copier.

It helped some, but the enlargements lacked depth and definition. Dissatisfied, Paige went back to the librarian's desk and asked again. "I thought the copier also scanned," he replied when she inquired again. Frustrated, Paige took her photocopies and lugubriously walked out of the library.

The outside air was much thicker than earlier, and as Paige descended the front library steps, large raindrops plummeted downward from dark clouds overhead. It wasn't unusual to have an afternoon thunderstorm, but this downpour was unexpected and unwelcomed. She ran and took shelter under the nearest store awning and waited until the rain let up a bit before darting across the street to the diner. There, she stepped inside and shook off like a wet dog after a romp through a pond.

"Paige, is it that you?"

She looked up from the puddle she'd deposited on the foyer floor. "Sorry, I've made a mess."

"When I saw Nate last night, he mentioned you were back in town."

"Maggie...how are you?"

"I'm good. How are you? I was so sorry to hear about your father," the well-endowed hostess said as she handed Paige a napkin.

"You back for long?"

"Till my parents' affairs are in order."

"We should all catch up...you...me...Nate."

"If there's time."

"Are you sitting or getting something to go?"

"I think I'll sit until I dry off. I'll be at the counter. It was nice seeing you."

Immediately, a young teenaged blonde with a ponytail bee-bopped her way along the counter with a menu and a pot of coffee. "Will you be eating anything?"

Famished, Paige ordered a grilled cheese and ham sandwich. As she waited for her order, she got to wondering what Maggie meant when she had said she *saw* Nate last night. He hadn't mentioned he was seeing anyone. *It wasn't as if she cared. His personal life was no concern of hers.* Whatever the reason, she wasn't imagining the stare down she was getting from Maggie.

Paige took one of the photocopies from her laptop case and mused while she waited for her sandwich. She and Maggie weren't exactly friends in high school, but they weren't enemies either. Why the hostility? She moved the picture, hoping that a change in lighting and angle would expose something. She scrunched her face and narrowed her eyes, nothing earth shattering appeared. Then suddenly it hit her. Of course, why hadn't she thought of it? Michael would have a scanner at his law office. It was just two blocks away. She'd come up with an acceptable excuse for her earlier rudeness and ask him for a favor.

When the rain ceased and the thunder faded into the distance, Paige paid her tab and left, only too happy to be out of the reach of Maggie's threatening glares. Energized and rejuvenated, she practically ran the entire way to Third and Main. Once there, she stood outside the law offices of Wilson & Wilson catching her breath before hesitantly placing her hand on the doorknob. As she did so, the door swung outward, throwing her off balance.

"Excuse me," said a gruff-looking man with a wild expression on his face and an unkempt salt-and-pepper beard.

Paige stepped backward as he pushed by like a bull escaping the slaughter house. Once he was out of sight, she entered through the open door.

Behind a small desk, a well-polished receptionist with manicured red nails looked up from a computer screen. "May I help you?"

"I was hoping Michael Wilson was in."

"Do you have an appointment?"

"I don't. I'm Paige Thompson, a friend." The receptionist looked her up and down before getting up from her chair and walking into a back office. Realizing she must look dreadful, Paige ran her fingers through her hair.

"Now this is unexpected. What brings you here?"

"I got caught in the rain. I'm a mess."

"You look enchanting, like an adorable mermaid."

Right. Paige rolled her eyes and inwardly laughed at the picture of herself flopping around like a wet fish. Which ironically, she felt like.

"Have you reconsidered my offer?" Hearing the hope in Michael's voice, she sighed inwardly with relief.

"No. But I was hoping you could help me."

"Anything."

"Do you have a scanner I could use? The library didn't have one."

"I do. Give me a few minutes to finish up with my client."

"Thank you. Do you have a ladies' room I could use?"

"Eve, please show Ms. Thompson to the ladies' room." He turned back to Paige. "You must be working on something very important."

She nodded as she gave him a vague look. Michael left the waiting area, disappearing down the hallway from which he had come. Paige sat and waited patiently for a long while.

Finally, a dark-haired woman in her fifties entered the waiting room and smiled at her as she put on a tan raincoat. Michael reemerged and motioned with his hand for Paige to come on in. They proceeded down a long, wide hallway, passing by several closed office doors. When they passed a door with the name plate FRANK WILSON on it, Paige heard the raised voices of two men. She couldn't quite make out what they were saying, but she recognized the tone. It was one of immense disdain. She turned to look at Michael, who seemed to be paying it no mind.

He ushered her along until they reached his office.

"Thank you so much for this," said Paige.

"I told you, if you needed anything while you were in town, I was your man!" He flashed her a big grin.

"You did say that."

"What're you working on? You were so determined when I ran into you earlier."

"It's in the formation stage. I can't disclose yet."

"Sounds mysterious," he said as he slapped his hand on the top of his desk chair.

"Sit…the scanner is in the corner. The Wi-Fi user ID and passcode are on the machine."

"This won't take long."

Michael picked up a yellow legal pad. "I've notes to give to Eve," he said and left his office.

Paige fired up her laptop, connected to the scanner, and then took the small white envelope containing her father's photos out. Carefully removing each, one by one, she scanned the photos, saved them to a file, and copied them to a flip drive. Then, before shutting down her laptop, she took a quick look at the file, reassuring herself that all the photos were there. Later, she'd enlarge, crop, and edit them. Mission complete, she closed her laptop and leaned back, letting her body melt into the mahogany, high-back, leather chair she'd been sitting in. Her eyes narrowed as she moved her neck from left to right several times, releasing all her pent-up angst.

"Hello, young lady," came a voice from the doorway of Michael's office. Paige slowly swiveled the mahogany chair around until she was face-to-face with a distinguished silver-haired man, with a tall, trim stature. She recognized the man's eyes. They had the same brilliant blue hue as Michael's.

She immediately hopped up. "Mr. Wilson! So nice to see you again. How are you?" *How long had he been standing there?*

"Have we met?"

"Paige Thompson," she said in her most composed voice as she extended her hand. "Emily and Nicholas's daughter."

"Of course, you look a lot like your mother. You poor thing." He took her hand and patted the top of it. "So awful…your father. Your mother…she's recovering?"

140

"Better every day."

"Great news! What are you doing here? Do you have an appointment with Michael? If there are questions about your father's will, I'm the one to see. Where's my son?" His tone changed from sympathetic to contentious.

"Michael stepped out a moment to speak with Eve. He was kind enough to let me use his office for a project I'm working on."

"That's right. You're the daughter who's a reporter."

"Photographer. I work for a news agency back home." A chill ran through her, causing her body to shutter and her shoulders to shrug involuntarily.

"There's no story here." His tone was stern.

"You've got it all wrong. Michael and I are acquaintances. He's helping me out."

"You remember, Paige, don't you, Dad?" Michael said as he walked in and stood next to her. Paige and I met at the hospital after her parents' accident."

"You didn't mention." Mr. Wilson looked at Michael disapprovingly, before softening his demeanor and turning his attentions back to Paige. "I'm sorry I startled you, dear. Give your mother my regards." As quickly as he had appeared, Mr. Wilson, disappeared. *Well, that was disturbing.* She found it hard to imagine her easy-going father and uptight Mr. Wilson ever being friends. They seemed polar opposites.

"I hope he didn't scare you." Michael looked down at her closed laptop. "He can be intimidating."

"Not at all," she lied. "But I don't think he likes me."

"But *I* like you." Michael put a friendly arm around her shoulder. "Your clothes are still damp."

"I should get home and change," said Paige as she rolled out of his embrace. "Thank you for your help."

"I couldn't help but overhear—acquaintances?"

"What?"

"You told my father we are acquaintances."

"Aren't we?"

"I was hoping by now you'd consider me a friend. Maybe a little more?"

"Of course, we're friends." Paige smiled and then turned away from him. She picked up her laptop. "I really do need to get going."

"You're on deadline. I'm holding you up. I understand. Let me walk you out."

As they walked the corridor back toward the lobby, Paige noticed that Mr. Wilson's office door was shut and angry voices were echoing once again. She slowed her gait, hoping to catch a word or two. Michael placed his hand on the middle of her back. She turned to look back at him as they passed the shut door. "Your father seems very passionate about his work."

"Is that your nice way of saying he's a loudmouth?"

"He seemed upset I was here."

"He's a very private man. Sometimes, borderline paranoid. It's been an adjustment coming home and working with him."

"You're not happy here?"

"It's still up in the air." He smiled at her as he held the lobby door to let her out. "But things are looking up."

"Remember we have a date, 6:00 p.m. tomorrow at Mahoney's."

"I'll try," were her final words as she walked out the door.

When Paige returned home, she found Todd in the kitchen, kneeling on the floor with a door hinge in one hand and a screwdriver in the other.

"I ran into Michael Wilson," said Paige.

"Where was that?" said Todd looking up from his crouched position.

"On my way to the library. Which…was a waste." She set her laptop on the table.

"Luckily, Michael let me use his office scanner. I also had a weird run in with Mr. Wilson while at his office."

"You do have an effect on people." Todd laughed.

"Stop it. I'm serious. I think he was really bothered… I was there."

Todd stood up. "Once this is realigned," he said holding onto the broken door, "I'm putting a dead bolt and chain on it."

Paige slipped the flip drive with her father's photos into her computer and opened the file.

"Oh my god!"

"What?"

"That man." Todd leaned in as she pointed to a large man with brown wavy hair, and a salt-and-pepper beard. That man...almost ran me over today."

"With a car?"

"No...not a car. At Wilson's law office. I was on my way in when the door burst open."

"Are you sure?"

"I'm certain. He sure was pissed about something," said Paige.

Todd closed the kitchen door, then opened it. "Perfect," he announced.

Paige looked away from her laptop. "You fixed it," then went right back to the screen and enlarged the next photo. "I don't know what this means, but it can't be a coincidence." She was so intent with the photos that she never noticed that Todd had left and returned with a power drill until a buzzing echoed throughout the kitchen. "Is that necessary?"

"Yes...the chain needs to be secure."

Paige turned. "The man in these photos...he's holding a shovel."

Todd lay the drill on the counter. "Looks like he's digging for something."

"Or burying something." Paige pointed at the corner of the screen. "We need to find this place."

"Where would we start?"

"Nathan seemed to think the egret photos were taken out at the reservoir," said Paige.

"We should start there."

"When I'm done, I still need to put a second chain on the front door," said Todd.

CHAPTER 20

WHILE TODD FINISHED UP THE repairs on the kitchen door, Paige's impatience got the best of her. What harm would it do, if she took a ride out to the Meadowbrook Reservoir, she rationalized.

She yelled out, "I've some errands to run," and she quickly left. After all, she needed no one's permission. She was more than capable of handling a walk in the woods by herself.

Twenty minutes later, Paige had located the east entrance to Meadowbrook Reservoir Woodlands Park, where she was greeted by a park ranger in khaki pants and shirt. After paying a small fee, another ranger waved her in and pointed her toward the main parking lot. On the far end of the large lot was a rustic two-story log cabin with a green tin roof. After pulling into a spot alongside a small boat trailer, Paige retrieved her camera and a pair of binoculars from the back seat and headed toward the building.

Situated near a long boat ramp and three docks, the lodge seemed to be the hub for the whole recreation area. The floating metal docks were lined with small aluminum boats and to the left of the them were twenty colorful kayaks and canoes for rent. A park directory hung on the side of the building, outlining the park rules and regulations, along with an extensive map of the seven-mile nature trail that encompassed the whole reservoir.

Paige stood on the dock and looked out across the large body of water. She would've loved spending all her time here as a child if it had existed. It was hard to believe this beautiful wonderland of fishing, boating, and hiking was once a forbidden marsh of skunk cabbage, cattails, and muck. Forbidden or not, Todd and she had spent a lot of time there when they were young. They would trek carefully along mushy trails in rubber boots till they reached the creek, where they would collect turtles, frogs, and toads as their father fished. It was always worth the muck because Cattail Creek was its own special kind of wonderland.

Of course, a trip to the marsh would never have been complete without taking a few cattails home with them. At night, serenaded by summer crickets, they would light the soft brown tops of the cattails, turning them into glowing torches. Paige enjoyed watching the smoke they produced, rise upward toward the heavens until it completely dissipated. Burning the cattails had a practical side too; the smoke helped keep annoying flying insects and blood-sucking mosquitoes away. Her musings were interrupted by the joyous laughter of children playing on nearby swings.

Paige studied the trail map she had picked up in the visitor's center. The trail started on the right side of the parking lot and then went through a wooded area and down a gentle incline to the edge of the water. From this point on, the trail followed the water's edge. Here, she paused to focus the lens of her camera on a pair of wading mallard ducks. As the colorful glossy green-headed male circled the malted tan female, she snapped several shots. Walkers, runners, and bikers passed behind her; and the sun glistened off the ebbing shallow water. For a moment, just one moment, she forgot why she was there before moving on.

Calculating that she needed to walk faster or she would be there all day, she picked up her pace until the trail veered right into a wooded area farther away from the water's edge. As she followed the trail deeper into the woods, she realized that she hadn't passed another person for half a mile. Though it was the middle of the day, it was eerily dark along this section of the trail, which was lined with thick underbrush and tall trees.

Paige stopped to take another look at the park map. Relieved, she hadn't deviated from the trail, she stashed the map back in her backpack. A large white-tailed deer jumped across the trail startling her. Gasping, her heart raced. She remained still as two yearlings followed after the first. Once the deer had disappeared from sight, Paige took to a slow jog. She moved along the trail until she came out of the dark wooded area back to the water's edge of reeds and cattails. She desperately wanted to pick a cattail, but that was against rule number five in the park manual: Observe nature but leave it untouched for others to enjoy.

She sat on a large log near the water's edge, catching her breath and wishing that she had brought a bottle of water with her. There was a small motor boat with two fishermen just off shore. From her seated position, she observed a small tree-covered island in the center of the reservoir. She took a closer look with her binoculars. She immediately recognized an area in the middle of the island from her father's photos. She zoomed in on the area and snapped a few shots. *I need a boat.* Paige walked back toward the ranger's lodge, hoping it wasn't too late to rent a boat.

The enthusiastic young park ranger inside the small office handed her a pamphlet with operation hours and rates. It was almost closing time. She'd have to come back another day to take a boat out to the island.

Nathan was sitting in his truck in front of the house when she arrived home from her jaunt. "Where the hell have you been?" were his first words.

"What're you doing here? Is something wrong?"

"Yes, something is wrong! You disappeared. You weren't answering."

"Why are you angry?"

"Todd was worried. He called me."

Todd emerged from the house. "Where were you? You've been gone for hours. You just can't do that."

"I went for a drive," said Paige.

"A drive," said Todd.

"Yes, I wanted to check out the reservoir."

"You went out there alone." There was a panic in Nathan's voice.

"Why not? I'm a big girl. I don't need you two Neanderthals telling me what to do!"

"We agreed we'd go out there together. You shouldn't have gone alone!" Todd shouted back.

"I couldn't wait."

"He's right. If you have no concern for your own safety, at least let someone know where you're going." Nathan chimed in.

Paige stood tall and placed her hands on her hips. "Well, if your department were doing a better job…" She stopped herself before saying something she didn't mean.

"You're impossible," said Nathan.

"Go to hell." Paige stomped up the porch steps and into the house.

Todd turned to Nathan. "She's always been impulsive."

"Do you know why she went out there?"

"She's convinced Dad's photos are key to his murder."

"Photos?"

"We showed them to you," said Todd.

"Oh, yeah," said Nathan.

"I better look at them again."

"There's one more thing."

"What?"

"After the break-in, we realized Dad's camera was missing."

"And neither of you thought to inform me." Nathan followed Todd into the house, through the living room, and into the kitchen.

"What do you two want?" Paige stared them down.

"I need to see your dad's photos again," said Nathan.

"You didn't seem too interested in them the first time I showed you," taunted Paige.

"Please…Paige." Nathan gave her a crooked glare. "There was a lot going on that day."

"You're right." Paige handed the photos to him.

"So this is why you went out there," said Nathan.

"Yes."

"I need to take these with me."

"I know." Paige gave him a tight-lipped smile as she closed her laptop.

"When were you going to tell *me* the camera was stolen?"

Paige looked at Todd. "You told him."

"We should've told him as soon as we knew," said Todd.

Paige looked down and away, and then she looked back up at Nathan. "It was me." She put a hand on her chest. "All me."

Nathan raised an eyebrow and looked Paige straight in the eye. "Is there anything else I should know?"

Paige pulled the photos from Nathan's hand. She pointed to a man in the background of one of the photos. "Just that I think I saw this man today, leaving Wilson and Wilson Law offices."

"And…"

Paige tightened her face and waved the photos at Nathan. "I think I found the spot where these were taken." She handed them back to Nathan. "Halfway around the reservoir trail. I sat on a log to rest along the water's edge… I think these were taken there. The background wooded area is part of a small island."

"I'll have it checked out. Promise me, you won't go back out there," said Nathan.

Paige turned away. "I'm exhausted. I think I walked…something like…ten miles today."

Nathan touched her arm. "Promise."

"I promise," said Paige as she turned back. *Sometimes, promises had to be made. And broken.*

CHAPTER 21

WHEN PAIGE FINALLY MADE HER way downstairs after a full night of sleep, Todd was walking out the front door. "Where you going?" Paige asked.

"Cate called. Mom's being moved from ICU to the rehab floor today," said Todd.

"You should've woken me up."

"You needed sleep."

"I'm up now. Give me a few minutes, I'll come with you."

Todd sat on the sofa and flipped on the television. He clicked through the channels until he found a station with the weather report. "Tropical Storm Martha has been upgraded to a category one hurricane as of eight this morning. At current, she is packing peak winds of eighty miles per hour and moving northeast on a track parallel to the coasts of Georgia and the Carolinas," said the handsome blond-haired meteorologist as he pointed to a large swirling mass out over the Atlantic Ocean. "As you can see here, some of the outer bands are reaching the outer banks of North Carolina. As the storm track brings Martha closer to shore, we expect significant wind and flood damage along the entire coastline. The outer banks of North Carolina are in for a beating."

Todd turned as Paige walked in the living room. "Did you hear about this hurricane moving up the coast?"

Paige stopped and looked at the television. "Hurricane Martha will continue to intensify over the next twenty-four hours and make a sharp turn toward the northeast on a path for the coast of New Jersey," said the weatherman.

"I thought it was headed out to sea," said Paige.

"The storm track changed," said Todd. He picked up the remote and turned off the television. Todd's cell phone rang. He reached in his pocket and checked his phone. "It's work. I've got to take this." He walked away into the kitchen.

"That was my supervisor. I need to get back home," said Todd.

"Did you explain how important it is for you to stay?"

"Of course I did. It'll only be for a few days. I've a mandatory training seminar. If I miss it, I might not get the promotion I'm hoping for. After all, it has been two weeks."

"When will you leave?"

"Tomorrow," answered Todd.

"Then we better get going," said Paige as she took a step toward the front door.

An orderly pushed Emily's wheelchair into the hospital third-floor elevator. Cate walked close behind, along with a uniformed police officer. The elevator went down two floors, and when its doors opened, Todd was pushing the elevator call button to go up to the third floor.

"Thanks for coming," said Cate as she approached Todd and Paige.

"We wanted to be here," said Paige as she watched Emily, the orderly, and police officer emerge out of the elevator.

"The doctor said after a few days in rehab, Mom can go home. I think she should come and stay with me when she's released," said Cate.

"That sounds like a good idea," said Todd. He walked over to Emily's chair and took her hand. "Hi, Mom. Sounds like you're doing much better."

Emily looked up. "I am. I can't wait to go home."

"Mom, I need to head back to Arizona," Todd explained. "Just for a few days. Then I'll be back."

"I understand." Emily looked from Todd to Cate. "You've all been wonderful. But you all have lives too."

"I thought I'd leave early tomorrow. Before the hurricane gets too close and they begin to shut down airports."

Todd, Cate, and Paige followed closely as the orderly pushed Emily's wheelchair down the corridor, turned the right corner, and pushed her into her new room. Officer Taylor positioned himself at the door. Paige looked around the brightly lit room. All of Emily's belongings were already there, including the fluffy small white stuffed puppy that Cate had bought in the gift shop. With the help of the orderly, Emily stood a moment before sitting back down into a tan high-back chair situated next to the bed.

"Why don't you kids get going?" said Emily.

Cate looked at her mom. "Are you sure?"

"You heard the nurse, I'm doing better. You don't need to worry. I have protection, and besides, I'll be going to physical therapy twice a day." Emily looked at Todd. "You have travel arrangements to make." She looked at Paige. "And what about your job?"

"I was hoping to get a few local assignments," said Paige.

"And, Cate, I'm sure you have plenty to catch up on at home."

"I do," said Cate. "Maybe you're right. I do need to freshen up the guest room for you."

CHAPTER 22

THE NEXT DAY, WHEN TODD left for Arizona, the winds had increased and the skies had darkened. And once again, Paige found herself drawn to the beach. She removed her sandals and walked to the water's edge. The winds blew her hair into a tangled mess as she watched the bands of swiftly moving clouds out over the churning ocean. She gathered her hair in one hand and clipped it onto the top of her head. The waves crashed on the shoreline sending a spray of salty water over her entire body. With each crashing wave, her feet sank deeper into the sand until they totally disappeared. Paige remained stationary as the water washed in, swirled around her ankles, and washed back out to sea.

She lifted her camera up and snapped her first of many shots as a large wave crested and rolled inward twenty yards out. She then turned and took a long panoramic of the coastline and quietly chuckled as an elderly couple strolling hand in hand, along the wet sand, jumped simultaneously when a foamy wave surrounded them. Her laugher turned into a smile as she realized they never let go of each other's hand. She sighed. *Sweet.*

Paige turned on the radio in her Jeep as she headed back to her parents' home. "All residents are strongly encouraged to have a plan of action and to prepare for long power outages. The latest National Hurricane Center update is predicting Hurricane Martha to make landfall somewhere between Maryland and New Jersey within sixteen to twenty-four hours." Paige knew better than to wait to prepare, but her preoccupation with chronicling the storm had taken a good portion of the day. When the tall oak in the front yard began swaying back and forth with each gust of wind, she finally decided she needed to get some provisions. More than once, while on assignment, as well as growing up at the Jersey Shore, she had witnessed firsthand the devastation a hurricane could leave behind.

As Paige pulled into the grocery store parking lot, she narrowly missed a food cart, which had been left behind in haste by an obviously anxious and overwhelmed elderly woman. The wind pushed the cart into the side of a dark green Range Rover. Paige grabbed it and rushed inside. She found the shelves nearly empty. She moved quickly up and down the aisles and then headed to the front of the store to check out. Long lines of impatient patrons snaked toward the cash registers.

Upon her return home, with a case of water and just one bag of nonperishables, Paige began a search for flashlights, candles, and matches. She retrieved firewood from the backyard, which had been split and stacked neatly by her father, and then organized her gathered supplies.

Feeling adequately prepared, she left the house again to check on her mother. As Paige walked by the nurses' station, they stared and whispered. She heard the words *dead body* and *suspect* as she passed. She faced forward and kept moving. She was happy to see an armed officer still posted outside her mother's room.

Now that her mother was getting up and about, Paige hoped she'd be up to answering some questions. Her plan was to start out with small simple questions, and if they didn't upset her too much, she'd hit her up with some tougher ones. She pushed in the door and was happily surprised to see her mother alone.

"Hi, Mom."

"Paige," said Emily as she looked up from her magazine.

"How are you?"

"A little sore from PT. But…who am I to complain? Just happy I'm getting around," answered Emily.

Paige nodded. "Can I ask you a few questions?"

"It sounds serious. About what?"

"Well," Paige began as she settled in. "I'm curious about yours and Dad's friendship with the Wilsons. How did you meet them?"

"We go way back. Actually, *Sarah and I* go way back. We went to high school together over in Collins. She was my best friend back then."

"And now?"

"We drifted apart after you kids came along."

"But you still consider them friends?"

"Of course. We were all young newlyweds together and we had a lot of fun."

"But Frank Wilson seems so…what's the word…"

"Angry? Mean? Arrogant?"

"Yes…all of it."

"He wasn't always that way. He was a nice man. Sometimes he still is."

"He is? What changed?"

"He likes to drink. Sarah said in the beginning it was drinks with clients, then it was a shot after a hard day at work, and soon he was coming home intoxicated. At first, your father and I didn't notice. Sarah was good at covering for him. After a time, she became distant, so far removed from the lighthearted, cheerful person she once was."

"Why didn't she leave him?"

"I guess she loved him…or at least cared enough…not to."

"But to live like that. I couldn't do it," said Paige.

"She was afraid. She hadn't worked in years and she had a small child to look out for."

"So…"

"You girls today…are so independent. You have options."

"Sarah had no options?"

"Her parents were deceased, and she has no siblings."

"Couldn't you help her?"

"Of course I tried. But the more I tried, the more closed off she got."

"Was he abusive?"

"I suspected he was getting hard to handle, but she wouldn't admit anything. Why do you ask? Is it because you had a date with Michael?" Emily smiled.

"Who told you?"

"Cate."

"Of course she did. It was nothing. Just dinner. And just like his father, he's a bit arrogant. Michael said he and Cate were friends? She acts like she doesn't know him."

"He was a part of her group of her friends in junior high."

"Actually, she seems to hate him," said Paige.

"It's a complicated story. But...I don't think Cate hates him."

"Why is everyone being evasive? Does this have something to do with Ryan Timmons?"

"When he disappeared, Cate took it hard. From what Sarah told me, Michael took it hard too."

"That's all?"

"Shortly after Ryan disappeared, Michael went away to boarding school. As far as I know, Cate and Michael lost touch. Nothing more."

"I don't know, Mom. I think there's something more there," said Paige.

"You'll have to ask your sister." Emily paused and looked out the window. She turned back. "When I think back, Sarah became more introverted after Michael went away. We lost touch. Then out of the blue, she called. We hadn't spoken in years. Frank was in the hospital. He'd had a heart attack. It was wonderful hearing from her. We spoke like we had when we were in high school, like no time had passed. We started to spend more time together."

"Did Dad and Mr. Wilson get along?"

"Mostly. They tried. I think Frank's still drinking. He's just gotten better at hiding it."

"I don't like Mr. Wilson. The man radiates bad vibes. Something else, I found some newspaper articles in Dad's study. Dad was in one of the clippings, standing behind Mr. Wilson at a rally against the Meadowbrook Reservoir. Was Dad opposed to the project?"

"No...I saw the article too and asked your dad what was going on. He adverted to it having something to do with his consulting on the project. He never clued me in."

"I took a ride out to the reservoir. It's beautiful."

"After it was completed, your dad spent a lot of time out there. He was proud of the work he'd done on the project. He called it his crowning achievement." Emily smiled.

"I found some photos Dad took out there," said Paige.

"Him and that camera." Emily shook her head. "He always had it with him. Just like you." Emily got a faraway look on her face. Paige realized her mother really didn't have an inkling as to what her father had been up to.

"Bet Mr. Wilson was happy when they discovered that body in the marsh," said Paige.

"What an awful thought," said Emily.

"But you have to admit. It did put a stop to the construction. I just meant the delay gave him more time to stop the project permanently."

"I suppose. But it makes no sense. Frank's president of the town's Chamber of Commerce. The reservoir has been good for the town. It's brought in tourists and new businesses."

"Maybe he knew there was a body out there."

"That's a stretch. Frank may be a drunk and a bad husband, but I don't believe he's capable of murder."

"I didn't say murder. But I think something was going on out there. And *Dad* got mixed up in it."

Emily threw back her head and laughed. "Your father was a straight arrow."

"I didn't mean that Dad was doing something illegal. I think he was on to something. Something that got him killed."

"Your father would disappear for hours, and when he'd come home, he'd shut himself up in the study. Especially, after Dusty disappeared. I should've pressed him more."

"You told me Dusty got hit by a car."

"He did…Your dad found him and took him to the animal hospital. I didn't get to say goodbye. Your dad said he was in a lot of pain and had him put down." Emily's voice pitched.

"Are you okay?" Paige asked as she took hold of her mother's hand. "I didn't mean to upset you."

"I miss him." Emily began to weep. Paige leaned in and hugged her. Emily held on tight and cried on her shoulder for several minutes. Then, Emily lifted her head and reached for a tissue. "I got your shirt wet."

"I'll change when I get home."

"I'd like to lay down. I'm feeling tired," said Emily as she pushed down on the arms of the chair and lifted herself up.

"Let me help you."

"I need to do this myself." Emily took two steps, sat on the edge of the bed, and then swung her legs up and lay her head on the pillow.

"Anything you need?"

"Can you stay till I fall asleep?"

"Yes," said Paige as she sat down in the chair. "I'll be right here."

"Just till I fall asleep," said Emily as she closed her eyes.

Paige squeezed her mother's hand and whispered, "Love you, Mom." Emily was sound asleep.

The winds had increased dramatically from earlier and rain began to fall just as Paige climbed into her SUV. She drove slower than normal, with caution, through an obstacle course of tree limbs and debris until she arrived back at her parents' home. She wished that Todd hadn't gone back to Arizona. But it was no big deal and this wasn't her first hurricane. Besides, what could happen when her personal protective entourage was parked in front of the house?

She'd noticed the undercover officer following her all day. Either Nathan or Todd had decided she needed looking after. *Typical.*

After double-checking all the doors and windows, Paige snuggled up on the couch with a soft fuzzy blanket and a hot cup of tea to watch the evening news. She listened as the seasoned newscaster announced that Hurricane Martha had become a category 2 hurricane with sustained winds of 96 to 110 miles per hour. As she sipped her tea, the lights flickered, and the television went dark. She struck a match and lit a jar candle on the coffee table in front of her, just as the power went out. The scent of vanilla filled the room and the light the candle gave off danced across the ceiling. Paige shimmied herself down and nestled under the cozy blanket for what could be a long night.

There was a bang on the front door. Paige startled awake. Had debris been flung against it? There it was again—a banging on the front door. "Give me a minute!" Paige shouted. She peeked out the side window to see who it was. *Nathan.*

Paige unlatched the chain and then turned the dead bolt. When she opened the wooden interior door, Nathan stood there holding the screen door. The wind caught it and swung it fully open. He desperately grabbed for it. Catching it just in time, so as not to break off its hinges.

"Hurry, hurry, get in here. The wind sure picked up," rushed Paige.

"You're okay. I called you several times. You didn't answer."

"Sorry, I dozed off."

"You're always worrying me."

"Why are you here? Your man is parked out front. Or didn't you think I'd notice?"

"There's no car out front. I don't have a man out there. I wasn't able to get further approval."

"Come on. I saw him. He followed me to the store and the hospital today."

"I'm telling you…it wasn't anyone from my department."

"But you told me you'd assigned a man to watch me. I thought he was following me. Not that I need it."

"Why didn't you just call?"

"Why would I call you? I thought you were having me followed."

"Well, that settles it. I'm not leaving here until this storm passes." Nathan moved to sit on the couch.

"Hold it. You're not sitting on my mother's couch all wet. I'll get a towel." As Paige walked away, she added, "Take those wet clothes off. I'll get something for you to put on."

Paige disappeared up the stairs with the flashlight. After a search of the bedrooms, she returned with a towel, one of Todd's old flannel shirts, and a pair of boxer shorts. "Here." She tried not to notice

Nathan's muscular bare chest and six-pack abs. As he reached down for the zipper on his jeans, Paige quickly turned away.

"Don't be a baby." He began to slowly slide his jeans downward. "Are you sure you don't want a peek?" He chuckled. "A lot has changed since the last time we went skinny dipping."

"I don't think your girlfriend would appreciate it."

"My girlfriend?"

"Yes. Maggie."

"Maggie who?"

"Maggie from the diner…are you dressed yet?"

Nathan tapped her on the shoulder. "It's safe now." Paige turned with her eyes still covered.

He pulled her hands away from her face. "See…"

She looked him up and down. "Better."

"Maggie Caldwell…is not my girlfriend," said Nathan as he made himself comfortable on the couch and pulled the fuzzy blanket up and over himself.

"She made it seem so."

"She's delusional. We went out for a short time when I first returned home. But that was years ago."

"Well, she's still got a thing for you. She made it very clear."

He looked up from his seated position. "Care to join me? It's nice…and warm under here."

"Don't mind if I do," said Paige as she yanked the blanket up off him and plopped herself down on the far end of the couch.

"You're right…nice and cozy."

CHAPTER 23

"STOP LOOKING AT ME." NATHAN was making Paige extremely fidgety and self-consciously aware of her desires.

"You're here. It's you...but it's not you. I know...I'm not making any sense."

Paige contorted her face, inwardly amused. "You sound surprised."

"You were always cute in your tomboyish way, but now, you're... let's just say...all grown up. You're beautiful."

Wow! He continued as her thoughts ran away. She pushed a piece of hair behind an ear as her cheeks warmed and her thoughts simmered. She'd never had a conversation like this with Nathan. They'd always done the brotherly, sisterly, teasing thing. He was her pal, her friend, her...she wasn't quite sure anymore. "It's just the candlelight. It hides my flaws."

"What flaws?"

"Everyone has flaws."

"I have flaws." He chuckled.

"You know what I mean. No one's perfect."

"I wish we hadn't lost touch. I've missed you. I'm to blame," said Nathan.

"It's no one's fault. It's called life. We grew up." She hesitated before adding, "You got engaged to Janine."

"I got engaged? Where are you getting your information? First, it's Maggie, now it's Janine. I hope you're better checking facts at your job."

"I got it from them. I saw Maggie at the diner yesterday. And Janine and I were in touch for a time after high school."

"Janine and I...it was never serious."

"I don't know what it is... You cast quite a spell on women."

"But not on you," he said as he pushed the sole of his foot against hers. "I'll admit, I was a little lost after you left... No one to get in trouble with. Janine was...she reminded me of you, of high school. Is that why you stopped calling? She was a nice girl...but she wasn't you."

"You and I were friends, and if she was your happiness, who was I to interfere?" said Paige.

"Friends...always...but haven't you ever wondered?" He strained through the darkness to see the expression on her face.

"Wondered?"

"Yeah...about us. Everyone assumed..."

"What does it matter?" She looked away. "You were here and I ended up there..."

"Maybe it wouldn't have worked...then. But what about now?" Paige heard his words, but they didn't register.

Now? She could feel his eyes on her. He stretched out his leg until his toes skimmed over the calf of her leg. A chill ran through her. She moved her eyes to meet his.

"Yeah, now. The girl who left here, she wasn't the settling down kind. Her heart was full of adventure. She was a dreamer. I knew that and I accepted it. Perhaps now, your dreams may bring you closer to home."

"Dreams can change," said Paige.

"Let's hope."

Paige pulled her leg away from Nathan's touch and sat up.

"I've said too much. Don't be upset."

"I'm not." She stood, then looked down, and took a deep breath. "I'll be right back. Why don't you start a fire? It's chilly in here." *That was close.*

"Good idea. It doesn't look like the lights will be coming back on anytime soon."

After a few minutes spent in the kitchen, foraging, Paige emerged with an opened bottle of wine, two glasses, and a plate of cheese. "Look what I found."

"Can I help?" asked Nathan as he approached and took the plate.

"Nice job on the fire," said Paige. The fire place was blazing. Golden flames flickered across the room.

"I think it'll be warmer over there." Nathan pointed to the blanket he had placed in front of the fireplace.

"Let's not forget there's a hurricane howling outside and a killer on the loose," said Paige.

"There's nothing we can do about that right now. It's best for us to stay put."

"Stay put. You mean right there?" Paige pointed toward the fireplace. "On that blanket?"

"Why not? It'll be like old times, camping out," said Nathan.

"Except, we won't be looking up at the stars."

"We'll pretend."

Paige nodded as she expertly balanced the bottle of wine in one hand and the two glasses in the other. She squatted down on the blanket. Nathan sat down close to her and whispered in her ear, "Listen." The only sounds one could hear were the pinging of rain as it pelted the windows, the whistling of the wind as it gusted outside rattling the doors, and the popping of the crackling fire. "It's kind of awesome…"

"It is…but are we supposed to be enjoying it?"

"We're just making the best of things."

"To the best of things." Paige lifted the bottle and filled their glasses. "I hope you like red."

"I'm more of a beer guy."

"I can check the fridge," said Paige as she started to stand.

He pulled her back down by the hand. "No need." He took a sip from his glass. "I like wine too."

"Are you hungry?" She pierced a cube of cheddar with a toothpick and held it out. His eyes followed her every move.

"What? Is there something…on my face."

"No…just looking. This is nice."

Paige turned away, not knowing if it was the heat from the fireplace or his staring that was causing her cheeks to warm again. She turned back. "You're right. It's nice…nice not to have to pretend to be someone I'm not."

"You've never put on pretenses for me."

"That's it…exactly…we can just sit here and be…or we can be silly like school children." The words flowed from Paige's mouth. She hadn't felt this comfortable with anyone else, ever; except Nathan, maybe. Perhaps they always were, always meant to be. They had just been too stubborn to see it.

"You're the most real person I've ever met. You're the smartest, funniest, most exasperatingly perfect person," said Nathan. A flicker of light from the fireplace, danced across his face. Paige tapped her unpolished fingernails on the stem of her wine glass. Why was she so nervous? Why couldn't she think straight? There was nothing to be nervous about; it was Nathan. Her pal, her friend, her…she wasn't used to thinking about him that way. He placed a hand on her thigh as he laughed. She hadn't heard a word he'd said for the last two minutes. Had he been telling a joke? She didn't know.

"Are you all right?" He leaned in toward her.

She nodded. "Yes…Yes." *Am I all right?* Paige wasn't sure. She was suddenly overcome with emotion and embarrassment. Perhaps, it was the wine that was making her head swirl, though she'd only drank one glass. Nothing was wrong…for the first time in years, everything felt right.

"Are you sure?" He lifted her chin with his index finger until her eyes met his. He softly whispered, "Paige."

"Yes." Her voice was low and sultry.

"I tried to find a replacement for what we had, but nothing came close…no one came close." She nodded several times. He took the glass from her hand, set it down on the lower edge of the fireplace, and leaned in closer.

Without warning, Paige kicked her left leg out, vigorously shook it, and then tapped her heal on the floor. She looked at Nathan. "Charlie horse!" She burst out laughing. "I'm sorry."

"I hate when that happens. Put your leg here." She swung around and placed her leg on his knee. He gently kneaded and massaged her calf muscle. "Better?"

"It's getting there," said Paige. She looked up into his face. *So serious.* "You're good at this."

"Lots of practice," said Nathan.

"Practice with Charlie horses or massages?"

"Both," he replied with a grin bordering on cockiness. Though her calf muscle had relaxed, he continued rubbing it, and she let him. Slowly his hand left her calf and moved up to her thigh and she didn't think to tell him to stop. He looked down at his hand. "Sorry." He quickly moved it.

Paige took his hand. "It's okay." She gave him a shy, closed-lip smile. He held on to her hand and nudged closer. Their shoulders barely touching, an electric current swept through Paige's body. She leaned back into his shoulder, letting her head rest against his. "What if it's not what we imagined? What if we ruin everything?"

"I'm willing to take the chance," he replied as he placed his hands on her torso and turned her body toward his. He touched the tip of her nose with his index finger and then slowly moved it down to her top lip. As he gently traced her mouth with his finger, her lips parted. His lips were soft and warm on hers. She was paralyzed for a heartbeat.

He pulled back and looked at her from an arm's length. Nervously, she ran her tongue along her top lip. Her heart racing; her breath quickened at the anticipation of his next kiss. The feelings he aroused in her were alien; it had been so long since her heart and body had dared to feel. She tried desperately to hide her true thoughts, afraid to look in his eyes for fear he would see how vulnerable she was to his touch.

Her defenses melted as his strong arms drew her in and he kissed her once again, harder, with more intent. She kissed him back with a hunger that matched his. His lips left hers, moved down her neck, and settled in the softness of her breasts. Her mind went blank. All reason was out the window. Paige pushed all her thoughts and fears aside, telling herself it was worth the chance, and jumped in with both feet.

Exhausted, with sweat the only thing between them, they curled up together. Within moments, Nathan was asleep. Unable to close her eyes, Paige's head was dizzy with her circling thoughts. Only three weeks ago, Nathan was just an old childhood friend she remembered with great fondness...and now, their bodies were intertwined. What if it was just the hurricane raging outside that had trapped them together or her recent heartbreak with Jeremy making her vulnerable. Or simply, adrenaline and lust pushing them on.

When they awakened in the morning, still tangled in each other's arms, the worst of the storm had passed. Nathan placed a kiss on her forehead and drew her back in.

"Morning," he whispered in her ear.

"Morning," she hesitantly replied. "We better see if there's any damage to the house."

"I'd prefer to stay right here." Nathan squeezed her tight as he nuzzled his face in her blond mane and moved his hands slowly over her soft, naked skin. Paige's body responded to his touch and she found herself lost once again.

Nathan's portable radio sounded, interrupting their rising passions. They unclenched and lay there listening as the call went out for all officers to report to headquarters. "I need to go in," said Nathan.

"I know," said Paige as she sat up and slipped her tee back on. She was suddenly keenly aware of her nakedness.

"I don't want to go," said Nathan as he scrambled to his feet.

Paige opened the front door and looked out as he put his damp clothes back on. The wind was still howling, but not hurricane force, and the air was warm, almost tropical. The lawn was littered with broken tree branches and leaves, and a large oak tree had uprooted in the Brown's front yard and landed on their garage roof. She took a step out onto the porch and looked up at her own roof. The house seemed intake. She stepped back in as heavy rain began to fall once again.

Nathan walked over and stood next to Paige in the doorway. "I wish I could stay. I'm sorry." He put an arm around her. She placed her head on his shoulder. They stared out in silence.

"I get it. You've a job to do," said Paige.

He turned her around to face him. "Paige..." He looked down into her eyes. "Paige..."

"Yes..." She placed her hands on his hips and looked up.

"Stay inside. I imagine there are a lot of downed trees and wires. Lock the door behind me. I'll be back as soon as I can." He gave her a small kiss on the lips, then another, and another. "I need to go... before I never leave."

"Be careful...I...I...I'll be here," said Paige.

Nathan grabbed his portable radio and keys off the entrance table, gave her one last kiss, and left. She remained stationary for quite some time, deep in thought, until her mind began to reel and crazy thoughts began to creep back in. She wasn't sure if the real damage had occurred inside or outside the house. Logic told her she may have just made one of the biggest mistakes of her life. But her heart...and her anatomy...felt differently.

CHAPTER 24

PAIGE STRETCHED OUT IN FRONT of the fireplace. All that remained of the roaring fire from the night before was a smoldering pile of ashy embers. She drew in a deep breath and pulled the cover up to her neck. Nathan's scent lingered on the blanket and in the air. She closed her eyes and imagined his hands tracing her body once again. She wanted to hold on to the feeling, to the tingle that remained in her body, for as long as possible. She took another deep breath and felt relieved to be alone. *Don't be a silly girl!* She rolled to her left, she rolled to her right, and then she got up and wandered into the kitchen.

Paige turned on the faucet and ran her fingers through the stream of water. Cupping her hands, she let them fill with cold water and splashed her face and then repeated the process. She dried her face and hands with a dish towel. Refreshed and her eyes now wide open, she grabbed an apple off the counter before returning to the living room. She went straight to the front window and peered out. The world outside had stopped. Not a neighbor, not an animal was to be seen.

She supposed they were all still sheltered in place. *Now what?* She began opening all the blinds in the living room. The daylight brightened the room a bit. The blanket where she and Nathan had made love the night before was still in front of the fireplace. It was time to put it away. To stop fantasizing that something real had happened. She folded the crumpled blanket and placed it on the end of the couch. Then she took the brass fire poker from its stand and stirred the cooling ashes. *Done.*

Paige picked up the house phone receiver and listened—no dial tone. Alone and feeling cut off from the world, Paige picked up her cell phone from the coffee table and dialed Cate. A recording came on. "Your call cannot be completed at this time. Please try again later." She slipped on her sneakers and stepped outside. The rain had finally stopped and patches of blue sky poked through the gray clouds. She walked around the yard picking up large branches and piled them near the curb.

By the time she had finished cleaning up the cluttered yard, the sun was bright, the sky a vibrant blue, and there was not a cloud for miles. It was as if the storm had never happened. She looked upward and found herself smiling at a mockingbird sitting on a sagging electrical wire. It happily sang a tune oblivious to the fact that a hurricane had swept through the night before. If it hadn't been for the broken tree limbs and green leaves scattered across the sidewalks, streets, and lawns, Paige herself would not have known. But there had been a storm, and now she was left alone to deal with the damages.

Bored and curious, Paige set out on a walk around the neighborhood. Ultimately, she hoped some exercise would stop her mind from racing. But, wildly, vivid memories continued to flash through her mind. She blushed with embarrassment at the memory of Nathan's hungry kisses and feverish touch. She could still smell him, taste him. Paige tried not to overanalyze the situation. It must've been the wine and candlelight. He had made her feel safe and protected, but that was no reason for letting go like that! How was she ever going to look at him? What would she say the next time she saw him? Maybe she should call him; that'd be much easier. Tell him it been a wonderful night, but her job and life were in Virginia, and a long-distance relationship just wouldn't work. *Now who's jumping the gun? A relationship?* It was just sex! Right! Better not say that. He'd think she was a slut. She'd just tell him he was a wonderful man, that they just got caught up in the danger, and it was the ambiance of the evening. *He's a man. It probably was just sex!*

Several blocks away from her parents' home, Paige came upon a giant maple tree which was uprooted and lying across the roadway. Power lines dangled from a nearby pole. Seeing that a power company truck was just arriving, she thought it best to turn around and go back home. She needed to grab her camera and come back out. She'd been so self-absorbed that she'd almost forgotten work.

Paige dug in and ran as if running for her life. Ten minutes later, she was home, sweaty and tired—happily too tired to think about Nathan anymore. She flicked the light switch on as she entered the house. The power was still out. She checked the phone line, there was still no dial tone. She checked her cell phone, no calls. Worst of all, her cell had only one bar of power left and no electric to recharge it.

After a quick cold shower, Paige gathered more kindling and firewood just in case there was another night without power. Once that was done, she jumped in her SUV and made her way around downed trees and through road detours to the hospital. The hospital would have their backup generator running and she wanted to check on her mom.

"I'm making out just fine without power, Mom. Please, don't worry. Nathan stayed at the house last night."

"Guess things are back to the way they used to be." Cate had stayed the night at the hospital.

"What's that supposed to mean?" Paige asked.

"Nothing! Just you and Nathan did everything together as kids. You were the two musketeers."

"Oh."

"Little sensitive, aren't we? I've seen the way you look at him."

"What are you talking about?"

"Come on, admit it…you like him…you want him."

"Yuck." Paige waved off the remark.

"Are you telling me you've never had romantic thoughts about Nathan?"

"Furthest thing from my mind." Paige lied and turned away from Cate.

"I need to get going," said Paige.

"You just got here. What's so important?" Cate asked.

"I've been given a work assignment."

"Does that mean you're leaving town?" Emily asked.

"No. Actually, it's here. I've been chronicling the before and after of Hurricane Martha and the Jersey Shore. It makes sense, I'm already here," said Paige.

"I think that's wonderful," said Emily.

"So…you understand?"

Emily reached out. Paige took her hand. "Of course. Be on your way. I'm not going anywhere."

Paige kissed her mother's cheek. "Thanks for understanding." Paige unplugged her charging cell phone from the wall outlet. "I'm sorry, Cate. I hope you understand too."

When Paige arrived home a midsized black sedan with tinted windows was parked in front of the house. She hesitated a moment as she surveyed her surroundings. The neighborhood was still dark, not a light could be seen. Mrs. Reilly's shades were up and as usual she was looking out. Relieved to see another human being, Paige got out of her Jeep and waved to Mrs. Reilly. The driver's side door of the sedan opened.

"I tried to call you last night and this morning. It went right to voice mail. I thought something was wrong," said Michael.

"The storm must've knocked out cell service. I'm sorry I didn't get back to you. Things have been a little crazy around here. I totally forgot."

"Gee, you sure know how to make a man feel wanted."

"Sorry. Would you like to come in for a minute?" Paige unlocked the front door. "First there was the break-in, then Todd left town, and then last night, the hurricane…I really am sorry."

"I've been worried, rightfully so, I see. What was that you said about a break-in?"

"A few nights ago, someone kicked in the back door."

"You were home!" There was the sound of surprise in his voice.

"Yes."

"I thought you were staying nights at the hospital with your mom." He moved closer to her.

"Not anymore. Mom's doing much better. They've moved her to rehab. Looks like she'll be well enough to come home soon."

"That's wonderful. Mother will be happy to hear she's doing so well." Michael took her hands in both of his. "The intruder…didn't hurt you, did he?"

"Todd and I surprised them. Whoever it was ran off."

"Did you call the police?" The usual sparkle in Michael's eyes was gone.

"They came out, looked around, and took a report. But you know how that goes—no witnesses, no evidence..." He loosened his grip. She slowly pulled her hands away. "It's on record, but without anything to go on, what can they do?"

"Your neighbors...they didn't see or hear anything?"

"Not that I'm aware of," said Paige.

"I'm just glad you're okay. You should've called me."

"There was no reason to bother you. Todd was here."

"Now that I know you're fine, I need to head to my office. It's closed for the day, but I still need to check on things. I'll call you. You promised me a drink."

"I don't believe I did," countered Paige.

"You're right, but I'd like to take you out again. I wasn't quite myself when we had dinner. How about giving a guy a second chance?" His eyes met hers.

"We'll see." Paige smiled. Michael said all the right things; but the words lacked something. What did he want with her anyways? Why was he being so persistent about them getting together? And why the inquisition about the break-in?

They stepped outside together. "I appreciate your coming by." Paige saw from the corner of her eye Nathan's truck pulling up in front of the house. Her heart began to race, and Michael caught her off guard with a kiss on her lips. She stepped back away from him.

"Michael! Don't!"

"But...I thought..."

"You've been very kind. I thought you understood."

"I thought you were just playing hard to get."

"No..."

"I better go," said Michael. "Sorry for the misunderstanding."

Paige looked away. Why was Nathan just sitting there in his truck? Finally, he got out and strutted up the sidewalk toward them. She couldn't read his expression; she could only imagine what he was thinking. "Just checking in. I have a few follow-up questions, Ms.

Thompson." He didn't sound like himself. "Do you have a minute now or should I come back?" His eyes pierced right through her.

"Mr. Wilson was just leaving, Detective," Paige said, following suit.

"I can stay," Michael interrupted.

"No need. I'm sure I'm in good hands with Detective Edgemont here."

"Sure?"

"Yes."

Michael stepped down off the porch and then turned back to look at Paige. "I'll call you."

He nodded at Nathan as he walked past him.

Once he was out of ear shot, Nathan asked, "What the hell's going on? I'll call you!"

"Michael stopped by to see if I was okay. No big deal, his mother and mine are friends. But you know that."

"He kissed you."

"Well, that was unexpected."

"He kissed you," Nathan repeated.

"He misunderstood. We went out to dinner...as friends. He thought..."

"I didn't like it."

"What does it matter? I didn't ask for it!"

"That's who you had dinner with the other night?"

"Yes...and it's really not your business."

"Well...I don't think he just wants to be friends. Besides, men and women can't just be friends."

"Really? You and I have been friends for as long as I can remember."

"That's different. We were kids when we met. With men, it's always about sex, whether they say it or not."

"Is that what happened last night? We're not kids anymore. So you're saying we can't be friends. That we're not friends. Only boys and girls can be friends." Nathan stood there with a puzzled expression, listening to Paige ramble on.

"That's not what I'm saying."

"Then what are you saying?"

"I didn't like it."

"Like what?"

Nathan shook his head from side to side. "You've got me so... confused. I can't think straight." What a comfort it was to know she was not the only one confused. "I don't know what I was thinking. Has the power come back on?"

"Not yet. Soon, I hope," said Paige.

"There are downed power lines all over town," said Nathan.

"I saw."

"You went out?"

"For a walk around the neighborhood, then to the hospital." Nathan gave her a look. "I was worried about Mom."

"If power is not restored by dark, there may be a curfew."

"Okay, I won't go out after dark."

"You do know I care about you...about what happens to you?"

"And I care about you. Always have." After a long pause Paige added, "I always will."

"That sounds like goodbye," said Nathan.

"I'm just saying what you're saying. I care about you."

"And?"

"I'm not sure about last night...maybe it shouldn't have happened." Paige regretted the words as soon as they left her lips.

He looked away. "You like him, don't you? He's a rich, fancy lawyer with lots of money."

Paige turned Nathan around by the arm. "You know...that's not important to me." *Why am I defending myself to him?* He was supposed to know her better than anyone.

"You've been away a long time...maybe you've changed."

"You don't really believe that," countered Paige. He said nothing, but the blank expression on his face was infuriating. "You're being an ass. Go back to work and leave me alone." Paige stepped backward through the door and slammed it shut. *What the hell...who the hell...does he think he is?* Confused, saddened, and angered, Paige watched out the picture window as his truck pulled away. It was true, she'd been away for many years, perhaps too many. She wasn't sure whether she should be flattered that he was jealous or worried that there was a side to him that she didn't know. *Why did Michael have to come by and ruin everything?*

CHAPTER 25

IT WASN'T AS IF SHE could tell Nathan why she had had dinner with Michael. That she's doing some investigating of her own. He'd probably have her locked up. She'd have to accept for the time being that he was mad. *It was kind of cute.* Paige turned away from the window just as the crystal table lamp next to the couch flickered, then totally went out once again. *Come on. Really.* Paige shook her head, huffed like a disappointed mare, and threw her hands up. *Could this day get any worse?* The bulb flickered again and to Paige's great relief, remained illuminated.

With the power back on, Paige now could see what was going on in the rest of the world. She lowered herself into her father's brown leather recliner, picked up the remote, and turned on the television. It took a few minutes for the cable to reboot, but when it did, the first thing she heard was an update on hurricane damage. "These images are from the height of the hurricane. As you can see, there's been extensive flooding in many beach side communities along the Jersey Coast," reported a young brunette in hip waders as she trudged through flood waters on Ocean Avenue in the nearby town of Belmar. The camera shot expanded to expose a broken, tattered boardwalk behind her. Paige intently watched and listened. "Hurricane Martha has left a good portion of the New York/New Jersey Metropolitan area without power."

Paige sprang up out of her chair, grabbed her camera bag, got in her Jeep, and drove toward the shore. An assignment was exactly what she needed.

Parking three blocks from Ocean Avenue, she walked around orange barricades and then hopscotched her way to the boardwalk. Only stopping once, momentarily, to take a picture of a house which had lost half its roof. Most of Ocean Avenue was covered with a thick layer of sand, with low-lying areas still flooded. Sections of the boardwalk were splintered and upended. While other sections looked like a fresh coat of powdery snow had rained down on them.

She trudged through the soft, wind-swept sand until she reached the inlet jetty that jutted out from the shoreline. She stepped up onto one of the many large gray boulders that made up the jetty.

Then step by step, she carefully maneuvered from one boulder to another, gingerly stepping on the wet, slippery rocks. At forty yards out, she stopped, planted her feet, and looked out at the angry, churning sea. Paige removed the lens cap from her camera, adjusted the zoom, and patiently waited for the perfect shot.

Seagulls soared overhead, diving and swooping downward, scavenging for food along the water's edge. Ten-foot waves repeatedly crashed into the jetty drenching Paige with a heavy mist of salty water. She wiped the stinging water from her eyes and then violently shook her head, from side to side, like a wet dog after a bath.

Determined, Paige continued watching as waves rolled in, crested and crashed hard on the shore, and then rolled back out to sea. Hearing squeals and screams, Paige twisted around.

Several brazen teens ran along the wet sand, darting back and forth from the water to the dunes. One stopped, bent over, and picked up a large conch shell. A rare find along the Jersey Shore, but not that usual after a hurricane had passed through, churning up the ocean's depths, bringing all its treasures to the surface. The young man held the shell to his ear. His face lit up, and Paige believed it was because he was hearing the sounds of the ocean coming from the shell. The first time she'd done it, she was amazed.

A large grayish seagull dove down, narrowly missing her. It then flew upward with an enormous clam in its beak. The gull dropped the clam and it smashed on a rock, cracking open into several pieces. Swooping back down, the gull landed and began to feast. Paige seized the moment and was able to capture an incredible picture of the gull as it spread its wings and went airborne once again.

Her cell phone rang. Hurriedly, she fumbled through her camera case, pulled out her cell, and answered it on the fourth ring. "Hello."

"Paige Thompson?"

"Yes." The call dropped. She checked the ID caller. She didn't recognize the number.

She tried to call it back. There was no service. That was her cue to pack it in. Paige began leaping from rock to rock, heading back toward dry sand. Unexpectedly, her right foot slipped out from under her, causing her to wobble from side to side. Then splat, she fell forward, off the rocks, planting her face-first, into the sand. Paige spit the gritty white substance from her mouth, wiped her face with a sleeve, and pushed herself up onto all fours.

Realizing just how lucky she was to have landed in the sand and not on a rock, she sat where she landed and gathered herself. She tried to wipe some of the sand off, but it had adhered to her wet clothes, and nothing short of jumping in the ocean would get it all off.

CHAPTER 26

PAIGE POSITIONED HERSELF AT HER father's desk with a cup of hot tea to take the chill out of her bones and finish her work assignment. She tapped her fingers on the edge of her laptop as the storm photos downloaded. Once loaded, she methodically edited and organized the photos, added captions, and emailed them off to her supervisor at the Williamstown Courier. She shut down her laptop and set it aside. *Now to get back on track. Forget Nathan Edgemont exists.*

"The hurricane has been all over the news here. I tried to call several times," said Todd.

"Cell service has been spotty. Most of the area is without power. I'm lucky. The power came back on quickly here," said Paige.

"How'd Mom make out?"

"Good. Cate stayed with her last night."

"Hey…any news on the investigation?"

"There's nothing new."

"Nothing?"

"Yup…so I'm doing my own thing."

"Like what?"

"Trying to connect with some of Dad's friends and colleagues, mostly just nosing around."

"Please be careful."

"I've been looking for Dad's journal. Where'd you put it?"

"Back where I got it. What's going on?"

"Nothing…"

"You're up to something," said Todd.

"I never had a chance to read it."

"That's all?"

"Yes."

"Okay, got to go…work. I'm glad you got through the storm without much damage," said Todd.

Easy for him to say, thought Paige as she hung up and a vivid flash of her and Nathan grabbed her attention. *Stop. There's no time for that.*

Paige retrieved her father's journal, took a squat on the couch, and began to read. The first entry was dated June 2, 1978: "Finally, all moved in. The new house is a big undertaking. I'm hoping the utilities won't be too much. Emily is happy, that's what matters."

As she flipped through the next fourteen years of scattered entries chronicling not only her father's life but her family's, Paige began to see her father differently. As a child, all she knew was that he was her dad and in her eyes, he was all knowing and invincible. As she read his words, she discovered he was also a vulnerable man, who worried about his finances, his work, his family, and his friends, just as she did.

When Paige came across her father's entry on May 1, 1991, she paused, pondered, and reread it: "I hope I did the right thing. My family is my everything. I pray for forgiveness. What's done is done." The entry had a haunting tone to it and Paige couldn't image what her father would need forgiveness for. Had he done, like so many other men, perhaps, cheated on his wife? *No, not my dad.*

The next day's entry read: "Cate's very upset. Heard her crying last night. I wish there was something I could do. Emily said she'd handle it. A classmate of hers has been missing for two days. I think she has a crush on the boy. Definitely Emily's territory." Paige thought back to what her mom had said about Cate and Michael once running in the same circles and how they both were upset when Ryan Timmons went missing. *This must be what Mom was talking about.*

Hungry for more information, she read the next entry dated May 5, 1991: "The Police are still searching for Ryan. Relieved to know my three children are all in their beds. Can't begin to imagine the distress and grief Ryan's parents are feeling."

On May 25, 1991, Nicholas Thompson wrote, "Memorial Day. Took the family to the beach. What a mistake, had to park blocks away. Forgot how crazy the first official weekend of summer can be at the Shore. Todd and Paige had fun. Thought a change might cheer up Cate."

Paige felt compelled to call Cate. "Where are you?" she asked.

"I'm home. What's up?"

"Thought we could catch up."

"Now?"

"Yes."

"I've a ton of things to do here at home," said Cate.

"Okay, I'll let you go…but first…thank you for taking such good care of Mom."

"You noticed," said Cate.

"You're a good sister. I should've said so sooner," said Paige.

"Thank you."

"I'm sorry," said Paige.

"For what?"

"For misjudging you. For thinking everything has always been so easy for you."

"What are you talking about?"

"I've been going through some of Dad's things…trying to find clues."

"You found something?"

"I found out something about you…I didn't know."

"I don't know what you mean?"

"Ryan Timmons."

"That was a long time ago."

"It must've brought back bad memories when his body was discovered."

"Of course."

"Was it a relief to finally know what happened?"

"No…I had hoped that someday I'd find out he'd run away. Why are you asking about this now?"

"I don't remember anything about this."

"You were too young to understand at the time. He was in my class. You didn't know him."

"Was he your boyfriend?"

"No…let it go."

"Mom said you, Ryan, and Michael were all friends before Ryan disappeared. Is that why you don't like Michael?"

"This is about Michael. He put you up to this, didn't he? I want nothing to do with that man…and you shouldn't either."

"So…why don't you explain it to me."

"There's nothing to explain. Ryan disappeared, then Michael went away. You do the math."

"You think Michael had something to do with Ryan's disappearance."

"It crossed my mind."

"Maybe like you, he was upset."

"It seemed convenient…the way he went away to boarding school."

"How come you never talked about this?"

"People did plenty of talking at the time. Now…I'd just like to forget."

The connection was lost. *She hung up on me.* Paige hadn't intended on upsetting Cate. She just wanted to understand and perhaps put some of the pieces together. She sent Cate a text message: "I'm sorry."

Picking the journal back up, she skimmed over the next few years which were full of ordinary moments: Cate's high school graduation, Todd's football and baseball games, and her junior high school years. With a special mention of her stint in the drama club, when she played Jo in her junior high's production of *Little Women*. Paige always had thought her father was too busy to really notice what was going on in his children's lives, but apparently, she had gotten it all wrong. He may've been a quiet man, but he definitely was paying attention.

After hours of reading, the muscles in her back and legs began to cramp. She stood and stretched to her left side, then her right. Then she bent forward from her waist and touched the floor.

Now that she was limber, she moved to the front window. Dusk was setting in with the sun low in the western sky. The neighborhood still abandoned, she closed the curtains and double-checked the locks and deadbolts on the front and back doors.

Paige settled back on the couch with some toast and tea. *Why hasn't Nathan called? Probably still mad,* she thought. *I don't want to hear from him anyways.* She covered her legs with a blanket and began to read where she'd left off.

On March 8, 2011, her father wrote, "Ran into Robert Gilbert. He asked I call his office and make an appointment to come in about a consulting job. Big project coming up. I'm considering it. Will run it by Emme first."

His next entry was dated May 3, 2011: "It's good to be working with Robert again. Emily had lunch with Sarah today."

On June 15, 2012, the entry read, "Human remains were unearthed at the reservoir site today. Project shut down. Don't know how long shut down will last."

On September 10, 2012: "Had lunch with Robert today. No word from the State yet on when construction can resume."

Paige jumped in place when the doorbell sounded. Quickly, she scurried to the front door. She moved the corner of the window curtain and took a peek. Then unlocked and opened the door. "Are you here to apologize?" she asked as Nathan walked through the door.

"What?"

"This morning? Remember?"

"Oh that. It's been a long day." He wrapped his arms around her like nothing had happened. *Just like a man. Forget what happened. Move on. You're too sensitive.* She melted into his chest. "I'm sorry, I overreacted," he whispered in her ear. His breath was warm and she shuddered.

"Are you hungry? I can make something."

"I can't stay."

"You can't?"

"Most of town is still without power. I'll be working all night," said Nathan.

"You could've just called," said Paige.

"I needed to see you." He gently placed a kiss on her lips. Paige smiled, nibbled on her bottom lip, and gazed up into his eyes. "Everything good here? What've you been up to?"

"Finished a work assignment. Most of the day I've been reading Dad's journal."

"What journal?"

"The one we found hidden…" Paige stopped and looked away.

"You can't keep things from me," said Nathan as he turned her back around. "It might be helpful."

"It's personal…I want to read it first." She gave him a look. "You understand."

"I get it. Promise, if you find anything relevant, you'll hand it over."

"Of course."

"I put a rush on the ballistics," said Nathan.

"The results aren't back yet?"

"The lab has a backlog. The hurricane didn't help any either."

"Anything else?"

"We found an abandoned pickup. It's being towed to the impound lot."

"Is it the one?"

"The owner reported it stolen the day before your parents' accident."

"I was hoping…by now, there'd be more," said Paige.

"It takes time. The truck needs to be gone over."

"The waiting is hard."

"What about your dad's journal? Anything?"

"Maybe…does the name Robert Gilbert mean anything to you?" Paige hesitated.

"No. Why?"

"My dad did some consulting for his company. He and Dad were close."

Nathan cocked his head sideways and looked her straight in the eye. Paige shrugged. "It's just a hunch. Dad mentions him quite a few times in his journal. From what I've read so far, Dad trusted him. He may know something."

"I trust your instincts… I'll take a look at him," said Nathan as he headed toward the kitchen. Paige followed and watched as he opened the back door, stepped out onto the deck, and looked around the backyard. He stepped back inside, locked the door, turned the deadbolt, and hooked the chain. "There's a curfew downtown. The power is out there."

"Sure…you don't want something to eat?"

Nathan picked up a large red apple off the counter. "Maybe I'll take one of these. Can I have two?"

"Take as many as you want," said Paige.

"I wish I could stay."

Their hands brushed and their fingers entwined. "You be safe," said Paige.

"Keep all your doors locked. I'm hoping to get a man assigned to your house for the night." Nathan gave her a lingering kiss, then stepped out through the door. She locked it behind him, slid the deadbolt, and hooked the chain in place.

Paige picked up her father's journal and continued to read. On May 5, 2017, her father made a long entry: "What a beautiful spring day. Went out to the reservoir for an early morning walk. Took some great photos. Ended my walk at the docks, where I saw Frank Wilson and one of his handymen bringing in his boat. He said the bass weren't biting. Odd, didn't see any fishing gear in the boat. Frank was in a hurry to leave."

His next entry was the following day: "Made prints of yesterday's photos. My favorite is that of a majestic, white egret. I captured Frank's boat off in the distance moored near the island."

On May 22, 2017, he wrote, "I was followed today by a blue van. Lost it in the parking lot of Stop-N-Go. Circled back around, found it, and tailed van to alley behind Wilson's law firm. Two men got out and entered a rear door to Luigi's Pizza. Maybe I'm being paranoid."

Paige flipped through the last few blank pages, hoping to find just a few more words. Her father's final journal entry was dated June 14, 2017: "I found Dusty early this morning lifeless in the backyard. His throat was slit. I buried him in the far corner of the yard, near the fence, before Emily saw. He was a good dog. I'll miss him. I hate not telling Emily the truth. Don't want to upset her. It's time to confront this head on. It's getting too close to home. I did this, I need to fix it. I'm tired of the haunting nightmares." *That's it. Really, Dad!*

Paige closed the journal, placed it on the coffee table, and silently tried to process what she'd just read. *Why so vague?* She took a sip of tea, and as she placed the cup back on the table, her cell phone vibrated. She read the text message from Nathan. "A patrol car will be making rounds in your neighborhood all through the night." For once, she was thankful for Nathan's vigilance. She messaged him back. "Stay safe. I'm home with all the doors and windows locked." Even though her eyes were tired from reading and her mind dizzy from thinking, she knew she'd never fall asleep.

CHAPTER 27

PAIGE SPRANG UP OFF THE couch with the first sunlight the next morning. Even after two cups of coffee and a shower, she was still tired from lack of sleep. But no matter how tired she was, she had made up her mind somewhere in the darkness of the night that she'd take a trip back to the reservoir. Just to see for herself what her father saw.

It was the perfect time to further investigate what her father had been up to, absolutely perfect, with no one around to tell her to be careful or it was a bad idea. The further west she drove from the coast, the less storm damage she encountered, and as luck would have it, she found the park's front gate open and the parking lot empty.

She grabbed her backpack and camera from the backseat and headed toward the ranger station, where two young rangers were dragging a green canoe out of an aluminum storage shed. She watched as they placed the canoe on the sandy edge of the water next to several different colored kayaks. Then returned to the shed and repeated the process several more times. When they had finished, the water's edge was laced with a colorful rainbow of red, yellow, green, and blue.

As planned, Paige rented a kayak and set out on her expedition. The large body of water was a bit choppy but navigable. An experienced adventurer, she guided the slick kayak over the water's surface, the paddles cutting through the water, propelling it forward.

At the center of the reservoir, she slowed the vessel. The shoreline now at a distance, she observed on the far right a patch of tall greenish, yellow marsh grass populated with large pockets of cattails. She watched the chocolate brown, bushy tops of the cattails sway back and forth ever so gently in a hypnotic waltz. For a few moments, she was able to clear out all chaotic thoughts and just be. A gentle breeze swept across the open waters, cooling her brow. She wished to stay a bit longer enjoying the peace and serenity, but she was determined and would not be sidetracked. Paige was certain the answer to the mystery surrounding her father's death was out there somewhere. She supposed her father may've stumbled upon the men while out on a nature hike. But there was always the possibility that he had been following them.

What could be out there that even the knowledge of would jeopardize his life? Paige pointed the nose of the kayak toward the small island and paddled till she came to a shallow, where she jumped out with a splash, into a foot of water. A large water moccasin swam by making her squirm and then disappeared into the shadows along the island's edge. Quickly, she dragged the kayak up onto the shore and secured it. There was a narrow trail leading up the sloping shore into the brush. With her backpack of detecting supplies over one shoulder and her camera slung over the other, she walked upward and followed the muddy trail along the outer edge of the island.

Coming upon an open area surrounded by thick bushes, Paige cautiously stepped off the path and into it. Thinking this might be the spot, she stood in its center, slowly twirling around, surveying the area. She recognized a tall forked oak tree and stopped. She took three steps back and then unzipped her backpack to remove her folding camping spade along with her father's photos.

She looked at the photos and then looked at the tree. They definitely matched. The ground was covered with brown decaying leaves and the soil was soft from the recent rain fall. Paige stomped around with the bottom of her foot, feeling for a spot where the ground might be loose. The soil gave. Using the spade as a rake, she pushed the leaves aside, then slowly and methodically began to dig. With all her strength, she dug, moving shovel after shovel of dirt until large mounds of earth surrounded her. Her fortitude began to fizzle as the morning progressed and she found nothing.

As exhaustion was setting in, her shovel hit something and a clanging rang out. She gently tapped the shovel on the hard object. Then she bent over and brushed away the surrounding dirt with her gloved hand. She huffed. *Damn it.* It was only a beer bottle. She tossed the bottle aside as she uprighted herself. Her back spasmed and she wrenched as it tightened. Afraid to make any sudden movements, she bent from her waist, to the left and then the right. It was then that something small and round caught her attention. Could it help solve the puzzle, she didn't know, but nonetheless, she placed the button into a clear plastic bag and put it her backpack. *Perhaps it was from one of the men in the photos,* she thought. With a renewed sense of purpose, she began to dig once again, this time in the area of the button. Sweat dripped from her forehead, her armpits smelled of perspiration, and the back of her neck began to smart from sunburn, but she pressed on. The payoff being the discovery of a small black piece of a plastic bag with a jagged edge. She tucked it away with the button and continued. Next, a long army-green canvas strap fell to the ground as she flung a shovelful of dirt. She stopped to examine it. It was faded and weathered and similar to the straps of her own backpack. It was at this point that Paige got down into the hole on all fours and dug carefully sweeping the surface, like a paleontologist unearthing the fossil of a dinosaur.

When her hand slid over a flat surface, she paused. Then traced the outside edge of the object with an index finger. She pried around the object with the point of her spade until she was able to get under it and remove what appeared to be a backpack in its entirety minus one strap. Paige sat back in the dirt, easily unzipped it, and pulled out a calculus book. Written on the inside cover of the book was the name Ryan Timmons. Paige's mind began to go into overdrive. A backpack belonging to Ryan would've fallen apart from being buried for more than two decades. It was dirty, but it wasn't rotting, nor decayed. *Why wasn't it found when his body was discovered? How? It makes no sense.*

With the sun now low in the west and dusk not far behind, it was time to head back to the ranger station. Paige recalled reading a sign that indicated all boats "must" to be returned before dusk. If she left now, she'd just make it. She placed Ryan's backpack in a white plastic garbage bag, filled in the large holes she'd dug as best she could, and then kicked some leaves over the area.

Chapter 28

Nathan's pickup was parked in front of her parents' home when she returned. She gave him a quick wave as she pulled her Jeep into the drive. When she pushed open her driver's side door, he was standing right next to her vehicle.

"Where've you been?"

"What? You said not to go out after dark. It's barely dark." She replied with a nonchalant attitude.

"Why do you insist on not listening to me. Have you no common sense? And why didn't you answer your cell?"

"I didn't hear it."

"Well...where were you?"

"You're not my father." Paige turned her back to Nathan, unlocked the front door, and waved him in. "I'll explain once we're inside." She realized he was just trying to protect her and found it somewhat appealing, but she was an independent woman and struggled to balance the two ideals.

He shook his head in frustration. "Paige, you will be the death of me. I got worried when you weren't here."

Paige was happy to find the power still on. There'd be no need for all the firewood or the half-burnt candles scattered throughout the living room. Nothing to cloud her judgement like the other night. Nathan followed her in and made himself comfortable on the couch.

He stared at her feet. "Your shoes are muddy. Your knees filthy."

Looking down, Paige replied, "I was hiking at the reservoir. The trail was muddy."

"What would possess you to go back out there?"

"I was bored. Besides, I had unfinished business out there."

"It couldn't wait?"

189

"No, it couldn't! I kept thinking about my father's photos. I needed to see for myself."

"I asked you to stay here. It's dangerous for you to go anywhere by yourself."

"Why is that…what aren't you telling me?"

"Is that a shovel… I see in your backpack? I know you have a story… You might as well tell me."

"I rented a kayak and went out to the island in the center of the reservoir."

"By yourself! Are you crazy?"

"Stop saying that… I'm not crazy. I know exactly what I'm doing."

"You have no business digging around out there. You're lucky you didn't get yourself arrested for destroying park property." Paige pulled out the small plastic bag from her backpack and shoved it in his face.

"A button and a strap," remarked Nathan. "What am I supposed to do with these?"

"Not much, without this," said Paige as she opened the white trash bag.

"Now what…a dead rat?"

"No…Ryan Timmons's backpack!" Nathan stepped and leaned forward to see inside the large white trash bag Paige so proudly displayed to him. "I never dreamed I'd actually find anything out there."

"Found something or not, you should've never been out there! How'd you know?"

"My dad's photos. You have them."

"The photos of the bird? I handed them off to the lab."

"That was dumb," boasted Paige. "I blew up the images."

"You could've clued me in."

"Of course. I just thought…"

"You thought what? Paige, you shouldn't be investigating this on your own. You took a dangerous chance. What if someone saw you? Or worse, followed you?"

"I was careful. No one saw me, except two park rangers."

"You need to stop playing Nancy Drew and let me do my job." Grabbing onto her hands, he looked her straight in the face. "I can't do my job if I'm worrying about your safety."

"Then...don't worry."

"Easier said than done," he said.

"I think we should put"—Paige pointed back and forth between herself and Nathan—"whatever this is between you and me...on hold." She put her hands together and then dramatically parted them. "A separation of church and state."

"You're right...we should. It's the best thing for now. Excuse me, I need to make a call," said Nathan. He left the room.

When he returned, he continued, "Bad things keep happening around your family. And now you may've contaminated a crime scene."

"That wasn't my intention. I was just curious."

"I have a team on the way over to get your statement and pick up the items you found. Tell them exactly how you came across Ryan Timmons's backpack. This is part of an active investigation."

"I just wanted to help."

"You have...but enough is enough. I've no one available to watch this house tonight. That means I'll be staying here."

"You just agreed... We're putting us on hold," said Paige.

"We are. But it's my job to serve and protect."

"So...this is only the job?"

"Yup."

Paige put her hands on his chest and pushed him toward the door. "Then you should be out there like any other officer."

"You expect me to sit in my truck all night. I'm not any other officer."

"Tonight...you are! Please go. All I want to do is take a hot shower and go to bed. Alone."

Paige found it difficult to sleep knowing Nathan was so near. That night she dreamt of his strong arms wrapped around her, his heated kisses gliding over her skin, and their bodies entwined like a braided pretzel. She longed to feel his touch again. But her pride and common sense wouldn't let her give in to her desires.

Just as the sun poked over the horizon, Paige awoke and looked out her bedroom window. Nathan was still there, looking extremely uncomfortable, with his head slumped against the driver's side window. Her heart melt at the sight. She hated herself for being so intolerant the night before; he was first and foremost her oldest and dearest friend.

Paige gently tapped on the truck window. His eyes brightened and he sat up straight. Nathan rolled down the window. Paige handed him a large ceramic mug of coffee. "I'm sorry. Please forgive me," she said.

"Nothing to be sorry for. Do you think I can use the bathroom?"

Paige moved to open the truck door. "Please...come back in." His eyes were red and his hair a matted mess.

"Want to nap on the couch? Or shower? Whichever will make you feel better. Do both, do neither. I'm just so sorry that you sat out here all night because of me."

"Don't be so hard on yourself. It was my choice."

"You stayed because you were looking out for me. I was only thinking of myself."

"I think I'll take you up on that couch. I just need to shut my eyes for a bit."

Within moments of stretching his long legs out on the sofa, he was asleep. While he napped, Paige busied herself in the kitchen making breakfast. The least she could do was make him something hearty to eat. A half hour into his nap, the alarm on Nathan's cell phone went off and he jumped up off the couch.

"I need to go," he shouted toward the kitchen.

Paige emerged with a plate of pancakes. "I made breakfast."

"Thanks, but I need to get to roll call."

"See you later?" She called after him as he sprinted out the front door.

Turning, he gave her one last look. "I'll check back in. Please try to stay out of trouble."

Paige stared at the closed door. Then sat down on the couch to eat the pancakes. Picking up the remote, she turned on the television to watch the 7:00 a.m. news. When the news ended, she caught up on work emails and calls, and then sent a text message to Nathan inviting him to dinner.

He accepted her invitation, replying he'd be over by six. *Maybe I should tell him everything.*

Paige answered her phone on the second ring. "Hello."

"Is this Paige Thompson?

"Yes. Who's calling?"

"Mary Gilbert. I'm returning your call."

"Mrs. Gilbert, thank you for getting back to me."

"Your message said you are Nicholas Thompson's daughter. I read about your father's accident in the paper. I'm sorry for your loss. How can I help you?"

"While going through my father's papers, I came across your husband's name and number. I was unable to reach Mr. Gilbert at his office. I hope it wasn't out of line that I called your home."

"My husband is away on business." Paige heard two men speaking in the background.

"When will he be back? It's important that I speak with him," said Paige.

There was a silence for a moment. "It's up in the air."

"If you hear from him…please give him my number."

"I'll ask him to call you. But I can't promise. The other line is ringing," said Mrs. Gilbert. Paige didn't hear a phone ringing. *Click.* She stared down at her phone. She may've not known Mrs. Gilbert, but she knew when she was being blown off. Why'd she even bother to call her back? thought Paige whose instincts began to tingle.

CHAPTER 29

PAIGE SLOWED HER VEHICLE IN front of a large white home with forest green shutters, encircled with a wooden porch with ceiling fans on Steeplechase Road. A sign on the eight-foot-high black wrought-iron gate read, "The Gilberts." There was a red BMW in the drive. She pulled her Jeep a little further up the road, parked it, and got out. After crossing the maple-lined street, Paige sauntered along the cement sidewalk, casually trying to peek through the tall hedge of boxwoods that surrounded the entire residence.

The side door to the house opened; and a tall, husky, mustached man stepped out, followed by a woman dressed in a tailored navy pantsuit. Together they descended the porch steps. The man halted and took a stance once they reached the side driveway. The well-groomed woman in her fifties continued across the drive toward a detached three-car garage.

One of the overhead garage doors opened. The woman walked through the opening and disappeared inside.

Paige separated the branches of the hedge on the far side of the property and squeezed her body through. She crouched low to the ground. Her eyes moved across the yard, from left to right. She slowly crept toward the back of the house. When she reached the porch, she crawled up the four wooden steps to the porch landing. There she paused, drawing in a deep breath. She exhaled, then turned and looked. The hedges were now thirty yards behind.

She inhaled deeply and exhaled once more before moving closer to the exterior wall of the house. Pressed up against the shingles, she checked her surroundings before advancing. No one had noticed her, or so she hoped. She poked her head up and peered in through the kitchen window. There was a large steaming pot on the stove, and the kitchen table was set for three.

She moved to the dining room window and looked in. The room was empty. There was a loud bang of a noise. Paige's body shuddered. It was the side door slamming shut. She ducked down. Her heart raced and her body remained motionless as the sound of footsteps drew closer. A man and woman were talking. She strained to hear.

"We shouldn't have come back," said Mrs. Gilbert.

"We couldn't stay away forever. I've a business to run," said Robert Gilbert.

"You should tell the police what you know."

Paige's ears perked up. *Police!* Did she dare? She moved her head up closer to the window's ledge and then slowly, with fingers crossed, looked in. She let out her held breath. The couple was standing near the stove with their backs to her and there was a handgun on the counter.

"Tell them what? All I have are my suspicions and a few cryptic words I overheard. With the new alarm system...and the security guard...we'll be fine. You called Nick's daughter back?"

"Just as you said. I told her you were away on business."

"Did she say what she wanted?"

"To speak with you. She said she came across your name in her father's papers." Mrs. Gilbert stirred the simmering pot before turning toward her husband.

Robert Gilbert took his wife's hand. "Please, dear...don't worry."

"I can't help it! You could be next," she whimpered, stepped into his arms, and laid her head on his shoulder. He wrapped his arms around her.

"It's handled." He rocked her in her arms and then released her. "Something sure smells good."

"It's nothing special. Just soup," said Mrs. Gilbert as she turned back to the stove and began ladling the liquid into two ceramic bowls. She picked up one bowl and handed it to her husband.

Paige quickly squatted down. She scanned the yard as she struggled with what to do next. Should she knock on the door, confront them, and ask them why they lied to her? Risk being arrested for trespassing or being tackled by the big goon who was guarding the drive. Or do the responsible thing: tell Nate and let the police ask the questions.

There was an elongated shadow of a person across the side lawn. Beads of sweat gathered on her forehead. She remained still with her body pressed against the house. Then, like a cornered cat, Paige began crawling backward away from the house and down the porch steps.

She looked again. The shadow was near the corner of the house. She stopped and held her breath. When the shadow moved and then totally disappeared, Paige let out a sigh and leapt to her feet. Then scurried across the side yard, pushed through the hedges, and ran, not looking back until she was in the driver's seat of her vehicle. She turned on the engine and called Nathan.

When the call went straight to voice mail, Paige left him no message. *What am I doing? He'll kill me if he knows what I'd been up to.*

Keeping one eye in the rearview mirror all the while, Paige put her Jeep in gear and drove away. Once she was a safe distance from the Gilberts' home, she pulled her vehicle to the curb to breathe and think. As she reflected by the side of the road, a caravan of power trucks passed, reminding her she needed to take more photos of the damage left behind by the hurricane for the next installment of her work assignment.

Paige spent the remainder of the morning driving around Meadowbrook making notes and taking additional photos of damaged homes and businesses. Once her job assignment was done and filed with the paper, Paige headed out to the grocery store.

She parked in the east lot, grabbed a shopping cart, and went in to purchase something that would wow Nathan. Nothing elaborate, she was no Rachel Ray in the kitchen. She picked out two thick, marbleized ribeye steaks, romaine lettuce, parmesan cheese, and Caesar dressing, and then checked out.

As she exited through the automatic doors, she had the uneasy feeling that someone was following her. She turned her head ever so slightly as she rounded the left corner of the building. She quickened her pace. The man behind her quicken his. Nervously, Paige looked for her Jeep.

There was a man standing next to it. What was he doing? She pulled her cell out of her jacket pocket and hit redial, then stopped, and turned. "Why are you following me?" She demanded.

"I'm not following you, miss. My car is parked over there." The short man in a plaid shirt pointed at a midsized white car and passed her. She turned her attentions toward her Jeep. The man was gone. With a sigh of relief, she placed her bag of groceries in the back compartment of her SUV.

It all happened so fast. A dark sack slipped over her head and a strong arm restrained her from behind. She screamed. A hand was placed over her mouth. She heard a vehicle pull up. It stopped, its engine still running. Paige tried biting the hand that covered her mouth. She got a mouthful of cloth instead. The man was much taller and stronger than she. Thrashing her arms in darkness and kicking at air, she struggled to free herself. One assailant lifted her by her ankles, the other by her arms. They flung her. She landed hard inside the rear section of the cargo van.

One of her attackers jumped in on top of her, putting his entire body weight on her lower back. "Hurry up, stupid. Let's get out of here." She kicked her legs up and down, trying to get the heavy man off her. The engine revved and the van took off with a screech.

After what might have been a fifteen-minute ride but felt longer, the van stopped. Paige heard the driver's door open. Her heart rate increased, extreme panic set in, and she prayed. The driver slid the side door panel open. "How yah making out?"

"She's a biter." The man remained seated on top of her.

"Catch." The driver tossed a roll of silver duct tape. "We've a long ride." The big man caught it with one hand. "Tape her mouth first. I can't stand her screams."

CHAPTER 30

PAIGE HAD INVITED NATHAN FOR dinner; he was sure of that fact. But her Jeep wasn't in the drive when he arrived at precisely 6:00 p.m. The Paige he knew never would've invited him over just to stand him up. Had she gotten carried away with her work assignment? She had mentioned that she was going out in the afternoon. What had she said? He tried to recall her exact words. She was taking a ride through downtown and then would be following Ocean Avenue up the coast a bit to take storm damage photos. He pulled out his cell. There was a missed call at 4:06 p.m. from Paige. It had gone to voice mail. He listened. The message was muffled. What was she saying? "Why are you following me?" What kind of message is that?

He called her cell. It went right to voice mail. Before jumping to any outlandish conclusions, he called her sister. She may have stopped at the rehab to see her mother, but Cate hadn't heard from Paige all day.

Nathan waited another five minutes before trying her cell again. The call went straight to voice mail once again. Now he was worried. He got out of his truck and walked around the house. He looked in through a kitchen window. There were no signs of dinner preparations.

There was nothing to indicate foul play either; still, he couldn't shake the feeling that something wasn't right. If he remembered correctly the Thompsons had always hidden a house key in the backyard. To his great relief, it was still there, under the garden gnome with the blue cap, half embedded in the soil from years of being untouched.

Once inside, he did a quick but thorough walk through. The blanket he and Paige had lain on was folded on the couch. His mind flashed back to the other night when he had finally fulfilled his lifelong dream. He had been in love with Paige since he was twelve and had let the dream of "them" go when she went away to college and didn't return to Meadowbrook. But now she was back, and he had a second chance.

Nathan blinked and his mind returned to reality. He put a call into dispatch to see if any accidents or incidents involving Paige had been reported and asked for a detailed account of the daily patrol in the neighborhood surrounding the Thompson home. Just as he had requested, a patrol car had made a sweep at least once an hour and at random intervals, paying close attention to the Thompson property. At this point, he couldn't involve the department any further. It wasn't as if Paige had been missing for any length of time; he just couldn't find her. The chief would laugh him out of the office if he asked that an APB be put out on his girlfriend. Or was it…friend?

Paige had been nosing around investigating her father's death. He should've stopped her. But she was a force to be reckoned with. Before setting out to look for Paige, he wrote her a short note saying to stay put if she returned home. He signed it, "Love, Nathan," left it on the kitchen table, and then headed out of the neighborhood toward downtown Meadowbrook.

If someone was interested in photographing storm damage, where would one start? Or in other words, where would Paige start? The marquee at the movie theatre had been blown off. That would be a logical place to start, thought Nathan.

A public works employee confirmed that there had been a blonde taking candid snaps of the cleanup efforts in the early afternoon. Their description of the woman made him believe it was Paige. Maybe she was still in the area? He searched for her Jeep in the town parking lot. He found nothing.

With no sight of Paige or her Jeep, he headed toward the shore area and Ocean Avenue. He drove up the coast to the Highlands and back to Meadowbrook. He'd hoped to find her with a broken-down vehicle on the shoulder of the road, but he didn't. Out of options, he took a drive through the hospital parking lot. It was worth a shot, he told himself.

Nathan called in some favors from his friends on the force, a little unofficial help. He met with the officers in the parking lot behind Town Hall and gave them a description of Paige and her vehicle. They could hear the urgency in his voice. If Nathan thought something was wrong, then they would help.

After several hours, Nathan received the call he'd been waiting for but didn't want. Paige's Jeep had been found at the local grocery store, but she was not in the store. Of course, why hadn't he thought of it; she had been going to cook him dinner.

The back hatch of the Jeep was ajar and a grocery bag was inside. The steaks, which had fallen out, had turned brown from the heat of the hot August afternoon indicating they'd been there for hours.

Internalizing his panic, Nathan called the department chief and asked an all-points bulletin be put out on Paige. The request was granted as more officers arrived on scene. The officers spread out, searching the lot and questioning employees and patrons. Meanwhile, Nathan went inside the store to check surveillance tapes.

The store manager led Nathan to an upstairs office where two large monitors with six quadrants each sat on a tiny desk. In front of the monitors sat a small man with narrow eyes and a large belly that hung over his belt named Tim. Tim explained that the monitor on the left was in-store surveillance and the monitor on the right covered the front and back exits and the parking lot.

"Pull up all of today's footage from 1:00 p.m. on," directed Nathan.

"Inside or out?"

"Start with inside."

They watched as at 3:56 p.m., Paige perused rib-eye steaks in the meat department before choosing two. She put them in her shopping cart. Then she walked down the baking aisle toward the front registers and checked out at 4:03 p.m., at register five. She was smiling as she made small talk with the young sandy-haired clerk ringing up her order.

The camera at the front exit caught her image next, showing her walk out, then disappearing from camera's view.

"There's a blind spot once you turn that corner," explained Tim.

"There must be another camera on the side parking lot," said Nathan.

"Yeah. Give me a minute."

"Stop. That's her." Nathan took a deep breath as the image of Paige appeared on the screen. "Slow the tape down," he said as he placed his right hand on Tim's left shoulder. "Why is she turning around? Who's she talking to? Is there audio?"

"No."

"Can you stop it? Now go back. Someone is near her, there's a shadow. We need to find that person." With his cell phone, Nathan took a picture of the still screen showing an average-looking man, with brown hair, wearing khaki shorts and a white polo shirt. "Now, let's see the rest."

When the video resumed, Paige was turning and then walked toward her Jeep. They watched as she opened the rear compartment and placed the brown, paper, grocery bag inside. A navy cargo van pulled up, obstructing the view of Paige. When it pulled away, she was gone.

Nathan stood there, stunned.

"Where is she?" Tim asked.

"Can you zoom in on that license tag?"

"No. This isn't exactly FBI equipment we've got here. It's a grocery store. We're looking for shoplifters."

"Don't be a wise ass. I need a copy of all the footage showing that blonde. Do you understand? I need it ASAP."

"Sorry." Tim sat up straight. "It'll take a little time, but I got it."

"Good, I'll be back in twenty."

Nathan went downstairs and outside to where his team of officers was searching the parking lot. "Any witnesses?" he asked Detective McGuire.

"Haven't found any."

"There may not be any. This vehicle's been here almost three hours. When will CIU get here? We need them to sweep the SUV for prints."

"On the way."

"Keep me informed," ordered Nathan.

As promised in exactly twenty minutes, Nathan reappeared at the surveillance room door.

Tim promptly placed a DVD in his hand. "Thank you. You did good work today," Nathan said as he closed his hand around the DVD and extended his other. He ran back down the steps, through the electronic glass doors, jumped in this truck, and was off to the crime lab with the DVD. He was not about to place Paige's life in anyone's hands but his own.

After logging in the DVD at the crime lab, Nathan stopped at the rehab facility to inform Cate, face-to-face, of Paige's disappearance. He also briefed the officer stationed outside of Emily Thompson's room of the situation at hand. Understandably shaken, Cate asked that they not say anything to her mother at this point.

While he waited for the lab to enhance the surveillance video and for officers to report in, Nathan went back to Paige's parents' home in hopes that in retracing her steps, he'd learn something helpful. He searched Mr. Thompson's study, which he'd never have done without a search warrant, except in this case. *Finding Paige is all that matters and if that means bending a few rules, then let it be,* thought Nathan.

He picked up the folder containing the reservoir newspaper articles which was hanging off the corner of the desk. He gave them a quick look through, set them aside, and moved on.

Next, he opened Nicholas Thompson's leather-bound journal that sat in the center of the desk. On the last written page was an entry dated June 14, 2017: "I was followed today by a blue van. Lost it in the parking lot of Stop-N-Go. Circled back around and tailed van to alley behind Wilson's law firm."

His phone rang. It was the crime lab. They were able to enlarge the license plate on the blue cargo van. The plate had been run. The van was register to Wilson and Wilson Law.

CHAPTER 31

NATHAN FORCIBLY CLANGED THE BRASS knocker on Judge Brown's door until she opened it. It was early, before 7:00 a.m., but the search warrant for the law offices of Wilson and Wilson *had* to be signed right away.

"Judge Brown…sorry to disturb. Has the chief called you yet?"

"He did. Come in Detective Edgemont," replied Judge Brown. She put on a pair of readers and scanned the papers Nathan handed her. "You're sure? Frank Wilson is well-respected and a damn good lawyer."

"I'm sure, and if I'm wrong, I'll deal with it. But right now, a young woman has disappeared and Wilson's company van was placed at the scene. We need this, I need this," said Nathan.

Judge Brown signed the warrant and handed it back to Nathan. "Keep me informed."

"Got it," said Nathan before dashing out the door and jumping into an idling cruiser.

It was 7:30 a.m. as Lisa Templeton, a small-framed brunette, slid her key in the front door lock of Wilson and Wilson Law. Nathan and four officers descended upon her.

"Miss…we have a search warrant for these premises," said Nathan.

The young woman tentatively took the document. "I need to call Mr. Wilson."

"There's no time for that. These papers allow us in."

She unfolded the papers with her shaking hands and carefully read. Then she looked up. "Okay." She finished turning the key in the lock and opened the door. The four officers entered and spread out, each taking an office to search while Nathan grilled Lisa about any and all vehicles the firm owned. She only knew of two vehicles used by the firm. There was the one leased for Michael Wilson and the one leased for Frank Wilson.

"I want to know about the company van. I can take you in to the station," threatened Nathan.

"I'm just the receptionist," Lisa insisted. "Perhaps you should speak to Mr. Wilson's secretary."

"You seem to be the only one here right now, so I'm asking you," said Nathan.

"I'm new. I don't know." Lisa searched her purse for a tissue as she turned into a blubbering wreak of a person. Nathan didn't have time to waste. Every minute that passed could be Paige's last minute on earth.

Amy Cooper, Mr. Wilson's secretary, arrived at 7:50 a.m. She picked up the front desk phone. "I'm calling Mr. Wilson," she stated.

"Go right ahead." *Nothing would make me happier than looking into Frank Wilson's eyes.* "I'd like to know what he has to say about the van that this firm owns."

"Is that what all the fuss is about? That crappy old piece of junk the firm bought to haul boxes of files back and forth to our storage unit? We haven't used that van in months. It's parked out back. See, its right over there." She pointed out the conference room window to an empty lot. "Well, it *was* there, last I looked."

"Who has access to the van?"

"Anyone at the firm can use it. The keys are kept in the front office file cabinet. The Wilsons have always been nice about letting employees use it."

"Who would've taken it?"

"I don't know."

"Guess," Nathan insisted.

"Like I said, to the best of my knowledge, the van was still parked out back. Mr. Wilson did say last week that a friend of his might be using it to move. But I didn't give anyone the keys." She opened the file drawer. "The keys are missing," she said with surprise.

As she closed the drawer, Frank Wilson walked through the front door in a huff. "What the hell is going on here? Amy? Answer me."

"They have a search warrant," she stammered.

"Why didn't you call me?"

"I did. I left you a message. They were here when I got in."

"Who let them in?" Wilson yelled.

"I did," Lisa timidly replied as she broke out in tears again.

"I want to see the search warrant." Frank Wilson grabbed the warrant from Detective Edgemont's hand and quickly scanned it.

"This warrant is only relevant to any and all documents associated with vehicles owned by this firm. It looks like you've overstepped your authority. I represent my employees, and you won't be questioning my staff any further without legal representation."

"If I were you, I wouldn't be worrying about your employees. The van is registered to your firm. Where is it?"

"It's usually parked out back. Stop the bullshit. Why are you here?" demanded Mr. Wilson.

"Paige Thompson has been abducted. Your company van was placed at the scene."

"Paige has been abducted?" a voice came from behind Nathan. It was Michael Wilson.

"Like it's news to you."

"What can I do to help?" Michael asked.

Nathan assessed Michael's demeanor. He appeared to be sincere. "I need to know where the van is."

"It's kept behind the building."

"It's not there."

"It's not?"

"Where is it?"

"Beats me," answered Michael.

"I'll need a list of any and all persons who have had access to the van in the last month."

Again, Michael seemed to be genuinely surprised. "Amy, put a list together of all persons using the van and give it to Detective Edgemont."

"She's my secretary and I'll tell her what and when to do something," Frank Wilson fired back.

"Can I speak to you, Dad? In your office." Michael looked at his father. "Please."

The two gentlemen exited the front reception area and walked down the hall. They entered Mr. Wilson's locked office and closed the door behind them. "I don't understand why you won't cooperate with such a minor request," Michael asked.

"That detective is out of control. Right now, it's a small request. Next thing you know, he'll be accusing us of something."

"Do we have something to hide?"

"Of course not."

"Really, Dad?" Michael had a look of disgust on his face. "It wouldn't be the first time you circumvented the law to help yourself or a client."

"You're imagining things, just like you did when you were a child."

"I'm not going to argue with you about the past. Paige Thompson is missing. Her parents are friends of yours. And I care about her."

"They're your mother's friends and all they do is interfere."

"I knew you had issues, but I never imaged you were totally heartless. How can you be so…unconcerned?"

"Oh, I'm concerned. Concerned you're sweet on her and getting soft." Mr. Wilson had an evil glint in his eyes as his forehead crinkled. "You've always been a pussy."

"I'm just saying it doesn't hurt to cooperate with the police or at least pretend to be cooperative. Then they'll go away," Michael reasoned.

"Perhaps you're right." The Wilsons emerged from their sequester and went back to the lobby. Calmly, Frank Wilson instructed his secretary to give the list of names to Detective Edgemont.

"Next time, I may just drag you into the station for questioning," Nathan spoke at Mr. Wilson.

Nathan added Michael and Frank Wilson to the list of names and emailed it to the station to be run through the police database. Both Wilsons and their employees all came back with clean records. But that doesn't rule them out as suspects, thought Nathan. It just means they haven't been caught yet. Nathan assigned a detail to keep a watchful eye on Frank Wilson.

Amy, Wilson's secretary, had mentioned that the firm had a storage locker, and Nathan put an investigator on assignment to locate it. It wouldn't be the first time that a criminal had used a public storage unit to conceal a crime. In the meanwhile, Nathan called the building department, the tax assessor's office, and the fire bureau looking for information for property owned by, leased by, or used by either Wilson and Wilson Law or the Wilson family. As he went through the motions of the investigation, he reminded himself that Paige was a smart, strong, resourceful woman who wouldn't go down without a fight. He hoped that it was enough that she was still alive and that he'd be rescuing her body, not recovering it.

It had been twenty-four hours and still no sign of Paige, when the officer assigned to tailing Frank Wilson reported in at 3:56 p.m. "Frank Wilson left his office at 1:12 p.m. He drove a silver BMW, plate WJK287, registered to him. He stopped at the court house, remained inside for forty-two minutes and then went back to his law office. He remains inside."

"Any other activity going on?" Nathan asked.

"At 2:15 p.m., Wilson's secretary left, entered Luigi's Pizza next door, carrying what appeared to be a take-out order. She reentered Wilson and Wilson. At 3:00 p.m., there was an express delivery at the rear door."

"Stay on him," ordered Nathan as he pulled up to the Wilson residence on Maple Avenue to find the front door locked and the blinds down. The home looked eerily shut up. He rang the doorbell. No answer. He rang it again. He was certain he heard someone moving around inside.

He took his fist and pound on the thick wooden door. Finally, he saw a pair of eyes peering out from behind a blind.

"Who is it?" a female voice called out.

"Mrs. Wilson. It's Detective Edgemont of the Meadowbrook Police Department."

"Let me see your badge." Nathan unclipped his shield from his belt and held it out.

"Anyone can buy one of those at the five and dime. Let me see a photo ID."

Nathan pulled out his ID and held it up to the window. He heard the deadbolt click. The door opened three inches, held in place by a steel chain.

"What do you want?" She spoke in a voice so low it was barely audible.

"Paige Thompson is missing. I was hoping you could help us by answering some questions."

"Emily's daughter?"

"Yes." Mrs. Wilson undid the chain and let him in.

"I'm sorry to disturb you. Are you all right?" She had a bruise on her right cheek and an ace bandaged wrist.

"Oh this." She twisted her wrist to hold up her hand in front of her body. "Just a tennis injury. How can I help? I don't really know her. I'm friends with her mother."

"Does your husband have any dealings with the Thompsons?"

"Yes."

"Can you elaborate on that."

"The Thompsons are clients of Frank's. Emily is one of my dearest friends."

"Any animosity between your husband and Nicholas Thompson?" Nathan asked as he recollected the entry he had recently read in Nicholas Thompson's journal.

"Not that I'm aware of."

"And your son?"

"I'm not involved in my son's business…or my husband's."

"Your husband's firm owns a blue van. Does he ever loan it out or bring it home?"

"He did bring it home a few nights ago. One of his handymen took it the next day."

Sarah Wilson paused and sighed. "I was just going to have a cup of tea, care to join me? It gets very lonely around here."

"His handyman?" Nathan followed her and sat down at the dining room table as directed.

Sarah Wilson had a quiet dignity about her as she sat a tea cup in front of him. She was reserved and well-maintained. Nathan felt like he had just walked into the home of a Stepford wife. Every hair on her head was in place, a string of pearls adorned her neck, and her home was immaculate.

"My husband has two men who help around the yard and run errands for him."

"So they work for the firm?"

"No. They work for Frank, not the firm."

"Do you know their names?"

"Jack and Sam," she replied.

"Do you know their last names?"

"I'm not sure. I believe one of their last names is Lewis. My husband referred to one of them as Lewis once."

"Where's your husband now?"

"He should be at the office."

"Did he have plans to travel outside of Meadowbrook today?"

"He doesn't run his daily itinerary by me. I thought you were here about Paige. Why all the questions about Frank? Is he in trouble? He's doesn't mean to be…" She stopped, picked up her tea cup, and took a sip. She sat the tea cup back down and continued, "His work is stressful."

"You've been very helpful." Nathan stood to leave. "Thank you for the tea."

"I'm not sure how I helped. But it was nice to have company."

"Are you sure you're all right?"

"I'm fine enough," she calmly and matter-of-factly stated.

"Here's my card. You can always call me. There's help if you want it." Sarah Wilson took the card and tucked it away in the inside pocket of a cookbook and then escorted Detective Edgemont to the door.

Nathan walked away wishing he could do something to help her. But she had to ask for his help and he needed to focus all his attentions on finding Paige. Mr. Wilson was not the upstanding man he presented himself to be; he was abusive, manipulative, and, from the looks of it, a wife beater.

CHAPTER 32

FRANK WILSON PEERED OUT THE third-story window of his downtown office. Below, an unmarked police vehicle was positioned with two undercover officers in it. Periodically, the officer in the shotgun seat would get out, stroll the sidewalk, and disappear from view. Minutes later, he'd get back in. The charade continued all afternoon as Frank Wilson carried on business as usual.

Amy tapped on Mr. Wilson's closed office door.

"Come in," he called out.

"It's just after five. I'm leaving for the day. Anything you need before I go?"

"Is my son still here?"

"He left at three. Said he had a new client to see."

"Thank you, Amy. Could you please lock up the front when you go?"

"I guess that means you'll be having another late night."

"Looks that way."

"See you in the morning," said Amy, shutting the door behind her.

Frank remained seated, with an elbow on the desk. He rested his chin on the palm of his hand and contemplated. After a short time, he picked up his desk phone and redialed the last number.

"Are we good?" he asked. He nodded and listened. Without speaking another word, he replaced the phone receiver back in place, took a small key from his top desk drawer, and unlocked the file cabinet next to his desk. He reached into the top drawer and retrieved a 38 pistol. After tucking the pistol in his waist band, Frank Wilson locked his office door and left.

He walked down the hall toward the rear of the building and exited into a dimly lit stairwell. Passing by the first-floor landing, he continued on to the basement. The basement was big and open and continued on farther than one would've expected. As he crossed the space, one could hear voices and the clanging of pots overhead. An aroma of garlic, onion, and tomato permeated the air. Frank made his way to the far side of the dingy basement, stepped through a doorway, and took the seven upward steps to the rear door landing of Luigi's Italian Restaurant.

He took a glance in the direction of the kitchen. The cooks were too busy prepping for the dinner rush to notice him. He removed a greasy apron from a laundry bin next to the door. He slipped the apron over his head and down around his neck and then cracked the rear door to the alley. Just as he had requested, there was a white Honda waiting for him. He closed the door.

Before opening it again, he took a Yankees ball cap off the coat rack and placed it on his head. The driver's side door of the Honda was unlocked. Nonchalantly, he got in and reached down, feeling around under the floor mat for the ignition key. "Ahh...ha," he muttered as he found it.

Frank Wilson's car zoomed through the arched wrought-iron gate of his family's old homestead. The car tires kicking up a cloud of dust as he drove the long dirt drive toward the main house. The structure was dark. He drove past the house and turned behind it. The car came to an abrupt stop in front of a large weathered wooden barn. He had never planned on keeping the run-down piece of property, but over the years, it had come in handy. He got hastily out and beat on the barn door. It immediately swung open. Frank returned to his car and drove through the opening. The barn door closed behind him. Jack slammed down a large metal bar with a thud and locked it in place. It was a typical barn with bales of hay piled high, an overhead loft, and animal stalls, though empty, along both side walls.

"Where is she?" bellowed Frank Wilson.

"We've locked her in the root cellar, just like you said," replied Jack, a husky tall man with thick shaggy brown hair.

"You haven't hurt her, have you, Jack?"

"Not yet, but I'd like to. She's a feisty bitch."

"You'll get your chance when I'm done with her." Frank followed Jack to the root cellar hatch. He watched as Jack reached down and lifted the heavy metal cellar door upward. The two men descended into the musty, damp, dungeon-like cellar. Jack reached back up, closing the door above them. Frank pulled a black ski mask down over his face. "I always hated the smell down here. It hasn't changed much since my grandfather used to lock me in here."

Jack flicked on a large flashlight, pointing it in the direction of the far-left corner. "Don't mind the blood. I had to rough her up a bit to get her here. But she's alive."

Paige lifted her sagging head to look in the direction of the light. Her eyes grew wide when she saw the masked man approaching. She could only make a grumbled sound as she struggled to speak through the saliva-soaked handkerchief gagging her mouth.

"You just couldn't mind your own business." Frank slid the gag out and down to her chin.

"Who're you trying to fool? I know it's you, Mr. Wilson. You had my father killed," she slurred.

"Don't be silly. I didn't have your father killed. I killed him myself. I do my own dirty work." He pulled the mask off his head. There was a cold, wicked look in his eyes as he spoke those haunting words.

"You and my father were friends!"

"Friends? Honey, we were much more than that. Your father was a smart man. Too smart. Said he was going to the police even though it'd implicate him. I knew if given time, he'd break. So I took care of the problem before the problem took care of me."

"You're a monster!"

"You have no idea. But you'll find out soon enough. First, I need to know who you told."

"Everyone! I can assure you…there are people looking for me."

"Well, then, I best get started. Jack, you get upstairs and make sure we don't have company. I'll persuade this child into telling me what I need to know."

"Okay," Jack answered as he walked away.

Paige loudly screamed. "Don't go. Don't leave me here with this creep!" Unwavered by her emotional plea, Jack continued up the ladder to the barn above.

Defiantly, Paige spat at Frank Wilson. "You think you're so smart. You and your generation have no respect for your elders," he said as he backhanded her across the cheek.

Paige's head and neck wrenched with the force of the blow. Tears of pain released from her eyes, the stinging sensation lingering on her cheek.

"Now what do you have to say for yourself?"

Paige looked up through misty eyes. "Not a damn thing." His backhand connected with her cheek once again. This time she was prepared, moving her body with the smack. The blow knocked her and the old wooden chair over on its side. With a loud snap, the back of the chair cracked. Paige licked her lips. With a taste of salty blood on her tongue, she lay there in the dirt, gathering her strength. *Ouch!* The toe of his hard leather shoe dug into her thigh. She looked upward and locked eyes with Frank Wilson. It was at this moment Paige recognized and took her chance. She kicked upward with the heel of her foot, smashing it into his knee cap. He toppled forward landing on the dirt floor next to her. She yanked her tied hands apart with all her strength. The back of the splintered chair fell apart, and she was free of it. With her hands still tied behind her back, she struggled to her knees, uprighted herself, and kicked him in the groin.

"You bitch," he roared in excruciating pain.

While he lay there holding his balls and whimpering in agony, Paige stopped, stepped through her tied hands, and picked up the baton flashlight. She hit Frank across the back of the skull and then took off running toward the ladder. She momentarily glanced back as she placed her foot on the bottom rung. Frank Wilson was still on the root cellar floor holding himself. She clambered to the top of the ladder and pushed the root cellar door upward with the force of a charging rhino. It popped up and open. Holding the flashlight out in front of her, ready to defend, she crawled out and into the barn. She knew that somewhere in the dimly lit structure was Jack.

"Hey!" Jack turned his attentions away from the front barn door as Paige made a break for the back. He took off after her. Paige deviated from her original plan as Jack closed in and made her way up the loft ladder. Once in the hayloft, she ran to the open gable window, closed her eyes, took a short breath, and jumped out. She landed like a cat on all fours, rolled, scrambled to her feet, and began a full-out sprint toward the pasture. Dusk had settled in. On the far side of the pasture were acres—as far as one could see—of tall, thick rows of mature corn.

Even though Jack started to fall behind, she continued at her top speed until she was making her way through the cornfield. Finally, under the coverage of the tall stalks, she slowed to catch her breath. She remained stationary.

Just when she thought she could rest a moment, she heard the rumble of an engine. It was getting louder with each passing second. Across the open pasture, a small pickup roared toward her. Where had that come from? She took off running again. As she ran deeper into the field, the engine sounds got louder. She zigged and zagged through the maze of corn, searching for a place to crouch down and hide. It was dark in the field, but she didn't dare turn on the flashlight for fear of giving away her position. Suddenly, there was silence. Now what? She remained still, listening. Her heart wildly pounded in her chest. She did some yoga breathing, in and out, trying to calm herself.

"There you are!" Jack was behind her. He grabbed her shoulders. "I got you now." He called out to Sam, "Over here." Paige swung around, thrashing at him with the flashlight. He grabbed it and yanked, pulling her forward. She let go of the flashlight and he stumbled back a step. As he tried to regain his footing, she turned and ran right into Sam.

Paige was no match for the two of them. They lifted her up off the ground with ease. She kicked her legs and swung her arms. "Put me down!" Against all her protests, they carried her through and out of the cornfield. Once they were back in the pasture, Jack tied her legs as Sam held her arms in a vice-like grip.

"Why should Wilson have all the fun?" Sam said as they lifted her feet up off the ground. "When was the last time you had a piece of ass like this?"

"Never," answered Jack.

Sam ran his right hand slowly across her heaving breasts. "It sure is tempting."

"Wilson isn't the type of man you cross and live. We better not keep him waiting," reminded Jack.

They bound her hands behind her back once again and then picked her up and bounced her into the rear cargo area of the small vehicle. Paige landed with a thud. A sharp pain shot through the back of her head as it made contact with the metal truck bed. Sam throttled the engine and vehicle shot off across the landscape.

Paige strained her neck, trying to lift her head above the side walls of the cargo bed. She was able to hold it up just long enough to see headlights far off in the distance. *Help is coming!* she thought as she took a deep breath, looked toward the heavens, and prayed. It was a clear night. A shooting star cascaded across the dark sky, bringing her back to thoughts of Nathan, the beach, and her youthful dreams. She made one final wish. And in an odd way, putting it out there, and making that one final wish, calmed her. Now, she could clear her mind and wait for her next opportunity to escape. More than death, she worried Jack and Sam would carry out their ugly threats to rape her before delivering her back to Frank Wilson.

The headlights she had seen off in the distance were getting brighter. "You didn't tell anyone?" Jack asked.

"Nope," said Sam.

"We better hide her," said Jack.

While Sam and Jack were distracted by the oncoming vehicle, Paige struggled and wiggled her hands and fingers behind her back. One hand slipped out, then the other. As she loosened the ropes around her ankles, the truck came to an abrupt stop.

Frank Wilson shouted at them as the vehicle passed through the doorway into the barn.

"Where the hell have you two been? You better have that bitch with you!" He stood in the center of the barn with a pistol in his right hand. "Someone is going to pay for letting her escape."

"You're the one who let her get away, not us," answered Jack.

"I'm not in the mood." Wilson rubbed a large bump on the back of his balding head.

"We got her. She's in the back," said Sam.

Before Sam could retrieve Paige, they heard a car horn blast outside the front barn door and then shouts. "Dad, I know you're in there."

Michael. So he was involved. He must've been playing me all along, thought Paige. *I know I was playing him.* Jack headed toward the front door as Sam struggled to lift Paige.

"Where're you going?" Frank Wilson asked Jack as he walked away.

"Letting him in," replied Jack. "He's making too much noise."

"Make sure he's alone."

Sam lowered the back tailgate and pulled Paige out by her ankles. She landed butt first on the dusty floor of the barn and let out a grunt. Though her hands were untied, she kept them behind her back so as to not let on. Quickly, she pushed herself up to a standing position and swung at Sam, her fist hitting him square in the jaw. Dazed, he closed his eyes and shook his head. Paige began to hop toward the rear barn door.

As the front barn door swung outward, Michael rushed in. "Dad, what the hell are you up to? What's she doing here?" Paige turned and looked at Michael.

"You mean your noisy little girlfriend? Are you blind, son? She was using you...to get to me."

"You...demented old fool! Do you have to destroy everything, everyone, I care about? You ruined...my mother, killed my best friend, and now, Paige." Jack and Sam crept backward and away. Michael ran to Paige, who had almost made it through the rear door. "Are you okay?"

"No," shouted Paige.

Michael turned and moved at his father. "Stay back," Frank shouted as he pointed the thirty-eight at him. "That's far enough." Frozen in place, Paige inhaled sharply.

"What? You're going to kill me too?" Michael tauntingly spoke at his father.

"I don't want to, but I will, if I have to. I didn't kill Ryan. He was hit by a car. I just helped cover it up."

"Then who?"

"Ask Miss Smarty Pants over there." Frank Wilson pointed at Paige.

"I don't know who did it," said Paige.

"Then I'll tell you. It was your father!"

"No...you did it!" Paige screamed and pointed at Frank Wilson. "You...buried Ryan's body out there in the marsh."

"Won't deny that. But I was covering up your father's mess."

Paige collapsed into a heap.

"If it was an accident...why the cover up?" Michael pushed.

"Do you remember that day, son?"

"Like yesterday."

"You and Ryan...in the garage drinking my scotch."

"Yeah...you sent him home. And he was never seen again. You made me...believe it was my...fault." Michael beat his fist on his chest. "My fault."

"It was your fault. You two stole my scotch. It was unfortunate...that your father"—he looked at Paige—"happened along and accidently hit him. But I wasn't going to jail because of two stupid kids."

"You're not making any sense," said Michael.

"I sent Ryan home, he wandered into the street...well...you've got the picture."

"My father would've called for help," said Paige.

"He did. He called me," said Frank Wilson.

"You...you told my father not to report it," said Paige.

"Client–lawyer privilege," he smugly added as he advanced closer to Michael and Paige.

"Everything was good until your father wanted to clear his conscience. I couldn't have that."

"So…what's the plan, Dad?"

"She knows too much," said Frank.

Michael leapt toward his father, grabbing at the pistol. The two wrestled for what seemed like minutes but was really only seconds. Paige sat in the dirt, watching in disbelief.

The pistol went off. Paige screamed. Michael collapsed to one knee, holding his left hand on his gut. His white shirt turned red.

"Don't just stand there! Grab them or you'll be next," ordered Frank Wilson to Jack and Sam who had disappeared. "Where are you two? Get them." Wilson's anger erupted.

Sam lunged at Paige. She scrambled to her feet and tried to limp away, her feet still entangled in ropes. Sam tackled her from behind, planting her, face first, in the dirt. As pain shot through her body, she tried to crawl her way out from under him. The weight of his body kept her from moving. He lay on top of her until she stopped struggling. He placed a knee in the center of her back, holding her in place. Jack walked over with a new rope. This time the ropes were tight. She lay there on her belly as Jack, Sam, and Frank scurried around. She arched her back, straining to move to see what they were doing. To see if Michael was still alive, she wiggled and squirmed, inching her way, and turning herself. Finally, she was in a position where she could see Michael. He was slumped forward and tied to a wooden column in the center of the barn. She shook her head back and forth trying to get his attention. There was no response.

Paige lay on the barn floor, in total darkness, listening for footsteps and whispers, and waiting for the hammer to come down. Then there was quiet. Besides the crickets chirping, there were no sounds. The silence was unbearable. At least when she heard them moving around, she knew where they were. Maybe it was better this way; she wouldn't know when it was coming. Fatigued from struggling to free herself, Paige gave in to it and closed her eyes. Just for a short time, she told herself. She needed to conserve her energy for the next round.

How long had she been out? She didn't know. She opened her eyes when she heard a crackling sound and smelled smoke. There was a glow all around her. The men were gone.

She shouted at Michael. "Wake up! The barn is on fire." He didn't move. Paige wiggled like a snake, moving herself across the dirt on her belly until she reached him. She nudged at him with the top of her head. "Hey, it's me. I know you're in pain. Please…wake up. I need you to wake up." Paige noticed Michael was tied with only one rope around the barn pole. They must've thought he was dead. It was slight, but his chest was moving in and out. She positioned herself behind him. With her teeth, she bit and pulled at the knot. She was able to loosen it enough that he fell over sideways. The jolt woke him. "You're alive. Michael, we need to get out of here. Can you untie me?"

"Paige, what happened?"

"Your father shot you. We need to get out of here. The barn is on fire. Untie my hands. Once I'm free, I can help you up. We can get out of here."

Michael began working at Paige's ties. Once her hands were free, she quickly untied her feet and stood. She tried to help Michael up.

"I can't make it," Michael whispered shakily. "Go without me."

"You can. Try," she ordered him. He struggled to stand as she pulled him up by his two arms. He let out a moan of pain as he held onto his bloody gut.

"We can do this." Paige surveyed the barn, looking for a way out. The fire had encircled them. The barn was filling with smoke. Their only way out would be through a wall of flames.

"I got it!" Paige coughed and gasped. "The root cellar…we'll be ten feet underground. It might give us a chance." Paige quickly removed her blouse and ripped off the sleeves. "Here."

She handed a sleeve to Michael. "Hold this over your nose and mouth." She threw what was left of her blouse back on. She held the other sleeve over her own mouth and nose. "Let's go. Move it." She guided Michael as flames shot through the rafters above them.

It was a major undertaking supporting Michael's 6'2" frame while moving toward the root cellar. They moved slowly but steady.

The smoke was surrounding and thickening. Their visibility diminishing. "We need to get close to the floor. Do you think you can crawl?"

"I'll try," answered Michael.

Like soldiers crawling under barred wire, they moved, hugging the ground as flames danced overhead. They kept low, their faces covered, until they reached the metal root cellar door. Beat up and exhausted, Paige refused to give in. With both adrenaline and desperation driving her, she reached deep inside and found the strength she needed to lift the heavy door. "You need to go first. I'll close the door once we're in," said Paige.

Michael turned his body and began moving backward down the wooden ladder. He didn't speak, just slithered. After three rungs, he lost his grip and tumbled downward, letting out an anguished cry of pain as his body crashed hard on the dirt floor. "Are you okay?" called Paige from above. There was no response.

She threw herself into the opening and pulled the root cellar door down with a loud bang, shutting them in. As she drew near the bottom rung, she leapt over Michael's sprawled-out body and got down on one knee. "Are you with me?" Michael let out a low grumble.

Paige's eyes adjusted to the darkness and she was now able to see Michael's blood-soaked shirt. She placed a hand on the center of his chest. He was still alive, but for how long?

She ripped his expensive dress shirt open. Blood still oozed from his gut.

Reacting, she did the only thing she could, placed her hands over the wound, and applied pressure. Paige took a deep breath in of the stale, damp, smoke-free air and prayed that she had made the right decision. The last place she wanted to be was back in the root cellar where she'd been held prisoner for the last day and a half. Her survival instincts told her this was the only option, but was it? *Too late to rethink it.*

CHAPTER 33

IN AN EFFORT TO KEEP Michael conscious and herself sane, Paige rambled, "Stay with me. We're safe now. I'm sure someone will see the smoke. The fire department will come."

Michael's eyes opened. "Paige, I'm sorry." Paige leaned in closer to hear. "He's my father."

"Don't let him get to you. It's not your fault."

Michael blinked. "Ryan was my friend. That day…after school. He dared me… We took a bottle of scotch from the liquor cabinet." Michael paused and his eyes shut. When his eyes opened again, he continued, "It tasted like crap…"

"You two wouldn't be the first to steal their parents' liquor. It was a long time ago. Don't think about it. We all do stupid things… when I get out of here… I'm going to make things right…with." Paige got thoughtful as she recalled the petty things she'd said to Cate; how instead of accepting they were different, she'd let it drive them apart. Maybe her mom was right, out of every bad thing, no matter how bad, some good comes. Suddenly, her thoughts shifted, and the haunting words Frank Wilson had spouted about her father consumed her. It just didn't sound like the man she knew—the man who had raised her to be honest, trustworthy, kind, and resilient. She knew there was more to the story. She vowed that once she got out of this death trap, she'd track Wilson down herself and get the answers she needed, but until that time, she wouldn't breathe a word to anyone about it. Frank Wilson was a monster and capable of anything, even framing her father.

"We were surprised by my dad. He never got home that early," Michael picked up where he had stopped. "We tried to play it off, but Dad knew we were up to something." Michael paused and took a gasping breath, determined to tell his story. "He asked what we were doing. We tried not to laugh, but the alcohol had kicked in. We bust out laughing."

"Sounds like harmless kid stuff."

"It was. We tried to bullshit our way out of it. He saw the bottle on the workbench behind us. One minute we were laughing, the next I was flying across the room."

"Oh, Michael."

"The worst pain I'd ever felt...till now. His words haunt me, 'You two want to be men.' I blame myself."

"I know he's your father, what an ass."

"I remember Ryan said, 'We just wanted to taste it.' Dad shoved the bottle in his face. Ryan cried. He forced him to drink. I got to my feet...grabbed the bottle. My father laughed. He'd lost it. It was as if the man in front of me was Mr. Hyde." Michael's breathing labored and he stopped.

"Conserve your energy. You can tell me later." Paige stood up. "Help will be here soon."

"I drank it...gagged on it." Paige looked down. Michael stopped. She listened for movement above. There were crackling and popping sounds overhead. Then suddenly, a loud thud rang out, "Did you hear that? Something heavy just fell on the cellar door."

Oblivious as to what was going on around them, Michael continued his story, "My father finished the bottle. My head was spinning. I passed out."

"What happened to Ryan?" Paige was caught up in his story.

"I never knew. When I woke...he was gone. Dad said he sent him home." Michael's words faltered. Paige felt his wrist for a pulse.

Michael drew in a deep breath. "It's my fault he's dead."

"It's not...it's your father's...and"—Paige hesitated—"my father's."

"The police came knocking on our door late that night. Ryan never made it home. I overheard. My dad told them we hadn't seen him. *He lied.* That's when I knew... I was certain my father had done something."

"You never told anyone?"

"No...Who would've believed me? I was a coward... I don't blame Cate for hating me..."

"She knew?"

"No..."

"So why would she hate you?"

"Ryan was gone... I felt guilty... I left. All our lives changed that day. You'll tell Cate I'm sorry..."

"You can tell her."

Michael closed his eyes and remained quiet for a long while. A time or two he tried to tell her more but struggled. He wanted to tell her that he'd fallen into a deep depression after Ryan disappeared. His mother had assumed it was because he had lost his best friend. School officials labeled him as withdrawn and sullen. The school psychologist suggested he get professional help. He began regular sessions with Dr. Goldstein, who suggested a change of scenery would be good. That's when his father happily shipped him off to prep school.

"Tell my mother I love her."

"I promise."

"He needs to pay for what he did."

"Is that why you came back? For revenge?"

Michael suddenly had a renewed strength. "I tried to put it all behind me. Then one day, I picked up the paper. There was an article about a body being uncovered in Cattail Marsh. My father must've had a coronary when they dug up Ryan's body."

"My father too," added Paige. She recalled an entry in her father's journal near the time of Ryan's disappearance. "I'll never drink again." Had he been drinking that night, is that why he called Frank Wilson and not the police?

Michael struggled to lift his head. "You need to lie still," reminded Paige.

"It was time to come home. Settle up with him. I didn't know about your father's involvement. Don't blame him. It was an accident. My father...he never should've kept your father from calling the authorities. He was only thinking about himself. It would've all come back on him. He forced Ryan to drink the scotch."

"I'm sorry for all the bad things I thought about you. I thought you were involved with Dad's death," said Paige.

"I did seek you out…that day, at the hospital. I knew my father had something to do with it."

"How?"

"I overheard your father and mine at the office. Your father said he couldn't do it anymore, that he was going to the police. I clearly heard him say Ryan's name. Then, my father threatened yours."

"If you'd gone to the police…he might still be alive."

"I know…I'm sorry! I hired a PI. He followed your father to the reservoir."

"You broke into my parents' home?"

"I thought you were at the hospital that night. I never meant to scare you. My PI—"

"Why didn't you just ask?"

"That was my plan. But then I got to know you… I was afraid you'd hate me, like Cate. I was pressuring my PI for results. He broke into your parents' home. When you started looking into your father's death, you started crossing over into my investigation of my father… which helped."

"How so?"

"My PI followed you." Michael stopped speaking.

"I knew I was being watched. Do you hear that? It's sirens. We're going to be okay."

Michael's head slumped forward. "We're saved," Paige rejoiced and grabbed his hand. His grip was soft.

"Stay with me," Paige pleaded. He didn't answer. She placed two fingers on his wrist and then his neck. His pulse was extremely weak. Paige quickly jumped into action, placing the palm of her hand in the center of his chest. She began compressions. Then she pinched his nose and did mouth-to-mouth breathing. She continued to rotate between compressions and breaths, intermittently feeling for a pulse. *Nothing.*

All her strength expired; Paige collapsed next to Michael's limp, lifeless body. She wiped a tear away as it spontaneously trickled down her face. She gently closed each of his eyes with the tip of an index finger. He seemed at peace. Perhaps, he was at last.

The air in her underground prison began to thicken with smoke. Paige didn't know how much time or air she had left. Now, alone, she prayed.

CHAPTER 34

WHEN THE TAX ASSESSOR CALLED Nathan, it'd been over thirty-six hours since Paige's abduction. He had located another property owned by Frank Wilson. According to the tax rolls, in 1992, Frank Wilson had inherited a large piece of farmland on Thoroughbred Lane, just off Double Tree Road. Nathan knew the area. It was to the west of Meadowbrook with rolling hills and horse farms. He was headed toward the Wilson farm when the fire call for the old estate came over the radio.

A mile away, he could see smoke and flames shooting high above the trees. When he arrived on the scene, the barn was fully engulfed and surrounded by several pumper trucks. Water shot downward from an aerial onto the barn roof. Plumes of smoke rose up into the late evening sky. Nathan barely put his truck in park before jumping from it. He sprinted toward the fire chief. "I believe there may be people inside. You need to send in a rescue team," he yelled frantically.

"Nobody's going in until we knock the fire down. It's not safe."

"I understand your position, but I'm respectfully requesting you rethink your strategy."

Clenching his fists, he fought back the urge to punch the chief.

"As soon as it's possible, I'll send in a search team. Now, get behind the fire line."

"You don't understand. There's a woman in there."

"The structure is too far gone. I'm not sending in my men. It's about to collapse."

Nathan reluctantly obeyed and moved behind the fire line. He couldn't just stand there, watching as the wooden building collapsed. Nearly out of his mind with panic, he ordered his men to search the house and surrounding areas, just in case. Maybe Paige wasn't inside the barn, though all the information he'd received over the last hour pointed to her being somewhere on the grounds.

Nathan grabbed an eight-pound fire axe off a truck and ran toward the main house. With a surge of energy, he vigorously swung at the heavy wooden door. As each swing of the axe connected with the door, he became more determined. Finally, the door broke open; Nathan was the first one in.

He made his way through the large house. The more hours that passed, the less chance of rescue. He couldn't bear it. It was Paige, the girl…the women…the love of his life. His sheer willfulness would keep her alive. It had to.

As Nathan and his men searched the house, he was keenly aware of the fire that raged out back. The house was dark, and the flames from the barn fire flickered through the windows, onto the walls, giving the whole house an eerie, haunted glow. He and his men went room to room, from first floor to second, opening every door, checking every closet, and looking under every bed. Nathan was so intent on his search that he ignored the loud crashing noise made by the barn roof as it collapsed inward, spending up a cloud of debris.

Nathan's portable went off. "Edgemont, all clear on the first floor." All clear on the second floor, thought Nathan in disappointment. He headed back down the stairs.

Two officers entered through the front door with a man in cuffs. "Look what we found hiding in the cornfield across the pasture," said Detective Charles.

"I didn't do anything. I was just watching."

Nathan double-timed it down the stairs and got in the man's face. "What's your name? Where…is she?" he demanded.

"Sam. Don't know who you're talking about."

"What were you doing out there?" Nathan shouted.

"I was watching. I like to watch fire," Sam stupidly replied.

"He wasn't out there watching. He ran when he saw us closing in," Officer Taylor added.

"The odor of gas on you tells me you weren't just watching. You better tell me where she is or you're going to regret it." Nathan grabbed the collar of his flannel shirt, brought him in close, and stared him in the eye. Several of the white buttons were missing from his raggedy shirt. Nathan released him, fighting back the urge to rough him up.

"Okay…Okay. I didn't hurt her. It was Wilson. He's crazy!"

"Where *is* she?"

"He made us set the place on fire. He shot his son."

"Michael. Michael Wilson? He was here?"

"Like I said, his father shot him. Left him for dead."

"What about the woman?"

"She's in the barn…tied up."

Nathan shoved Sam backward, thrusting him into the arms of the two officers, and then sprinted out the door. He ran through the fire line toward the collapsed barn and was stopped just short of flames by two firefighters, who pushed him back to safety.

"No one could survive that inferno," said Chief Donnelly. Nathan's knees weakened. He collapsed to the ground. "Medic. We need a medic."

An EMT ran to Nathan's aid. He took his BP and heart rate. Another EMT ran over with a stretcher and oxygen. Together they lifted Nathan up and onto the stretcher. They fitted a face piece over his mouth and nose. Nathan lay there, helplessly, for a short while breathing in oxygen as the fire department continued to pump water onto the collapsed barn.

"I feel better," said Nathan as he pulled off the facepiece and scrambled to his feet.

"Why aren't they going in?" Nathan asked Chief Donnelly. "I've information there are at least two people in there."

"A recovery team is preparing to go in now."

A fully geared-up recovery team, wearing self-contained breathing apparatus, entered the building. As they began digging through the rubble with axes and pike poles, Nathan anxiously paced back and forth outside the structure. He looked on as the overheated, exhausted team emerged fifteen minutes later and another team went in. He walked over to one of the team members at the cooling station. "What's going on in there? Any signs of victims?"

"It's too smoky to see much," a young firefighter answered.

Not being able to wait another minute, Nathan grabbed a set of turnout gear and air pack off a nearby truck. He dressed himself behind an ambulance, then walked up, and joined in with the next rescue team that was about to go in. As another exhausted team emerged, they handed off their tools to the waiting men.

Nathan had been a fire explorer back in high school and was familiar with the gear and air pack but had never actually been inside a live fire before. He stayed with the team, following what they did, poking and moving debris, as other firemen on a hose line, extinguished hot spots. They methodically moved through the building. It was hot and smoky. Even with the large scene lights, it was hard to see much, let alone anyone. There was a tap on Nathan's shoulder. It was the team leader signaling him it was time to get out.

He had seen for himself; no one could've survived. Nathan slowly walked away, his back to the barn, toward the cooling station. He took off his facepiece and helmet, and sat silently on a chair as a fan blew a fine mist of water over him and the firefighters.

Once cooled, Nathan breathed deeply in, stood, and walked away to the patrol car where Sam was being held. He yanked open the back door, pulling Sam out. "You better have a good lawyer. Cause the charges just went from arson to murder, and that means…life. If you don't want to die in prison…then you best tell me exactly where you left Michael Wilson and Paige Thompson in that building."

"I told you, it wasn't me. It was Frank Wilson. He shot his son. Jack tied him to the center support in the barn." Sam shut up quickly, he realized he'd slipped up. They hadn't known about Jack. Not till he opened his big mouth. Oh, well, he thought, he hadn't signed on for murder. It just snuck up on him. He was in deeper than he ever imaged. Wilson was a scary man, but life in prison trumped Wilson.

"Who's Jack?" Nathan asked.

"Frank Wilson's main man. He does all the dirty work."

"We'll get back to him in a minute."

"You're sure there was a girl in that barn when you set it on fire?"

"I'm sure. She was lying face down near Michael Wilson."

"Where is this Jack? Where is Wilson?"

229

"I don't know. They took off in a white Honda."

"Where would they go?"

"I don't know."

"Who is Jack? What's his last name?"

"I don't know."

"You think I'm stupid or something? What's Jack's last name?

Sam's forehead began to bead with sweat and his armpits perspire. "Lewis. Jack Lewis."

Nathan took Sam by the head and squeezed his jaw muscles. "I'm done with you for now." Then he shoved him back into the rear of the patrol car. There was no time to waste. Nathan ordered an APB on the white Honda, Frank Wilson, and Jack Lewis. If Paige was dead, then the men who were responsible were...going to pay.

CHAPTER 35

PAIGE CAREFULLY PLACED MICHAEL'S HEAD on the dirt floor, stood, and climbed up several rungs of the root cellar ladder. She reached out. Heat radiated off the metal door. Quickly, she went back down the ladder and felt around, hoping to find a piece of the chair that had held her hostage. Luckily, she found a broken piece. Back up the ladder she went. She pushed with all her reserved strength until her shoulders ached and her eyes watered. Still, not even a squeak or a budge.

As the fire department continued to search the collapsed barn, Nathan felt useless...hopeless...he couldn't bare it, to be there and not be able to help. When a report of a silver Lexus being carjacked by two men at the corner of Main and Caldwell came in, Nathan knew what he had to do. He had to pull himself together and catch Paige's killer.

The carjacking was a lucky break; they now had an approximate location of the suspects. A new APB went out for the silver Lexus, and within minutes, two patrol cars were in pursuit of it. Nathan joined the chase. Jack Lewis was in the driver's seat, recklessly driving through the streets of Meadowbrook as Frank Wilson held on tight in the passenger seat. The speed limit in downtown was twenty-five miles per hour, and Jack was pushing eighty. He weaved the Lexus in and out of, and around traffic, until he reached the Parkway South entrance, where the car made a sharp right turn and entered the highway.

The state police sent out a helicopter. It hoovered overtop, following the car as it reached a top speed of 120 miles per hour on the open highway. More police cruisers joined the chase. Boxed in on all sides, Jack challenged the limits of the Lexus.

He swerved the car around an eighteen-wheeler, almost hitting a dump truck, and lost control of it. The car went off the highway, crossed over the median, and down a grassy embankment. It flipped over three times before landing upside down, with its front grill lodged between two enormous elm trees. Nathan slowed his car and swung it around, stopping on the grassy side of the parkway. Three other cruisers pulled up alongside as Nathan sprang from his vehicle and ran down the steep hill toward the flipped car. Behind him, he heard an officer radioing for an ambulance and an extrication team. Rescuing them was the last thing on Nathan's mind.

Nathan peered in the driver's side window. Both airbags had deployed. He wasn't sure whether Jack was dead or just unconscious; either way, he didn't care. He walked around to the passenger side to check on Frank Wilson. He was barely conscious as he hung upside down, wedged in place by the airbag and seat belt. Blood dripped from a large gash on his forehead.

As Nathan leaned in closer, Wilson's eyes popped open. Wilson moaned and placed the open palm of his hand on the cracked glass.

"Did you really think you'd get away with kidnapping and murder?" Nathan asked him through the broken window.

Frank Wilson had a wicked grin pasted across his face. "I always get away with it."

Do the right thing, thought Nathan though every fiber of his being urged him to do otherwise—to take his revolver out and blow Frank Wilson away. But that wasn't who he was and that would make him no better than Frank Wilson.

Nathan pulled at the passenger-side door. "Why should I bother..." He held his words and yelled up the embankment. "Bring a crowbar. It's jammed." A barrage of men was already headed down the hill. Nathan stepped back and let the extrication team do its job. Jack was the first to be pulled out of the wreckage. His lifeless body was strapped on a stretcher and hauled up the hill.

The EMT's preliminary assessment of Frank Wilson found several cracked ribs, a punctured lung, several broken appendages, and a large contusion on his head. They tried to make him comfortable and keep him alive until he could be freed, which could take some time.

It would take a cutter, a spreader, and the full extrication team working in synchronization to cut him out.

Nathan had no patience to wait around. The accident was in the jurisdiction of the state police; there was nothing more for Nathan to do at the accident scene. Frank Wilson wasn't going anywhere, and the pull at his heart to be close to Paige was undeniable. He'd been so caught up in catching Frank Wilson that he'd not taken more than a minute to grieve for Paige. They'd just reconnected, and now she was gone. He turned his car lights and siren on, and he sped away, back to the barn fire.

Nathan found the fire completely knocked down and firefighters rummaging through the debris, working at extinguishing hot spots when he arrived back at the Wilson homestead. He first checked in with his department officers and then headed over to speak with Fire Chief Donnelly. "We've found no evidence of human remains. Perhaps you were misinformed or they were able to get out," said Chief Donnelly.

"You don't know how much I wish that were true," replied Nathan.

"My men are still searching, but they've found nothing."

Nathan's radio beeped. "Edgemont here."

"Frank Wilson died on the way to the hospital," reported Officer Taylor. "Thought you'd want to know."

"Thanks for the update," replied Nathan.

A shout from within the burned rubble, bellowed out, "over here." It was Lieutenant Morris. Two firefighters joined the lieutenant near the center of the barn. "Do you hear that?"

They listened intently. "There. Listen. It's coming from underground. Three short taps, three long…it's an SOS. Move those rafters. I'll hit up the chief," announced the lieutenant.

Nathan ran into the rubble, joining the firefighters and taking control. "You two lift that large beam. And you…help me with this." The root cellar door was exposed and the tapping sounds got louder.

Two large firefighters in full turnout gear yanked upward on the root cellar door handle. The door lifted and opened.

"Help him!" shouted Paige as she popped her head up from her underground sanctuary.

"Ma'am, you okay?"

"I'm not the one who needs help. Get Michael…he's been shot," implored Paige as a firefighter helped her up and out. Squinting, she shielded her eyes with a hand as they adjusted to the bright sunshine. When she moved her hand aside, there stood Nathan.

"I thought you were dead." He lifted her up off the ground, squeezed her tight, and then set her back down. Gently he took her face in his hands. "Are you hurt?"

"Banged up a bit."

"But you're okay?"

"Yes."

"You're here!"

"Yes."

"You're alive."

"Yes," was all she could manage.

"You're alive," Nathan repeated.

"Yes." Shyly, Paige looked up, inwardly hoping he wouldn't notice she was a shamble of a mess, from her dirty face and knotted hair down to her ripped, tattered, bloody clothes and shoeless feet.

"Look at you." He moved a wisp of hair out of an eye. Taking her crusty, blood-covered hands in his. "I'd almost given up hope. But you…somehow you, defied all the odds. You amaze me. Have I ever told you that?"

Paige managed a smile, though painful. "No one's ever told me that." He brushed a smudge of dirt from her cheek. "I knew you'd find me. I tried to save Michael. This is his blood," Paige said as she showed Nathan her hands. "I'm not sure…I would've survived if he hadn't showed up. I owe him my life." Nathan's eyes followed her every movement.

"They'll get him out. Let's get you over to a medic." Nathan picked her up. She wrapped her arms around his neck, holding tight, as he carried her through the debris and ashes.

"Frank Wilson. He killed my father...shot Michael. You shouldn't be here! Don't worry about me. He's out there...getting away."

"Slow down, listen to me. Wilson's dead. His partner Jack Lewis is dead," said Nathan as he placed her on a waiting stretcher.

"They are...How?"

"While they tried to run...there was an accident."

"There was another man, short, stocky, named Sam."

"He's in custody."

"Wilson confessed... He killed my father."

"He most likely killed Ryan Timmons and buried him in the marsh too," added Nathan. "His fingerprints were found on the inside edge of the backpack you found."

Paige got quiet. *What had Nathan just told her.* Frank Wilson and Jack were dead. Sam was in custody, and she was quite certain he had been too far away to hear Wilson's actuations against her father, and Michael, poor Michael, had passed away in the cellar. To the best of her knowledge, *she* was the only person left alive who knew how Ryan Timmons had met his demise, the *only* person who could implicate her father.

"That's a lucky break," abruptly Paige blurted. *He'll never know...just how lucky.*

"A break you almost died for."

"Please don't scold me...not now," said Paige as she lay back on the stretcher.

Nathan took hold of her hand. "I thought I'd lost you," he whispered in her ear.

Paige cracked the tiniest of smiles, "I'm not lost anymore," and closed her eyes.

THE END

ABOUT THE AUTHOR

LINDA BOWNIK-PANASUK IS A LIFELONG resident of New Jersey. She earned a BA in English from Widener University in Chester, PA. Her first novel, *Return to Cattail Marsh,* was inspired by her love of New Jersey, its shoreline, rivers, forests, and farmlands. She is never happier than when she's walking along the sandy beaches of the Jersey Shore.

Connect with Linda Bownik-Panasuk at http://cattailmarsh. blog or on her Facebook page, "Return to Cattail Marsh."